"THERE ARE DIFFERENCES BETWEEN SEDUCTION AND COURTSHIP."

Foxworth was clearly shocked by her candor, and Isabelle congratulated herself for making him think. Then he leered at her, and bells of warning began clanging in her ears.

"Will you school me on the differences, my lady?" he said, his deep voice as soft as velvet while he possessed himself of her hand. For a moment she was paralyzed, and then he laughed.

Jerking her hand away, Isabelle said, "I see plainly that you have the seduction part perfected, my lord, but that can hardly help you win a wife. Now, if you will excuse me?"

"Of course, my lady," he said, still chuckling as he rose and sauntered toward the door.

Isabelle had to force herself to look away from those broad shoulders, the trim waist, but when she glanced back, he had turned to laugh at her again. The coxcomb!

"Was there anything else, my lord?"

"Only this. Courtship is all well and good, my lady, but do not discount the effectiveness of seduction. . . ."

Other books by
Julia Parks

THE DEVIL AND MISS WEBSTER

HIS SAVING GRACE

A GIFT FOR A ROGUE

Julia Parks

ZEBRA BOOKS
Kensington Publishing Corp.
http://www.kensingtonbooks.com

For my family, especially my husband.
Thank you for your love and care while
I do what I love—writing.

One

The heavy door slammed shut, but the Earl of Foxworth only smiled, relieved to put an end to Camille's tedious tantrum. Discharging her services had proven the most costly dismissal of any of his previous mistresses, but it was only money, he thought, taking a deep breath of the crisp November air. He placed his fashionable beaver top hat on his head and strolled down the street, his step jaunty and his cane swinging from side to side.

"Good evening, my lord," said his coachman, who was waiting at the end of the street.

"Good evening, George," he replied. "Lovely evening, isn't it?"

The grizzled old coachman, who had been with his employer's father before serving the current earl, only grunted his response and pulled his collar about his neck more tightly.

"Rheumatics still bothering you, George?" asked the earl, standing on the step of the carriage with the door open.

"Not so I cannot do my job, m'lord," said the proud old man. "Where to now, m'lord?"

"I've a mind to go to the club, George, but I don't want to keep the horses standing all night. Just drop me off, and then you can take the carriage home."

"Very good, m'lord," replied the coachman, lifting

the reins and sending the team down the gaslit street toward St. James's and White's.

The Earl of Foxworth was a well-known figure throughout London. He spent the majority of the year at his town home in Mayfair and was a common sight in the fashionable world, often being spotted at the theater or opera. The footmen at White's men's club greeted him by name as he moved from one room to the next, making a desultory search for someone to share a bottle and a game of piquet or whist.

In the reading room, hunched over a newspaper, he spied his old friend, Thomas Vickers, Marquess of Dunham.

"Dunham, what the devil are you doing here at midnight, reading a newspaper?"

"Same thing you would be doing, Foxworth, if you were still wed," grumbled the tall, taciturn gentleman, shoving a stack of papers onto the floor to clean off a chair for his friend.

"Can't be that bad," said the earl, motioning to a footman to bring him a glass.

"My wife's sister is staying with us. She's trying to polish her up for the Season next spring."

"I see," said the earl, resting his chin on the silver handle of his cane. "Must say, I'm glad I will not have to deal with that sort of nonsense. Having two boys, all I will need to do when they come to town is drag them out of River Tick from time to time."

"But you've got years before you have to worry about that," said the marquess. "What are they now? Six? Eight?"

"Phillip is eleven and Robert is thirteen—only a year or two older than your daughters. How are they anyway?"

The man rolled his eyes. "Beautiful, quite intelligent, and maddening. Their squeals can damage a man's hearing from one side of the house to the other. I see them as little as possible, and when I do, I try to keep the topics too boring for them to express the least excitement."

Alex Havenhurst, the Earl of Foxworth, chuckled, giving his friend a sympathetic clap on the back. The footman appeared with another glass, and the earl helped himself to the Madeira his friend had ordered.

"Bring us a deck of cards and another bottle of this," he said, sending the servant away again.

"Do I want to play cards?" asked the marquess.

"You would do anything to take your mind off your troubles, wouldn't you?" asked the earl.

"Even playing cards with the best cardplayer in the club?" asked his friend with a grin.

"Even that. Just a friendly little game," said the earl, taking the deck of cards the servant presented on a silver tray and shuffling them expertly.

As the earl dealt the cards, the marquess asked, "What is keeping you in town so late in the year? Almost everyone has left for the country by now, either to their estates or hunting boxes, or to visit friends."

"There is no attraction for me at home," he said. "If I went there, my mother might decide to visit. As for my hunting box, that is where my mother resides now that my brother and his wife have given her a granddaughter."

"So you're staying in town for Christmas?"

"No, I'll go home when the boys are there; Foxworth Court is deuced empty without them there."

"Besides, you do have one interest keeping you in London—a very pretty interest. I spied you at the theater last week."

A flicker of emotion shadowed his eyes for a moment, but the Earl of Foxworth never allowed distractions to interfere with his cards, and he deftly swooped up the trick before saying firmly, "I assure you, there is nothing keeping me in London."

"Blast," muttered Dunham. Then he smiled and asked, "Not afraid someone will lure away that mistress of yours? She is a beauty; must make you nervous to think of leaving her to her own devices for a month or two."

"Not at all. As a matter of fact, do you want her? You can have her if you like. Perhaps then I could reclaim my house. To avoid a tiresome scene, I had to promise her the thing to be rid of her. Now, if I decide to embroil myself with another female, I shall be forced to buy another house. But if you were to take her off my hands . . ."

The marquess held up both hands in mock horror and said, "Oh no! I have quite enough females in my life. Besides, Amy would shoot me, and she's really quite a good shot, you know. I taught her myself."

"What has happened to the fairer sex?" sighed the earl, collecting another trick. "Mistresses who refuse to leave the love nest and ladies learning to shoot guns."

"The world is changing, my friend, and I'm afraid the only places the likes of you or me will find respite will be our clubs."

"A sad state of affairs," murmured the earl, collecting the next trick. "And when will you be adjourning to the country?"

"Not until the week before Christmas, I think. That's what Amy tells me anyway. Something about her sister again. At least her twin sister is unable to travel at the moment and so will not be able to pay us her annual visit; the bonus to that is, of course, that their dragon of a grandmother will also be absent, watching over this new great-grandchild."

"Ah, yes, I heard about Plimpton. A shame. He was a decent sort of chap, just not much of a horseman. So

Lady Anne has given him a posthumous heir?" asked the earl.

"No, she had a girl. Poor Plimpton. He couldn't even get lucky in death. Still, at least he doesn't have to put up with Lady Anne's sharp tongue anymore."

"I never understood why you held her in such dislike, Thomas. The Lady Anne is a perfect copy of your wife."

"Physically, perhaps, but whereas my Amy at least pretends to acquiesce to my requests, her sister takes delight in crossing swords with me at every turn. You of all people must remember how vexing she can be!"

"Pray do not ask me to recall," said Alex. "I dislike nothing so much as recalling vexing matters." Collecting the final trick, he gathered the cards and began to shuffle, his expression thoughtful.

"Something on your mind, Alex?"

"No, not really. Well, perhaps. I was just trying to recall the last time something did vex me. It seems to me that it has been ages since anything has troubled me. As a matter of fact, I cannot recall the last time anything affected me in the least."

The earl sat back without dealing the cards, causing his friend to frown.

"Not a bad thing, surely, to have your life so ordered. I would give my right arm to be able to say the same. Trouble with you, Alex, is that your life is too perfect—if one can rightly call that trouble."

"Sometimes trouble can be exhilarating," murmured the earl. Shrugging his shoulders, Alex again settled on his face the polite mask Society dictated. Sitting forward, he began to deal, his expression bland and emotionless.

But the marquess had known him too long to be fooled. Ignoring the neat stack of cards in front of him, he said, "You need an interest, old man—something besides a mistress. Why don't you marry again?"

Alex gave a snort of derision at this suggestion. "Are you completely dicked in the nob?" he asked amicably. "Just because you poor married sapskulls want some more company under the cat's paw . . ."

The marquess chuckled and shook his head, his long fingers closing over the cards. "You can't blame a fellow for trying. I tell you what, Alex, why don't you come over tomorrow night? My wife has planned some sort of card party with a late-night supper—one of her buffets, you know the sort of thing."

"What? Trying to pair me up with some young miss just out of the schoolroom?"

"Devil a bit. Just some old friends. To be truthful, I don't know precisely whom she has included in the guest list."

"No, no, I don't mean to question your choice of guests," said Alex. "I apologize; that was not well done of me. I would be happy to accept—if you don't think my inclusion will disturb Lady Dunham's seating arrangement."

"Not at all. She will be glad you're coming. What's more, I give you my word of honor. I will not let her partner you with some insipid chit of a girl."

"Good, because you know how I hate to lose."

"Do I? I don't recollect your ever having done so . . . at least, not to me," said the marquess, glancing at his cards with a grunt of resignation. Suddenly a gleam lit his pale green eyes, and he murmured, "It might be worth your wrath just to do so, but I give you my word. I'll see to it that your partner is some dull, matronly friend of Amy's."

Alex grinned at his friend and nodded, saying, "Well, as long as she is neither too dull nor too matronly. Very well, I accept your most generous invitation."

"Good, then we will expect you tomorrow night at eight."

* * *

By the time the Earl of Foxworth reached his house, the servants were beginning to stir, going about their morning duties, which the housekeeper, Mrs. Pratt, had assigned. Alex addressed each footman and maid by name as he made his way through the hall and up the stairs to his room. There he discovered his valet slumbering in a chair, looking as prim and proper as if he hadn't slept in his clothes, waiting for his master.

"Tompkins, wake up."

"What? Oh, I beg your pardon, my lord. I must have dozed off. It won't happen again," said the fussy little man, popping out of the chair and standing at attention.

"Nonsense. What you should have done, as I've told you time and again, is seek your bed at a reasonable hour. I am quite capable of getting undressed and putting myself to bed. It has been years since I have allowed myself to become so brandy-faced that I could not manage for myself."

The dainty clock on the mantel chimed the hour of eight, and the valet ignored his master's words and began removing Alex's coat.

This task completed, Alex pushed his hands away, saying crossly, "I can manage the rest. Just go to bed."

"I wouldn't think of shirking my duty, my lord. You are much too tired to be able to . . ." The little man kept up a running monologue as he bobbed around his master, working quickly until Alex was clad only in his unmentionables and a silk dressing gown.

"Now, my lord, will there be anything else?"

"No, no, I can ring . . . ah, here is my breakfast now. That will be all, Tompkins," said the earl, rolling his eyes as the valet ignored this dismissal, vying with the housekeeper for the privilege of serving his breakfast.

Mrs. Pratt, who had accompanied the footman into the room, busied herself setting a place on the small table beside the chair near the fire.

"Good morning, Mrs. Pratt. How are you today?" asked the earl, sitting down in the chair.

The gray-haired housekeeper slapped at the valet's hand and picked up the snowy napkin, placing it on the arm of the dark blue chair.

"I'm very well, my lord. Thank you for asking. Will there be anything else?"

"I don't think so," he replied, and she sketched a curtsy and retreated. "Oh, yes, there is one other thing, Mrs. Pratt. I will be leaving for the country tomorrow. I am going to visit my brother in Pixley for a few days, and then I will go on to Foxworth Court. Will you shut up the house here and see to it that everyone arrives at the Court safely?"

"It will be a pleasure, my lord. It will be good to be home again."

"Indeed it will, Mrs. Pratt. I find I am quite looking forward to it. Oh, and if you have any messages for your sister in Pixley, feel free to send them with me."

"You are so considerate, my lord," said the housekeeper.

"Will you be wanting me to accompany you to Pixley, my lord?" asked the valet.

"Yes, certainly, Tompkins. You don't suppose I can do without you, do you? So, you must get some rest. I order you to go to bed for the rest of the morning."

"Yes, my lord. Very good."

When the valet had closed the door to the dressing room, Mrs. Pratt walked back into the bedroom, her lined forehead drawn up in a frown.

"Is something bothering you, Mrs. Pratt?"

"I don't like to put myself forward, my lord," she began, looking down at the carpet and missing the gleam of amusement this falsehood brought to her master's eyes. "You know that I certainly don't like to plague you with inconsequential matters."

"You may say anything to me, Mrs. Pratt. You know that. We have been together too long. Why, I still recall the time you washed my mouth out with soap."

Shaking her plump finger at him, she smiled and said, "Now, you know you gave me no choice. But that was more years ago than either one of us cares to remember. No, my lord, it is just that you did tell me last year that I should have reminded you while we were still here in London, that you needed to buy presents for the servants and for your family."

Alex sat up and slapped his knee. "So I did, Mrs. Pratt, and you are quite right to remind me. I'm afraid I will have little time for it today, and I'm going out tonight. There is nothing for it. Have Tompkins wake me at eleven."

"Oh, that won't be enough sleep, my lord."

"It will have to do, Mrs. Pratt. Now, take this away if you will. I have more need of sleep than Cook's kidney pie."

"Very good, my lord," she said, going to the door and signaling to the footman who was waiting in the hall. While he gathered up the breakfast tray, Mrs. Pratt began to pull the curtains across the windows, leaving the room in somber shadows.

The earl was already crawling into bed, his eyes closing before she reached the door.

"Thank you, Mrs. Pratt. You're an angel."

"Good night, my lord."

Dressed in a black coat of exquisite cut and cloth, the Earl of Foxworth would have stood out in any crowded room. Adding his handsome features and dark, glistening hair to the tall, well-built form, he was enough to make any young lady's breath catch in her throat—as well as that of the older dames present in Lady Dunham's elegant Mayfair drawing room.

Amy Vickers, the Marchioness of Dunham, however, appeared immune to the earl's charms as she greeted him with a kiss on the cheek and a rap on the arm with her unfurled fan.

"You have been away from Polite Society for too long, my lord. You should not neglect us so."

Alex smiled down at the diminutive lady. "I can only blame my lamentable memory, my lady."

"Do not mean to say that you forgot where we live?" replied his hostess.

"No, not that, but if I had remembered how very lovely you are, nothing could have kept me away."

"A very pretty compliment, but one that I cannot credit, my lord. I think it is a fondness for low company that keeps you away from polite company. I know you have been in London for several months."

"That is true, I fear," he said.

"So you have no excuse for neglecting polite company," she said coyly.

"Have you been neglected, my dear Lady Dunham? Then I must beg your pardon most humbly. But perhaps the person you should be reprimanding is your husband?"

His comment earned him another rap with her fan and a titter of laughter, but her husband protested, "Here now, Alex, don't drag me into your squabble."

"Foxworth was merely making a jest, my dear." She took the earl's arm and led him into the room. "Now, you are acquainted with Lady Brisbane, I believe, but I daresay you have not been introduced to her charming daughter."

"I warn you, Amy, I'll not stand for any matchmaking," muttered the earl in a quick aside.

"La, sir, you quite mistake the matter. Penelope Brisbane is a charming girl, to be sure, but she is entirely too young for a man of such, uh, mature tastes."

"I am hardly in my dotage," he commented, causing her to stop and gaze up at him thoughtfully.

After a moment, the marchioness blinked slowly and smiled, saying sweetly, "No, not in your dotage, Foxworth, for you are the same age as my Thomas, or near enough. But it would not matter if you were nine and twenty instead of nine and thirty. . . ."

"I am just turned thirty-eight," he protested.

"As you will, but my point is, you are still not at all suitable for a girl like Miss Brisbane."

She turned to lead him in the opposite direction, and the earl balked, saying stiffly, "Nevertheless, I should like to meet this youthful paragon."

"Very well, if you insist, my lord," said the marchioness, turning back immediately.

Alex eyed her suspiciously, wondering if he had not just been cleverly outmaneuvered, but he made no accusation and followed along meekly as she led him toward a young woman with blond ringlets and bright blue eyes. She was tall and slender and reminded him of Grace, his brother's wife, although Miss Brisbane was dressed in the height of fashion, and his sister-in-law didn't care to keep up with the latest whim.

When the introductions had been made, the marchioness floated away, leaving the earl to the mercies of the young miss who batted her eyes at him.

"How do you find London, Miss Brisbane?"

Her brow puckered and she nibbled like a rabbit at her pursed lips before saying, "Our coachman knows the way, my lord."

"Ah, yes, of course," said Alex, his eyes glazing over.

Then he tried again. "Are you enjoying yourself in London?"

"Oh, yes, my lord. Mama has taken me to all sorts of parties, and Papa has bought me countless new gowns. What young lady would not like London?"

"Have you attended the theater?"

"Yes, but I fell asleep. It was a dreadfully long play about some crippled man. Most distressing, I assure you."

"Indeed, I understand many people find our Mr. Shakespeare difficult to endure," he replied, looking about him for a means of escape. Why on earth had he insisted to Lady Dunham that he wanted to meet the dim-witted Miss Brisbane? he wondered. She was a pretty thing, to be sure, rather like a china doll. She smiled up at him, and he returned the expression.

"Your papa's money is well spent, Miss Brisbane. Your gown is very beautiful. Or perhaps it is only the person inside the gown that lends it her beauty."

She blushed and giggled. Alex felt the muscle in his jaw tighten. He should have kept to the commonplace. The girl would be getting the wrong idea about him.

"Lord Foxworth, how delightful to see you again," said Lady Brisbane, inserting herself between the earl and her daughter.

"And you, my lady. It has been too long. I can hardly credit that your daughter is of an age to have a Season."

The matron giggled too, then she sobered and shooed her daughter away.

Fixing Alex with a tight little smile, Lady Brisbane said bluntly, "I cannot imagine why her ladyship wanted to introduce my daughter to you, my lord. You are hardly interested in conversing with her, and since you are not at all suitable, she is wasting her time speaking to you."

"I beg your pardon," he demanded, lifting his quizzing glass to his eye and staring.

The gesture that had quelled many a man had no effect on the starchy Lady Brisbane.

Heaving a sigh that made him worry she might pop out of her bodice, she explained tartly, "I brought my daughter to London to give her some town bronze before her first Season in the spring. If she should settle on a husband before then, then I shan't have to endure a spring Season at all."

"You speak very boldly, my lady, and your reasoning is flawed. If you hope to marry off your daughter quickly, then why would you discourage her from conversing with an eligible bachelor like myself?"

Lady Brisbane had never been the retiring sort, and she said, "Forgive my bluntness, my lord, but I understood that you were a man of great sense, so I see no reason to mince words with you. I do not mean to insult you, but you are not precisely an eligible parti."

"I find that hard to believe," said the earl, giving her a patronizing smile. "Since when is a man of breeding and wealth—though I blush to speak of my own good fortune—since when is he not considered an eligible parti?"

"First of all, you are a rogue and a rake. Everyone knows that you could have remarried any number of times, but you never came up to scratch."

"You really do believe in speaking bluntly, don't you, Lady Brisbane?" As he spoke, his eyes drifted over her lips, lingering there and causing her rouged cheeks to darken. Leaning closer, he whispered, "Not an unattractive trait, in my eyes."

The matron's voice squeaked, but she continued doggedly. "I do not believe in misleading people, if that is what you mean. If I thought you had changed your ways, I would encourage my daughter to seek you out,

but we both know that such an eventuality is highly unlikely. Therefore, my lord, I take leave to tell you that
you are hardly the sort of husband I am seeking for my
daughter, and I would prefer it if you would not waste
her time."

"Perhaps if you were to tell me what sort of husband
you and your charming daughter are hunting, I might
help you in your search," said the rogue, his dark eyes
locking on hers.

The tactic failed miserably on Lady Brisbane. "Very
well. I want Penelope to find a husband who will remain at home in the evening, who will engage in
rational conversation with her, and who will listen to
her."

"But I am all ears, my dear lady," he said softly.

Her lips pursed in annoyance, and she said tightly,
"What nonsense! You are the biggest rake in all of London. Polite Society has long since stricken you from its
list of eligible suitors."

Alex frowned down at her, cocking his head to one
side until she expelled an impatient breath and continued. "You may be quite handsome, wealthy, and
well-bred, but everyone knows you will never marry
again, that you have two heirs and prefer lightskirts to
ladies. There! I have shocked you with my plain speaking, but it had to be said. Now, if you will excuse
me . . ." With this, she turned on her heel and sailed
away, leaving the earl to gaze after her in astonishment.

"I should have warned you about that one, old boy.
Lady Brisbane is like a tigress where that daughter of
hers is concerned," said the Marquess of Dunham, appearing at his friend's shoulder and shaking his head.

Looking about them to make certain he was not
overheard, Lord Dunham whispered, "You remember
her from our salad days, don't you? She was the reign-
ing belle when we arrived in London that first time.

She was older than we were but still unwed. I wrote the most awful sonnets to her. Thank heaven she turned me down."

"You offered for her?" asked Alex, the frown disappearing and laughter spilling forth at his friend's sheepish nod.

"Yes, but do not tell Amy. She would have a fine time mocking me for that one!"

"Don't worry. Your secret is safe with me. We fellows must stick together." Alex glanced around the room before nodding toward a small knot of matrons enjoying a cozy gossip in one corner by the fire. "Who is that sitting in her pocket?"

"Colonel Sutter. They are, uh, very close. She keeps him on a tight rein. She's still a handsome woman, but I am ever so glad that I am not her husband."

"I can see why. That would mean you were the father of that insipid miss. Still, it might be amusing to pursue the child just to irritate Lady Brisbane. Excuse me."

"Forget her," said his friend, latching on to the earl's arm and guiding him in the opposite direction. "Come and meet my sister-in-law instead. She is a sweet child."

"Are you not afraid to introduce her to such a rake?" said Alex.

"Certainly not. You know I can best you on the field of honor," said Dunham with a chuckle.

"That was in our salad days," said Alex, poking an elbow at his friend's paunch. "I doubt you would have the advantage nowadays."

The tall man said, "And that is why we are not going to put it to the test. I prefer to rest on my laurels, if you don't mind. You must allow me that privilege. I don't have your dangerous reputation to pave my way."

"Dangerous reputation?" asked Alex as they approached a young lady dressed in white.

"Here is Lady Sophia, my youngest sister-in-law."

The dark beauty wrinkled her nose and said, "Must you always preface my introductions like that, Dunham?"

"Only as long as it is the truth," he said, tweaking a silky ringlet fondly. "Make your curtsy to Lord Foxworth, brat."

"How do you do, Lady Sophia?" said the earl, sweeping a bow over her hand.

"I do very well, my lord. I am pleased to make your acquaintance. My sister has mentioned you on numerous occasions. She was quite happy to hear that Dunham had snared you for her little soirée. I gather it was quite a coup, considering that you have practically become a hermit as far as Polite Society is concerned."

She took his arm and allowed him to stroll away, gazing up at him with twinkling eyes that caused the earl to wonder what else Lady Dunham had said about him.

The temptation was too much, and he said, "I hope Lady Dunham's comments have been favorable."

"In a manner of speaking, but she was quite careful to paint you as a truly despicable character. She fears I will become enamored of someone unsuitable. But don't worry, my other sister Anne, told me the truth about you. You do recall Anne, don't you, my lord?"

"Indeed," murmured the earl, feeling his collar tighten around his neck. After his grief for his wife had subsided, he had very nearly offered for Lady Anne, but she had terminated their understanding upon learning that he kept a mistress. He couldn't even recall which mistress had been indiscreet enough to hail him in Hyde Park when he had been driving out with the beautiful Lady Anne, but the result had proven disastrous. Glancing down at the sweet child on his arm, Alex felt his color heighten, and he decided it was time to change the subject.

"Are you looking forward to the Season, Lady Sophia?"

"Oh, yes, I adore parties and balls. And I love dancing. I believe I shall enjoy my Season excessively. Will you be in town for the Season, my lord?" she asked, tilting her head to one side in the most provocative manner.

"Undoubtedly, but I rarely attend the *ton* entertainments."

She pursed her lips, her eyes twinkling, as she murmured softly, "A shame, my lord. You really should not neglect your social responsibilities like that."

"It is kind of you to instruct me, Lady Sophia," he commented dryly, "but I have already had the same lecture from your sister."

"Well, I feel we are old friends, my lord. I mean, I have heard so much about you. But I should not chide you. No doubt you have your reasons. I suppose when one has such a reputation to uphold, one cannot be seen at such mundane activities as Almack's."

Alexander Havenhurst had been on the town too long not to recognize the challenge this impertinent chit was throwing at his head. But he was not about to pick up the gauntlet. He had too much respect for his friend, the Marquess of Dunham, to trifle with his sister-in-law. He dropped her arm and sketched a slight bow.

"I must bow to your superior wisdom, my lady. Now, I really must speak to your brother-in-law."

"Of course, my lord. I understand," she said with a saucy grin.

Alex paused, then shook his head and walked away. He would not be drawn into such an absurd conversation with a child just out of the schoolroom. Why, she couldn't be more than eighteen, practically young enough to be his daughter. The thought sobered him, and he had the overwhelming desire to call for his hat and leave. But the Earl of Foxworth was not a coward. He would remain, shrugging off the misguided flirtation of Lady Sophia and the insultingly brusque conversation of Lady Brisbane.

Perhaps he had avoided Polite Society for too long. There was a time when his wealth and breeding would have guaranteed him the entrée into any social gathering. Now, it seemed, his reputation as a rake had tarnished his eligibility.

Not that he cared. He had no desire to become a target for Society's matchmaking mothers. At eight and thirty, the last thing he wanted or needed was a new wife, especially some giggling girl half his age.

"Foxworth, I haven't seen you in donkey's years. What have you been doing with yourself? Good heavens! Is that gray in your hair?" demanded the wizened old crone, her fingers latching on to his elegant coat as she held him at arm's length and looked him up and down.

Alex managed to stifle the groan he felt welling up inside. Instead, he gave the octogenarian a tight little smile, detached one of her hands, and bowed over the gnarly appendage.

"Good evening, your grace. I had no idea I would have the pleasure of seeing you here tonight. I thought you were with Lady Anne in the country."

"No need now. She had her baby girl three weeks ago. She can manage by herself."

"I hope they are both well."

"Perfectly fit. Of course, it was a disappointment to everyone that she didn't have an heir for her late husband, but it can't be helped. Now the title and estates will go to that coxcomb cousin of her late husband, Nigel Baines."

"I see. Well, you must give Lady Anne my best when next you see her."

"Humph! I doubt she wants to hear from you, but I'll tell her all the same. It might help her get over the case of blue-devils she's fallen into since Plimpton died. Such a shame."

"Indeed," murmured Alex, looking about him for someone to come to his rescue. The only person who appeared to know he existed was Lady Brisbane, and she was hardly going to play the knight errant for him.

"Come along, my boy. You shall be my partner for cards. I cannot abide listening to foolish chatter when I play, and you take your gaming seriously. We'll be playing against Lady Brisbane and her old cicisbeo Colonel Sutter. They haven't a prayer," she chortled.

Four hours later, the Duchess of Charlton announced loudly that she was perfectly exhausted from the ordeal of beating Lady Brisbane and Colonel Sutter all to flinders. Cackling like the old hen she was, she rose from the table and ordered the earl to escort her to the top of the stairs, saying audaciously that she would enjoy pretending her evening was going to conclude with a handsome lord leading her off to the bedroom.

Alex offered his arm and helped the duchess up the winding staircase. He marveled at her: eighty years or better, and she still held herself erect and wasn't even breathing hard when they reached the top.

"Will you give me your arm the rest of the way?" she asked, glancing at him sideways.

Chuckling as they continued along the corridor, Alex said, "I believe you are playing the coquette with me, your grace."

"It wasn't so bad, was it, my boy?"

"What wasn't so bad?" Alex asked, keeping the gnarly

hand that rested on his sleeve covered by his other hand.

"Playing cards all night with an old woman," she said, glancing up at him, her eyes bright and alert in her wrinkled face. "This is it."

Alex stopped and leaned down, kissing her cheek.

"I cannot recall when I have been more diverted, Duchess."

"Very prettily said, Foxworth." Shaking her head, she murmured, "Ah, if I were only thirty years younger . . ."

"If you were thirty years younger, my dear Duchess, I would not have trusted myself to escort you to your chamber."

"Rogue," she replied, unfurling the fan that hung from her wrist and fanning herself vigorously.

He bowed over her hand, turning it at the last moment and placing an audacious kiss on her palm.

"Good night, Duchess."

"Good night, my dear Foxworth," she said, stepping into her room. She turned to close the door and grinned at him. "I always thought Anne was a fool, you know. Then again, Anne ain't the sort who would tolerate sharing."

She closed the door, and Alex headed back down the corridor, whistling under his breath.

"Very nicely done, my lord," said Lady Sophia, who was leaning against her door and had obviously watched the entire exchange.

"Is it not past your bedtime, Lady Sophia?"

"Not at all. I just wanted to make certain my grandmother didn't accost you. She is ruthless about getting her way."

"I think I could handle her," he replied.

"I'm sure you could. You know, I thought it very kind of you, being her partner all night. Some gentlemen would have balked at such an arrangement."

"Then they would have been wanting in both manners and judgment. Your grandmother used to terrify me when I was younger, but I now find her company very entertaining."

"I do too. Interesting, my lord, we have something in common."

"Yes, we do, Lady Sophia. You are about to seek your bed, and so am I. Good night."

"Good night, my lord."

Alex went down the stairs and found his hostess to bid her good night. She also thanked him for partnering her grandmother, and once again Alex protested that he had enjoyed every minute of it.

As he made his way home, he was pensive. He had enjoyed the evening, something he had not expected. It hadn't just been because of the duchess's company; he had enjoyed conversing with Lady Sophia, Thomas and his wife, and had even enjoyed crossing swords with Lady Brisbane. Perhaps he had been away from polite company for too long. Perhaps the restlessness he had begun to feel of late stemmed from keeping low company.

He had steered clear of Polite Society since he and Lady Anne had parted ways, not wanting to become embroiled in the desperate matchmaking schemes of young ladies or their mothers. It appeared that he had succeeded only too well in discouraging them, if Lady Brisbane and Lady Sophia were being truthful. Perhaps he had grown to an age where the matchmaking mamas no longer considered him suitable.

And perhaps it was time he reentered Polite Society.

Two

"I tell you, Mrs. Havenhurst, I cannot bear the thought of leading Abigail and Amanda through the pitfalls of a London Season. Surely you can sympathize with me."

"I haven't ever thought about it, my lady. I mean, Allie is still too young for me to worry about such things," said Grace Havenhurst, the Vicar of Pixley's pretty wife. Tweaking the golden curl of the toddler in her arms, she added, "Surely it cannot be so unpleasant."

"My dear Mrs. Havenhurst, you cannot have considered my daughters. I warrant Amanda will not be such a trial, but you of all people should know that Abigail thinks nothing of speaking her mind. I shudder to think . . ." The matron matched action to words, closing her eyes and giving a delicate tremor.

"Yes, Abigail can be outspoken, but she is not unreasonable, and I'm certain when you explain to her the importance of weighing her conversation, she will behave like a lady should. When she was my pupil, we often had to have discussions about her unruly tongue, but she is older now. She is more mature."

"Humph, I cannot share your confidence."

Setting her daughter on her feet and watching fondly as she toddled toward her nurse, the vicar's wife said, "Perhaps there is another way, Lady Amelia."

"I am willing to consider anything," said the distraught older woman. "Oh, I wish I had never come home from Italy. It is so lovely there, so warm and bright. The art, the food . . . oh, I should never have left. Italy is—"

"If we could return to the matter at hand?" asked Grace. With a petulant toss of her graying curls, the other matron nodded, and Grace continued. "I know someone who might be willing to take the girls in hand. She has an impeccable reputation and has brought out numerous young ladies with quite remarkable results."

"Oh, I don't know. A hired companion? My girls, after all, will be presented under the aegis of your brother-in-law, the Earl of Foxworth."

"I do remember that they are his wards, my lady," said Grace, giving her daughter over to her nurse and waving farewell to her little one before returning her attention to her visitor. "I just thought it would make things easier for you, my lady, but if you don't wish to engage Lady Isabelle's services . . ."

"Lady Isabelle? Not Lady Isabelle Fanshaw?"

"Yes, are you acquainted with her?"

"Why, yes, I met her three or perhaps four years ago. She was bringing out . . . oh, I forget, but I do remember she was accepted into the highest circles. I do not recall her family history. I heard something about her marriage to the plain Mr. Fanshaw being quite a disappointment."

"Yes, I did know that. I have been trying to engage Lady Isabelle for our little school. She taught in the village school in Spursden after her husband passed away. In the past five years or so, I believe she has been chaperoning young ladies during the Season."

"You mean as a paid companion?" asked Lady Amelia, her nose in the air. "I cannot imagine doing so."

"As to that, I haven't inquired about the financial arrangements. I would not be so inquisitive. I know that she agreed to sponsor Pamela Baxter last year since Pamela's mother was too ill to undergo the rigors of a London Season."

"Really? And did Miss Baxter 'take'?"

"Oh, yes, but Pamela is such a pretty, sweet girl. She wed a Viscount Eastcote last month."

"Viscount Eastcote? Why, his family is as wealthy as Croesus, and high sticklers too. You know, I believe I will write to my cousin, the Earl of Foxworth, about this Lady Isabelle. It might be just the thing for my girls."

"You might wish to simply ask him in person, Lady Amelia. Adam received a missive from Alex yesterday saying that he was coming for a short visit."

"What a good idea. Thank you, Mrs. Havenhurst."

"You're very welcome, my lady. Now, if you will excuse me?"

"Oh, certainly. I shan't keep you any longer. I know you have your parish duties to tend to."

"Quite," murmured Grace, whose plans to work in the garden of the vicarage had been interrupted by her visitor.

When Lady Amelia had gone, she knelt beside the flower bed and began pulling irises to separate the bulbs. A shadow fell across her, and she glanced up to discover her husband smiling down at her.

"I thought she would never leave," said the Honorable Adam Havenhurst, the Vicar of Pixley. He held out his hands and pulled his wife to her feet, pinning her arms behind her back as he swooped in for a kiss. "Hmm, nice."

"Only nice? You have the most unfortunate way of paying a lady a compliment, my love."

"When the lady is my wife, she should know how I

feel about kissing her without my having to tell her every time."

"Still, a girl likes to hear it said."

"Very well, my love. I will tell you that if I had the time, that nice little kiss would lead to an entire afternoon spent upstairs, holding you in my arms." He punctuated this statement with a passionate kiss that left both participants dizzy and clinging to each other.

"Almost three years, and I still cannot get enough of you, minx," he whispered, bowing his head so that their foreheads rested against each other.

"Oh, Adam, never let anyone tell you that you are not eloquent," she breathed, tilting her head up for another kiss.

"I would think after one child and another on the way, you two would at least have learned a little discipline," said a deep voice, causing them to spring apart.

"Alex! How wonderful to see you again," said the vicar, grasping his brother's hand and drawing him closer.

"And you, Adam. How is my loveliest sister-in-law?" he asked, kissing Grace on the cheek.

"I'm fine, Alex. I'm so glad you decided to pay us a visit. It's been too long."

"I know, more than four months. How is my little godchild?"

"You will not recognize Alexandra. She is talking and running all over the place."

"I expect nothing less from my namesake. Allie is a child of great beauty and superior intellect."

"Well, come into the house. Have you been to see Mother yet? No? Well, then you'll need something to fortify you. I still have some of that brandy you sent me last winter."

"Ah, the life of dissipation you lead here in the country," said the earl, clapping his brother on the back, "makes me feel positively decadent."

Dinner the next night was a family affair, held at the earl's hunting box, a twenty-room manor house that currently housed his mother, the Dowager Countess of Foxworth, and the large staff of servants she deemed necessary for her comfort. Even little Allie accompanied her parents, though she stayed in the fully equipped nursery during their meal, coming to the drawing room with her nurse afterward. She watched her uncle from her doting grandmother's lap, hiding her face whenever Alex spoke to her.

"You're a lucky man, Adam," said the earl.

"I am aware of that. Grace tells me so constantly," he replied with a laugh. His wife stuck out her tongue at him.

"It's not all one-sided," said the dowager countess. "Grace should count her own blessings. It's not every spinster who is lucky enough to have such an eligible parti as Adam was appear in the middle of nowhere."

"Mother," said the earl, a warning in his tone.

"But she is quite right, Alex," said Grace. "If Adam hadn't happened along, I would still be teaching at Dodwell's Academy, blissfully unaware of what I was missing."

"Quite right," said her mother-in-law. "Furthermore . . ."

"Allie want chockie."

The childish speech made the dowager countess forget her conversation with the adults as she gazed adoringly at her grandchild.

"I don't know if I have any chocolate bonbons left, my love. Let me see," said the silver-haired woman, opening an enamel box on the table by her elbow. "Oh, dear, I was afraid of that. Now, now, don't puddle up, sweeting. Come with me, I know where we can find some."

Alex shook his head in astonishment as he watched his self-centered mother rise, carrying the two-year-old child in her arms as they went in search of a treat.

"I never would have believed it," he said. "Is she always like that with Allie?"

"Always. I guess she has been longing for a little girl all these years, and now that she has one, she's enjoying every minute of it. She will come over in the morning sometimes and spend the entire day with the baby. I better go and help," said Adam, rising and following in the wake of his mother and daughter.

Grace smiled after her husband, turning her contented face on her brother-in-law, who was watching her intently. "I thought the novelty would fade, you know, but your mother seems to enjoy Allie more and more each day. It makes it quite easy to forgive her cutting remarks when she so obviously dotes on our daughter."

"Extraordinary. Well, she certainly never took any pains to get better acquainted with my boys. But then, they were just more of the same."

"Your boys are delightful. When they came to visit last summer, I thoroughly enjoyed them," she said, breaking off her conversation while the footman brought in the tea tray.

"Tea?"

The earl nodded and Grace poured out, handing him the delicate porcelain cup.

Balancing it on his knee, Alex said, "The boys wrote to tell me how much they enjoyed staying at the vicarage. I could tell from Phillip's letter that Adam had influenced him greatly in his studies. He is first in his class this term, you know."

"Yes, he wrote to Adam about it. You must be very proud," Grace said, sipping her own tea and watching the earl over the gold rim. After a moment of silence, she asked, "What brings you here, Alex? No one comes to Pixley at this time of year unless they are hunting mad. And do not try to tell me you have developed an interest in fox hunting, for I'll not believe you."

"No interest at all," he said, his dark eyes hooded and a frown creasing his brow. "I really cannot say, Grace. I have been seized by a . . . a disquiet, a restlessness, of late. Perhaps I am getting broody in my old age."

"Old? At eight and thirty? And you look to be closer to thirty than the other direction. Is that why you stayed in London so long? Looking for diversion?"

Alex rose and strolled to the window, gazing into the darkened garden, his fingers laced behind his back.

"I find the diversions London offers sadly flat these days, my dear. I thought perhaps it was the low company I kept, so I attended a card party at my friend's, the Marquess of Dunham's, house."

"And did that alleviate your restlessness?" she asked quietly.

He turned and faced her, the ghost of a smile on his lips.

"Not really. It pointed out one thing to me. A man who plays the rake too long can wear out his welcome in Polite Society."

"Never tell me you were made to feel unwelcome," said Grace.

Alex shook his head and wagged a finger at her. "Now, now, little mother, I know you didn't enjoy London, but it is not really such a wicked place. No, no, most of the guests there were surprised to see me, but they seemed pleased too. But one or two made mention of my reputation, claiming I was no longer the sought-after bachelor I once was. It seems the matchmakers have given up on me. I am now the sort of gentleman they warn their daughters about," he added with a little laugh as he strolled back to her side and resumed his seat.

"Well, given your rakish reputation, that is understandable, Alex," said Grace. "And don't tell me you haven't earned it, because I know from personal experience . . ."

"Yes, yes, let us not bring up something best left in the past," replied Alex.

Grace grinned at her brother-in-law and said, "Very well, let us return to the marquess's gathering. What was said, precisely?"

"It was nothing, forget I mentioned it. It was just Lady Brisbane, and who knows if she even knows what she's talking about. I mean, it could just be her own ideas about who is suitable for her daughter."

"Don't tell me you have formed a tendre for Lady Brisbane's daughter."

"Devil take me, I wouldn't want to spend five minutes with that empty-headed chit," said Alex.

"Then why should it upset you so? I should think you would be happy the grasping mamas are leaving you alone. I mean, it's not as if you are in the market for another wife," she said, her green eyes lighting with laughter.

The earl turned the full force of his dark eyes on her, and her breath caught in her throat.

"Oh, dear," she breathed.

"We really should go, my sweet," said the vicar, sweeping back into the room with his sleeping daughter in his arms.

"Yes, of course. I'll be there in a moment," said Grace, rising without taking her eyes from her brother-in-law's face.

He rose and executed a courtly bow over her hand.

"It's not as grave as all that," he whispered, his smile lighting his dark eyes. "I shall come about. If there's one sure wager in life, it is that I will find a way to get what I want. Well, most things," he said, leering at his sister-in-law and linking arms to follow his brother to their carriage.

At the door, he helped Grace into her fur-lined manteau and whispered into her ear, "Except you, of course. But then, I think I came along too late. If you had only met me before Adam, I might have had a chance."

"We shall never know," she replied, grinning at him and offering her cheek for a chaste kiss.

"Do not keep her talking all night, Alex. It's cold out here," called the vicar from the carriage where he held Allie, wrapped in a heavy blanket.

Grace stood on tiptoe to whisper into the earl's ear. "Come and see me tomorrow, Alex, and we'll discuss this matter. I shall give it some thought."

Alexander Havenhurst, the Earl of Foxworth, looked into his sister-in-law's kind eyes and smiled, the cares of the world sliding from his shoulders. He nodded and helped her into the carriage, where she snuggled up to her husband and little girl.

As the carriage rolled down the drive, Alex murmured, "I knew I needed to come to Pixley for a reason. Grace won't rest until she has seen me through this impasse."

Whistling, he returned to the warmth and light of Foxworth Manor.

"There is someone I want you to meet," said Grace, pulling her brother-in-law into the snug parlor of the little vicarage.

Alex looked around him, amazed as always at the

changes his brother and bride had made to the small house. The front parlor, which was reserved for parish members, was as tiny as ever, but once past this small room, the addition to the house had truly transformed the place. The family drawing room was large and snug with two sofas and several comfortable chairs. On one side of the stone fireplace was a wooden rocking chair, a gift to Grace when his godchild had been born. He glanced through an open door into his brother's study; he waved, but Adam was too engrossed in his work to notice the visitor.

"You must forgive him, Alex. When he is working on his sermon, he doesn't know the rest of the world exists."

"That all right. I'm glad he is happy in his work here. There was a time when I thought he had made the wrong decision, joining the clergy, but time has proven me wrong."

"Time changes many things," said Grace. She paused at the doorway to the morning room, which housed a varied selection of plants. "Now, I ask only that you hear me out. I know my idea may seem a bit drastic, but . . ."

"You are making the hair stand up on the back of my neck," said the earl. "If you don't want me to run away, you had better explain yourself."

"Very well, come this way."

She led him into the morning room, to the far end, where there was a small sofa and delicate chair. They were both covered in green silk, which made them blend in with the many potted plants his botany-mad sister-in-law had positioned all over the room. Seated on one end of the sofa, her back straight, not touching the back of the upholstery, was a petite, dark-haired woman. Alex judged her to be in her late twenties, but it was difficult to tell with the morning sun shining through the windows and casting her face in shadow.

"Alex, may I present Lady Isabelle Fanshaw. Lady Isabelle, this is my brother-in-law, the Earl of Foxworth."

As he bowed over her hand, he glanced up to find lively green eyes studying him. The expression carried him back to his days in leading strings when his nanny had been angry with him over some misdeed. He smiled broadly to cover this perplexing sensation.

"How do you do, Lady Isabelle?"

"Lord Foxworth," she said, inclining her head slightly.

Alex noted that Lady Isabelle did not appear ill at ease at all, and he frowned. He preferred being the one with all the answers. He looked to his sister-in-law for an explanation.

"All in good time," she said, smiling at him while she took her seat beside the other lady and indicated that he should take the chair.

"Lady Isabelle was thinking about teaching at Dodwell's Academy," said Grace.

"Only toying with the idea, Grace. I'm afraid I don't think I would be suited to teaching all the time. I enjoy my time away from the country too much."

"Do you not enjoy young people?" he asked politely, stifling a yawn.

She turned her green-eyed gaze on him, and he felt his face grow warm. Her eyes were fringed by long black lashes, and her lips were rosy and perfectly shaped for a kiss. Her porcelain complexion turned pink as he continued to stare; finally, she dropped her gaze. Alex dragged his eyes away, giving his sister-in-law a questioning glance.

She grinned and shook her head ever so slightly.

"Lady Isabelle has made it her mission in life to help young people, Alex."

"Really? In what way, my lady?" he asked, his amusement growing. The situation was too absurd not to be amusing.

"I would not put it in those terms, but I have been pleased to help several young couples find happiness."

Alex blinked. "In what way? Are you a seer? Do you read their fortunes?"

"Certainly not," said Grace. "Lady Isabelle has chaperoned several young ladies during their Seasons, and each one under her care has made an excellent match, matches that are not just suitable but promise happiness for the couple, too."

"You're a professional matchmaker?" said Alex, rising and frowning down at both ladies. "What folderol is this, Grace? I hardly expected you to bring in some Gypsylike fortune-teller!"

"If you would only listen . . ."

"I'm sorry, Grace, but I really don't think this was a good idea. I believe I should leave," said Lady Isabelle, rising to her full height of five foot two inches and glaring up at the tall earl. "I apologize, my lord. I didn't realize you were the person Mrs. Havenhurst wanted me to help. Really, Grace, his lordship doesn't need my help. Even with his reputation, I daresay he can find someone to accept him."

"Of course I can," he snapped.

"Yes. Oh, no decent young lady will look your way, but there will be others who are willing to overlook your . . . well, behavior. Good day, my lord," she said, her head held high as she walked past him.

Alex was never one to shrink from a challenge, and that is what he read in her eyes.

"Wait," he said, laying his hand on her arm. Lady Isabelle stared at that hand until he slowly removed it. She was quite powerful, he thought, for all her diminutive size.

"Why don't you admit it? You are simply unequal to the task," he said, taunting her.

"No, my lord. I am equal to the task, but in my experience, a man of your . . . experience, shall we say, cannot or will not change. Therefore, we would both be wasting our time," she said, walking away.

"Lady Isabelle," he drawled, lingering over her title with a raised brow, one that questioned and doubted.

"Please don't go, Lady Isabelle," said Grace, glaring at the earl as she trailed after the petite brunette.

Grace returned a moment later, her eyes flashing fire and her breasts heaving indignantly.

"I never thought you would forget your manners to the point where you would insult a guest in my home, Alex!"

"And I never thought you would come up with such a daft scheme," he snapped. "How could you suppose that I would hire some charlatan to . . . to what? It's not as if I will be turned away at the door should I decide to return to Polite Society. My rank alone will carry me through, and then it is just a matter of being a pattern card of good behavior."

"Indeed? And how long before your rakish ways land you in the suds again. You forget, Alex, that I have been on the receiving end of your rakish ways. They are so deeply ingrained, you didn't even recognize a lady when you saw one. So you will understand if I take leave to doubt you can behave like a pattern card of good behavior for any length of time."

"And your Lady Isabelle, is she going to instruct me?" he snarled.

Grace took several deep breaths, staring out the window for a moment. Alex knew how her temper ruled her head, and he grinned, but he covered his amusement. Any show of pleasure in their heated exchange might cause his impulsive sister-in-law to throw him out on his ear. Being married to his steadfast brother had changed Grace to some degree, but underneath she was as forthright as ever when her patience had been tried.

"First of all, Alex, Lady Isabelle has a kind heart. If she didn't think she could help you, she would never agree to my . . . daft scheme, as you call it. Now, of course, I daresay she will never agree. I thought of her because your cousin Amelia would like to hire Lady Isabelle as a chaperone for the twins next Season in London."

"For Abigail and Amanda? What is wrong with Amelia that she cannot see to her children?" demanded Alex. Grace pursed her lips and rolled her eyes, to which Alex chuckled. "Of course, I see what you mean. Amelia will be much too fatigued to endure the rigors of a Season with her daughters."

"Exactly. And unless you want your wards to remain unwed and forever hanging on your coattails, you'll see to it that they have their Season."

"And you truly think this Lady Isabelle's chaperonage will provide the twins with a successful Season?"

"She has spent the last five years with a different girl every year, and by Season's end, they are happily betrothed."

"Hmm, I suppose it would serve to keep the peace. The twins would go mad with their indolent mother guiding them."

"And you know that without a firm hand, Abigail's tongue will land her in the briars before the post horses have cooled down," said Grace.

"There is that," said the earl. "Oh, very well, I will go and speak to the Lady Isabelle, but only about taking my wards in hand next Season. My case is very different, and I shall make it plain to her that while I appreciate her past successes, I am not in need of her services myself."

"Be polite, Alex," said Grace, rising and placing a warning hand on his sleeve.

"Of course I shall be polite," he said. "I shall be my usual charming self, and she will be eating out of my hand in no time!"

"Lord Foxworth, Mrs. Fanshaw," announced the prim butler, standing to one side so Alex could enter the bright sitting room where Lady Isabelle Fanshaw was working on her mending.

She glanced up at her visitor, but she returned to her stitching without rising.

"Good morning, my lord," she said as if they hadn't already met at the vicarage earlier that morning.

"Good morning, Lady Isabelle," replied her visitor. "I hope I am not interrupting," he said, looking pointedly at her hands, which were busily whip-stitching the hem on a petticoat.

If he hoped to embarrass her by noticing the undergarment, he was sadly out of luck. With a little laugh, Isabelle finished the knot she was tying and clipped the threads, holding up the short, serviceable garment.

"My daughter is a great tomboy. I spend hours mending the tears in her clothes. Won't you be seated, my lord?"

"I didn't realize you had a daughter," he said as he sat, carefully smoothing his coat.

"Yes, Beth is seven years old and quite a handful, but I don't know what I would do without her." said Isabelle.

"I see."

"Benton," she called, and the butler immediately appeared. "Will you bring some refreshments?"

"Very good, madam."

Isabelle returned her attention to her guest. "Was there something you wished to say to me, Lord Foxworth?"

"Yes, I wished to beg your pardon for my rude behavior at the vicarage. My sister-in-law—"

"Is a wonderful lady, but she sometimes acts before she thinks. When you arrived, she had only just presented her scheme . . ."

"Exactly what I called it," said the earl.

"Well, it is the proper word. Who would think that you need a chaperone? What I mean is, you have been on the town for years and years."

"Well, not that many," he said with a little frown.

"No, no, I don't mean you are so old, but you have no need of my tutelage in proper behavior," she said, thinking that he was a prickly as a hedgehog. "After all, you have gotten along for years in the *ton*. If your reputation is, shall we say, tarnished, then you will simply have to make a push to shine it up a bit. It shouldn't take too long, a Season or two, perhaps."

"A Season or two," he murmured. The frown, which had fled, returned again, this time deepening as the idea sunk into his head. "I am not a very patient man."

"Most men are not," said Lady Isabelle. "But when one wants something, one must follow the rules. I'm afraid you have been breaking the rules for so long, my lord, it may take some time for Society to accept you back into the fold, to believe that you have reformed."

"Reformed? But I don't wish to reform. There's nothing wrong with me the way I am. I cannot pretend to be something I'm not."

"Of course not, my lord," she said, leaning over and actually patting the back of his hand as one would a distressed child. "But really, it is a matter of learned behavior, is it not? I mean, you must simply *act* the proper gentleman until Society once again believes you *are* a proper gentleman."

Her visitor scowled at her, but Benton appeared with the tea tray, and Isabelle busied herself with pouring out, allowing him time to assimilate their conversation.

"Sugar? No? Then milk?"

"No, thank you."

"Very wise of you, I think. For me, I must have both sugar and milk. I must confess, I really do not care for tea or coffee either. I drink it only because . . . well, it is one of those things one must do in order to fit in."

He paused with his cup halfway to his lips, one brow raised. "Is that supposed to be my first lesson?"

She chuckled at this, a dainty sound, modulated in tone to please rather than pierce the ear.

"I have not said I would school you, my lord," she replied.

"And I have not asked you to do so, my lady," he returned.

"Touché," she said, sipping the bitter brew.

"I really came to see if you would agree to chaperon my two wards, Abigail and Amanda Heart. Their mother, my cousin, believes the Season would be too much for her. Personally, I think the idea of spending any length of time with her twin daughters is too much for her."

"Yes, she came to speak to me yesterday about it. I told her I would consider it."

The earl looked around the snug sitting room, his gaze coming back to rest on Isabelle—those dark, penetrating eyes raking her from head to toe. She resisted the desire to look away from his regard. Self-preservation warned her that Lord Foxworth would consider such an action coquettish, giving him the advantage in this curious exchange.

He appeared to come to a decision, for he placed his cup and saucer on the table and stood, looming over her so that she had to throw her head back to see his handsome face.

"I am not a patient man," he announced. "When I want something, I don't want to wait around for it to happen for a year or two. Therefore, I have a proposal to make."

"Then would you please resume your seat, Lord Foxworth? I find it most uncomfortable looking up in this manner." There, she thought, that should put him in his place. He laughed, and she knew immediately that there was more to this handsome lord than mere arrogance. He also possessed a sense of humor and the confidence to laugh at himself. Such a man would make a formidable foe as well as a dangerously seductive friend.

Seated again, the earl said, "I want to reestablish my reputation. I have been restless of late, and seeing my old friends who are happy in their marriage, and my brother and his wife, well, I would like to find someone to share my own life. My sons are growing up, and I don't necessarily want another family, but a wife might be just the thing."

"I see. And do you have someone in mind?"

"Not exactly, and I don't want to make a hasty choice. I want to look around first, but I think I would find it very uncomfortable to suddenly begin attending Almack's and other such stuffy gatherings next Season. Therefore, I am thinking of holding a party of sorts at my country estate."

"I see."

He frowned again and said, "You don't approve? What could be better for meeting young ladies? 'Twould be informal and relaxed, and they needn't know they are being assessed."

"How flattering," she said. "How do you plan to lure these young ladies to your house, the house of a rogue and a rake?"

He was nonplussed by this, looking so downcast that Isabelle took pity on him. She paused, shaking her head at her own gullibility. It was incredible. Without even trying, he was charming her into helping him.

"There is another way," she began, smiling when he looked up, his eyes eagerly fixed on hers. "Can you persuade your mother to issue the invitations? Perhaps you could hold the party here in Pixley since everyone knows she has taken up permanent residence at Foxworth Manor."

"What a splendid idea!" he boomed. "And since you have been in London every Season of late, you can help make out the guest list, including those young ladies who would be suitable candidates for my scheme."

"No, no, my lord. I think you must turn to others for that, to people who know you and your tastes."

"Nonsense! There is no one else. Grace is the only one who knows me and knows about my plan, and she hasn't been in London in years. No, no, you must help me."

"Must I?" she said, trying for an imperious look but losing it in a girlish giggle. His eyes locked on hers, and Isabelle knew instantly that she had made a strategic mistake, allowing her guard to drop.

"Mama! Mama!"

Saved by her daughter, she thought as Beth rushed into the room, skidding to a halt when she spied their visitor.

"Come here, Beth, and make your curtsy to Lord Foxworth," she said, holding out her hands to the little girl.

Her smile polite and formal, the child dropped into

a perfect curtsy. Rising and cocking her head to one side, she said calmly, "Is that your horse in the stable yard, my lord?"

"If you are referring to the large gray, then yes, he is mine."

"What a beauty!" she breathed, her excitement and enthusiasm overtaking her manners. "What's his name?"

"I call him Bee, short for Behemoth, because he was such a huge colt. I never thought he'd be able to get his legs working together so he could stand up."

"Can I sit on him?"

"May I," corrected her mother.

"Then may I sit on him?"

"Perhaps later, when I am finished speaking to your mother."

"Oh, thank you, my lord," said the child, sitting down by his side.

"Beth, why don't you go to the kitchen for your tea. I will send for you when Lord Foxworth is leaving."

"Yes, ma'am," she said, grinning at the earl and skipping toward the door. Here she paused and said gravely, "You won't forget, will you?"

"My word of honor," replied the earl solemnly.

Another impish grin, and she was gone, leaving them alone again. Isabelle judged that the time had come to take matters in hand. She opened her mouth to speak, but her visitor beat her to it, his tone and attitude very much that of a man out to hire a new servant.

"Now, before we settle on an arrangement, there are a few things I must know about you, Lady Isabelle."

"Very well," she said, bracing herself.

"You call yourself Lady Isabelle, but your butler called you Mrs. Fanshaw. Why is that?"

"You are very observant, my lord. My servants have been with me forever. When my husband was alive, I used only Mrs. Fanshaw. I saw no reason to throw it in his face that my family was titled and his was not."

"And your family name?"

"Oh, the title is legitimate, Lord Foxworth, but I prefer to keep that to myself, if you don't mind. It is known by some people; that is why I am never questioned about it in London, and resuming it has smoothed my way as a chaperone. But, since my family did not approve of my marriage, and out of respect to my late husband, I choose not to use my family connections, nor do I associate with them."

"So you have no family?"

"None, except Beth."

"Very well, my lady. I will respect your wishes and not pry into your family history. I have only one other question. You appear to be quite comfortable here. Why go to the trouble of hiring out as a chaperone to the spoiled darlings of the *ton?*"

She bristled at his choice of words. The girls she chose to chaperone were hardly spoiled darlings. Two of them had been motherless, and the others had had mothers who were either too scatterbrained to be effective or too wrapped up in their own lives. But each girl had touched her heart in some way.

Isabelle took a deep breath. She could not tell this arrogant man such things. He would only laugh over her sentimentality or disbelieve her motives. So she decided to give him the one reason she thought he would believe.

"My daughter is seven years old. Before I know it, she will be ready for her own Season. If I remained here, buried in the country year after year, how many invitations would she receive when I took her to London for her own presentation? So you see, my reason is really quite selfish."

"I don't call it selfish to do what is best for your

daughter, Lady Isabelle. That is called being a good mother. Now, enough of my inquisition," he said, smiling when she heaved a sigh of relief. "Let us set a time when we can meet and discuss the guest list. And a ball. I want to give a great ball on Christmas Eve. My mother always used to do that at Foxworth Court. Who knows, perhaps I shall have an announcement to make by then."

"You are getting ahead of yourself, my lord. First you must learn how to court young ladies."

"Believe me, Lady Isabelle, if there is one thing I know how to do, it is how to court a lady."

"Just as there are differences between a lady and a lightskirt, my lord, there are also many differences between seduction and courtship."

He was clearly shocked by her candor, and Isabelle congratulated herself for making him think. Then he leered at her, and bells of warning began clanging in her ears.

Leaning forward, he possessed himself of her hand, holding it firmly but gently, and stroking her wrist with his thumb.

"Will you school me on the differences, my lady?" he said, his deep voice as soft as velvet, while his gaze penetrated her eyes, looking into her soul. She was paralyzed by those eyes, unable to look away. Then he laughed.

Jerking her hand away, Isabelle said, "I see plainly that you have the seduction part perfected, my lord, but that can hardly help you win a wife! Now, if you will excuse me?"

"Of course, my lady," he said, still chuckling as he rose and sauntered toward the door.

Isabelle had to force herself to look away from those broad shoulders, the trim waist, but when she looked back, he had turned to laugh at her again. He had known she couldn't resist watching him. The coxcomb!

"Was there anything else, my lord?"

"Two things. Which way is the kitchen?" When she frowned, he explained, "So I can fulfill my promise to your daughter."

"Benton will show you," she replied, happy the conversation had returned to a more sensible realm. "And the other thing, my lord?"

"Only this. Courtship is all well and good, my lady, but do not discount the effectiveness of seduction."

With this, he departed, leaving Isabelle to fume and fan herself with the next garment in her mending basket, a worn corset.

"The rake," she whispered, mopping her forehead with the satin-covered unmentionable. Suddenly she realized what she was holding and whipped it behind her back, her eyes flying to the doorway, certain the rogue had returned to find her fondling the delicate undergarment.

What was she thinking, agreeing to such an outrageous scheme? She should tell him she had changed her mind.

Isabelle rose halfway out of her chair, only to sink back down, a slight smile curving her lips. With a sigh, she picked up the corset and her needle and thread.

At least it would not be a dull Christmas!

Three

Riding home from the meeting with Lady Isabelle, Alex Havenhurst decided the country air had made him go mad. What else could explain taking a perfect stranger into his most personal confidence and deciding to throw a house party where he would undoubtedly be bored to death by mindless chits on the lookout for a wealthy, titled husband—namely him?

Foxworth Manor came into view, and Alex groaned. His mother would call her favorite physician to have him committed to Bedlam. As for her arranging the party, such an idea was ludicrous. She had spent too many years arranging her life to suit herself perfectly. She would be livid at having her household turned upside down.

"Courage, man," he muttered, earning a quizzical glance from the groom who ambled across the yard to take charge of Bee.

After dismounting, he stood watching as the groom, a man of some years, began to walk the big gelding up and down.

Alex stopped him after a moment and asked, "How many of you are here?"

"Here, m'lord?"

"Yes, how many people work here in the stables, looking after the horses and carriages?"

"Well, there's me, I'm Todd, and then there's Mr.

James, he's milady's coachman, and young Harry. He comes in from the village to polish the harnesses and clean the leather."

"That's it? How do you manage?"

"We don't mind a bit o' hard work, m'lord, an' th' stable is warm and dry in th' winter. Now, o' course, we've got your groom too."

"Speaking of Bottles, where is the man? He should be the one walking Bee."

"As to that, m'lord, I couldn't say," stammered the groom, his eyes shifting this way and that.

Alex frowned and started for the stable. Hearing a feminine squeal, he increased his pace and arrived in time to see his groom throw himself down on a laughing maid.

"Bottles, what is the meaning of this?"

Groom and maid scrambled to their feet, the maid tugging at her bodice to put her breasts back inside. Bottles, too, was using his hands for cover.

"I shall speak to you later. Go back to your duties in the house," said the earl.

The maid scurried away, leaving the groom to face his master alone.

"I'm sorry, m'lord. I didn't know you'd be returning so soon. We were just having a bit o' fun."

"Fun that takes her away from her work and leaves Todd to look after my horse. What do I pay you for?"

"I know, m'lord. It won't happen again."

"I should hope not. Besides, you do know who that was you were giving a tumble in the hay, don't you?"

"Her name is Penny, sir, and she's one o' the maids. That's all I know."

"Do you know that she doesn't live in because she goes home every night to the family farm to cook for her three brothers—her three very large brothers?" added Alex, relishing the way his groom's face paled.

"I . . . I didn't know."

"Well, unless you wish to find yourself saddled with a wife and three brothers-in-law, you'd best control yourself."

"Yes, m'lord!" came the fervent reply.

Alex turned on his heel and walked to the small set of rooms attached to the stables where his mother's old coachman lived. His knock was followed by an invitation to enter. Seeing his master in his parlor, the coachman made haste to clear off a spot for him to sit down.

Alex said, "No, don't worry, James. I'm not staying. It's just that I wanted you to know that I am going to host a party here at the Manor soon, and we'll need more room for grooms and such."

"That shouldn't be a problem, my lord. We'll just open up the old stone stable on the other end of the stable yard. It's been shut up for years, but I have made sure it's kept in good repair."

"How many horses and grooms can it house?"

"Oh, as many as a houseful of guests can bring, never you fear. When your father was alive, he and his friends would arrive with three or four hunters each, and there was always enough room."

"Very well, then I want you to hire some men locally to set everything to rights. Can you do that?"

"With pleasure, my lord. It'll be good to have the old place buzzing again."

"Thank you, James. If you need anything, let me know. When it's all ready, we'll send for some of the grooms from the Court."

"Very good, my lord."

Alex next stopped in the kitchens, where he found the three rulers of the household enjoying a cup of tea. The cook, the butler, and the housekeeper leapt to their feet when he entered, but he bade them sit down again as he pulled up another chair.

"I am glad to find you all together. I wanted to speak to you before I told my mother about my plans for the coming Christmas season. I know that you, Mrs. Teasley, will be glad to hear my proposal, because it will mean your sister will be coming to stay here at the Manor."

"That is welcome news, my lord. But what is the occasion?"

"I am going to hold a house party." At their collective gasp, which might have been anticipation or dread, Alex held up his hand for silence. "I know it will mean a great deal of work, and that is why I wish to bring my other staff to the Manor for the holidays. I have sent them on to Foxworth Court, but I will write to them today and tell them that they are to report here as soon as they can, to help ready the house and grounds, and to help serve once the guests arrive. What do you think?"

"Will all of them come?" asked Finley, his mother's youngish butler.

Alex knew immediately what he meant, and he said quickly, "No, not all of them. My butler, for instance, is too old for the rigors of a house party. Besides, his daughter lives near Foxworth Court and is expecting him for Christmas. My cook, too, has family there, though she'll send some of her helpers, who will report to you. The maids who come with your sister, Mrs. Pratt, will take their orders from you, Mrs. Teasley. You can work with your sister, can you not?"

"Of course, my lord. How wonderful to be together again," said the housekeeper.

"Good, and you, Finley, will be in charge of the footmen."

"Very good, my lord. I look forward to the challenge."

"Thank you. I will send for them today, and they should be arriving by the end of the week. I will contact the local shops to let them know that they should stock up for the coming holidays, and I shall tell them to let you have anything you need," said the earl, rising from the table.

The three servants also stood, waiting in silence until he had gone. Alex paused outside the kitchen door, grinning when they burst into animated conversation. He listened only long enough to make certain they were pleased at the prospect of the house party. Good, he thought. Now all he had to do was tell his mother.

The Dowager Countess of Foxworth was reclining on the satin striped sofa in her boudoir when he knocked on the door. She extended her hand for him to kiss and nodded to a spindly chair close to her feet.

Her nose wrinkled slightly, and she said, "Really, Alex, do you not know better than to enter a lady's chamber while reeking of the stable?"

"I didn't realize I reeked, Mother. Would you like me to go and change instead of staying and telling you my news?"

She heaved a sigh and shook her head, saying, "No, you might as well tell me while you are here."

"Good. I have decided to hold a house party for Christmas."

"Well, I shall attend if I am able to stand the strain, but I make no promises, my dear."

"I do hope you can stand the strain, Mother, since the party is going to be here at Foxworth Manor."

"Here!" she exclaimed, sitting bolt upright, her eyes flashing and all former signs of frailty gone. "You cannot possibly hold a house party here, Alexander! We have neither the room nor the staff for such an undertaking."

"As to that, I have already arranged for both staff and room, at least where the stables are concerned."

"But the people. Where are we to put all the guests and their servants?"

"Mother, this house has at least twenty bedchambers and an entire floor of rooms for servants. We can certainly accommodate twenty guests. If there are more, they can stay at the vicarage."

"At the vicarage? And put Grace out for your guests? I think not. No, we will manage. But please, Alex, do not invite any . . . well, undesirable types."

Alex grinned and crossed his heart. "I promise there will not be a lightskirt in the bunch, my lady."

"Only see how you speak to me," she moaned, falling back against the arm of the sofa and groping for her vinaigrette.

"I am sorry, Mother. And I promise the guest list shall meet with your approval." He rose and kissed her hand before strolling to the door. There, she asked the question he had been avoiding.

"What has made you decide to hold a house party, Alex?"

"Oh, just a whim, Mother. I thought it might be amusing. Now I have to go and write to Mrs. Pratt and to the boys. They'll be delighted to be spending Christmas here, near their uncle Adam and aunt Grace."

"And their grandmother," she said.

"Of course, and their grandmother."

Alex spent the remainder of the afternoon combing his memory for people suitable to invite to his house party. For the most part, his usual companions were too fast for such a party, nor were they likely to accept an invitation to such a tame diversion. What's more, his mother would certainly balk at the idea of putting her name on an invitation addressed to Lady Maria Phelpps or jolly Andy Remington.

There would be Thomas and Amy, and her youngest sister, the intriguing Lady Sophia. He needn't worry about the widowed Lady Anne, since she would still be at home with that new baby. As for the Duchess of Charlton, he penciled her in. At the Dunhams' card party, he had thoroughly enjoyed partnering the old dame at cards and had been greatly diverted by her acerbic tongue.

Beyond these, he considered Lady Brisbane and her daughter. It might be amusing to see if they would come. Lady Brisbane was one of the biggest gossips of the *ton*, and if she declared to the world that the Earl of Foxworth had reformed, then he could be certain the invitations would roll in next spring when the Season got under way. If he invited her, however, it meant inviting Colonel Sutter too. He was a stuffy bore, but he enjoyed fox hunting and might relish the chance to visit Leicestershire, which was known for its excellent hunting. He felt certain Squire Lambert would lend his pack of dogs for the thing.

Alex grimaced, the thought of hunting sitting poorly with him. He enjoyed riding, certainly, but he couldn't care less about doing it, helter-skelter, across the countryside, jumping every sort of barrier and endangering a piece of prime horseflesh. No, he would leave the hunt to the squire and the colonel. They could organize it if they wished.

"Why on earth would you wish to include the Duchess of Charlton?" asked Lady Foxworth, her nose sadly out of joint as she peered over his shoulder, studying her son's proposed guest list.

"Perhaps because she is witty and entertaining, Mother?"

"Not the last time I spoke to her. She had the audacity to criticize my hat."

"Which hat was that, Mother?" he asked, pretending a great interest.

"As if I can recall," she said, sailing around him and flouncing into the chair opposite his. "I believe it was the one the divine Longuement created for me. The one with the purple birds and ostrich plumes."

"Oh, that hat," said Alex, making a face.

"Wretched boy." She pouted for a moment, then asked, "Will you be including Adam and Grace?"

"They will be invited to every event, of course, but I daresay they will prefer to remain at home with little Alexandra. I was even thinking of asking if Phillip and Robert might stay with them. I think the boys would be happier there than with a houseful of strangers."

"You are probably right. Who else is on the list?"

"Cousin Amelia and the twins."

"Unavoidable, I suppose. After all, the girls will be coming out in the spring. This will give them a chance to practice their manners."

"Precisely what I thought. And then there is Lady Isabelle and her daughter, Beth."

"Lady Isabelle? I'm not acquainted with her. Who is her family?"

"As to that, I'm not certain," said Alex, debating on what story he should tell his mother. A half-truth, he decided, was the safest bet. "She is going to help Amelia chaperon the girls during the spring Season."

"Why? Is she some poor relation to Amelia's late husband?"

"No, I don't think so. It is just something she does in order to enjoy the Season more."

His mother's eyes narrowed. Alex could feel the

beads of perspiration popping out on his forehead as he strived for a blasé expression.

"She isn't one of your doxies, is she? Or is it her daughter? I'll not have them in my house if she is."

"Really, Mother?" he drawled. "In *your* house?"

She stiffened at his tone and said tightly, "Very well, if you are going to be odious about it. It is your house, but I will certainly refuse to have my name on the invitation if it is going to be one of your—"

"Oh, for heaven's sake, Mother, Lady Isabelle is as innocuous a female as you could ever meet. Her daughter is seven or eight years old. She is a great friend of Grace's, who introduced her to Amelia. I have met her only once," he lied.

"One of Grace's friends, you say?"

"That's right," he replied, watching the emotions warring on his mother's face. She still didn't quite approve of Grace, who had been teaching in her uncle's school until she wed Adam. The countess felt Grace was not good enough for her favorite son, but she had given her Allie, a fact that had earned Grace a new place of honor, to the doting grandmother's way of thinking.

"Very well," she said finally. "If you say she is Grace's friend, then I shan't question including her on the guest list."

"Thank you, Mother. And her daughter is about the same age as Lord and Lady Dunham's girls. They should get along famously."

"As to that, the children can stay in the nursery with their nannies and leave the rest of us in peace." A moment passed while the dowager countess searched for another complaint.

"Have you written to Mrs. Pratt at the Court?"

"Already posted and on its way, Mother. Was there anything else?" he asked.

"No, no, only do ask Grace to come over when it is time to write the invitations. I find handwritten ones so much more elegant than engraved, and Grace writes a pretty letter."

"I shall ride over there after dinner tonight."

"Thank you, dear. Now I must lie down. All this chatting has quite worn me down."

"Rest well, Mother," said the earl, returning to his list.

He read it over again and frowned. It seemed rather lopsided. Rising, he called for his horse to be saddled again. If Lady Isabelle was going to work for him, she might as well begin.

The ride to the neighboring village of Spursden took longer than Alex had thought it would after he stopped in Pixley to speak to the shopkeepers. Mr. and Mrs. Crane were the main merchants he needed to speak to, but he also felt it incumbent upon him to warn Mr. Gray, the blacksmith, and Miss Silverton, whose tiny shop was filled with luxuries like French soap and Irish linens. The servants might have reason to make purchases for the coming gathering at any one of these establishments.

By the time he had listened to all the latest gossip, for such was the true trade of Pixley's shops, the sun was beginning its descent toward the horizon. Frustrated, Alex turned his horse back toward Foxworth Manor. He certainly didn't want Lady Isabelle to think he had forgotten his manners so, that he would arrive at dinnertime!

"Why are we going to stay with that man, Mama?" asked the blue-eyed child, gazing at her mother from her little bed.

"We have been invited to a house party for Christmas, my love. You will stay in the nursery with the other children, and there will be all sorts of entertainments to amuse you."

"But I would rather stay with you, Mama."

"And so you shall. I will be staying at the Manor too. And you needn't worry that I shall abandon you. I'll come up every morning, and we'll spend time together."

"But it won't be the same as here, where it is just the two of us," said Beth, looking decidedly downcast.

"But, Beth, you must learn to make friends with other children, children from the best families. It won't be so many years until you are making your come-out, and you will be glad to have met some of the other young people when you get to London."

"If you say so, Mama. But we will come home for Boxing Day, won't we? We have to cook dinner for everyone, and I have something very special to give you."

"Have you now? And I have something for you too, but I warn you, you'll not coax so much as a hint out of me, little minx. And don't worry, we'll come home on Christmas Day. Now, close your eyes and go to sleep, my sweet. It's getting late, and you still have school tomorrow. Good night." She leaned over and kissed her daughter's smooth cheek.

"Good night, Mama."

Isabelle blew her a kiss at the door and then had to catch the one Beth sent her way. Smiling, she made her way downstairs to her own room, where the maid had lit the fire. Removing her gown, she slipped into a soft wool wrapper and sat down in the chair beside the fireplace. She picked up the book on the table, opening it, and then ignoring it as she lost herself in reverie.

What had she gotten herself into? she wondered. Accepting such a position! Tutoring a rogue like Lord

Foxworth! What was she thinking to have agreed to such a ludicrous scheme?

She should have put him off, told him she would have to think about it for a few days. But he had been so persuasive.

Isabelle frowned, biting at that lower lip as she always did when she wrestled with a problem. The truth of the matter was, it had not been his words that were so persuasive. Instead, it had been his handsome face. The confession brought a red stain to her cheeks.

She was not usually so foolish! How could she have let herself be taken in by the practiced charm and good looks of a known rake? She was not some green girl. She knew what two and two made.

Five? she thought, the idea making her giggle. Yes, the earl, his two sons, her, and Beth. That would make a family of five. What a preposterous notion! The thought made her laugh out loud, the sound too raucous to be coming from her own lips.

Isabelle rose and went to the dressing table, studying her image in the glass. She was not a green girl, that much was evident, but she would have to be very careful around the Earl of Foxworth. He was just the sort of man who would take advantage of a poor widow.

And just the sort a poor widow wanted to have take advantage of her!

"I don't see why I should include Miles Parker or the Forbes-Smyths. Parker is a bachelor himself, and the Forbes-Smyths have only sons."

"Remember our ruse," said Lady Isabelle patiently, glancing up from the list to watch the pacing earl over her spectacles. "And please, Lord Foxworth, do sit down before you wear out my carpets completely."

"Oh, very well. We will include Parker, whose reputation as a rake is almost as bad as mine, you know."

"Yes, we will use him as a contrast to you and your reformed character," she said, bowing her head and biting her lower lip to contain her laughter.

"I think you are enjoying this, Lady Isabelle," said the earl, scooting closer to her on the sofa and leaning down so that he could look up at her face.

It was too much for her, and she burst out laughing. He tried to muster up some indignation, but the sound was contagious, and he joined in. Their hilarity soon had Benton on his feet and peeking into the drawing room with raised brows. Swallowing their laughter, Isabelle and Alex sat up straight, sobering until they glanced at each other and fell into whoops all over again. Shaking his head, the prim butler disappeared.

"We have shocked Benton once again," whispered the earl.

"Oh, dear," she managed to get out before a fresh fit of the giggles overtook her.

She lifted her face and found he was just inches away from her, just inches away from her lips. She sobered instantly and pushed her spectacles back on her nose.

"Now we have enough gentlemen to balance the ladies," she said, her manner suddenly businesslike. He took his cue from her and settled back against the sofa, his demeanor casual. Isabelle ignored him and said, "Look over the list again and make certain every person has at least one other person they know well."

"Yes, they all know each other."

"Anyone else you wish to add?" asked Isabelle.

"All except this one," he said, taking the tablet from her, his hand covering hers in the process.

The touch didn't appear to effect the earl in the least, thought Isabelle, watching as he wrote down another name. She shook off the shiver of pleasure as she looked at the name.

"I left the duchess off because I am not at all certain she will come. Her granddaughter has just given birth and will be unable to travel, so I think the duchess will probably spend Christmas with her."

"Duchess?" said Lady Isabelle, her fingers trembling as she took the list back from him.

"Yes, the Duchess of Charlton. She's a regular old tartar, but I enjoy her company. Besides which, she will keep my mother in line," he added with a chuckle.

"I should think so," murmured Isabelle.

"What's wrong? Do you not care for the duchess?"

"No, it's not that. I have not met her, really. Not in many years."

"Well, neither had I, but I played cards with her two weeks ago, and I must admit, her observations tickled me. I think she'll be just the one to add a touch of spice to what might turn into a dull gathering."

"A dull gathering?" commented Isabelle, frowning at him. "You have some of England's finest families represented on this list, my lord."

"Breeding does not always equate with interesting," he said, his dark eyes raking her audaciously. "Well, one type of breeding may . . ."

Looking over her spectacles at him, Lady Isabelle said primly, "That is exactly the sort of conversation you must avoid, my lord, if you are going to mend your tarnished reputation."

"But I'm not hosting the house party yet," he replied, his manner as impudent as ever.

"No, but unless we practice avoiding those old habits, they will pop out at the most inappropriate times."

"Is that so, my lady? And what bad habits of yours pop out at the most inappropriate times?" he murmured, his eyes coming to rest on her lips.

Smiling sweetly, she batted her eyes. "My bad habit is that I am able to resist tired and tawdry rogues without the least effort. And another is that I speak my mind no matter what. And I must tell you, my lord, I find your manners tiresome and offensive."

The earl sat back again, flicking a piece of lint off his coat without the least appearance of interest in her words. He favored her with a polite, detached smile.

"That's better. Now, perhaps we should discuss what is polite and what is not polite when conversing with a young, gently reared lady. I fear you have little experience with them."

"I fear I am about to gain that experience, and I hope I shan't perish from boredom."

With an unladylike snort, Lady Isabelle rounded on him. "The first thing you must do, my lord, is decide what you want. Do you want to go shopping for a wife in the brothel or in the drawing room?"

"You know the answer to that. If I didn't want a proper wife, I wouldn't be planning this blasted party, would I?"

She pursed her lips and narrowed her eyes, spearing him with her gaze until she was satisfied. Then she picked up the paper and studied it again.

"Just for your information though," said the earl while gazing at the ceiling, "the nicer brothels usually have drawing rooms too."

Slowly, she turned to look at him, shaking her head in mock annoyance. Wide-eyed, he returned her stare.

"Well, they do," he said, grinning at her now.

Isabelle Fanshaw thought she was past being captivated by a man, but she was wrong. Her shoulders shaking, she burst out laughing again until she was leaning against him, weak and winded.

"You are a rogue," she managed to say, gazing up at him fondly. She glanced away under his warm regard, her manner severe again. "You know such an exchange will never do when your guests arrive, don't you?"

"Yes, Lady Schoolmistress, I am aware of that. I will behave when I must, but sometimes, when it is just you and I, I may have to let my hair down. Surely there is no harm in that."

"But it is that sort of habit you must break, my lord."

"Very well, Isabelle," he said, taking her hand and holding it against his heart. "I swear I will try to keep my conversation forever commonplace and proper if you will allow me one boon."

Extracting her hand, she asked, "What is that?"

"That you will call me Alex . . ." He captured her hand again and continued doggedly. "And you will allow me to call you Isabelle whenever we are in private."

"Well, I suppose that will be all right. But only when we are in private."

He lifted her hand to his lips, turning it over and giving her palm a butterfly kiss before releasing it.

"Done!" he said, leaning back on the sofa and raising his arms, lacing his hands behind his head.

"A gentleman would never sit like that in the presence of a lady," she said, very properly keeping her gaze on the paper in her lap.

"Ah, but an Alex would sit this way in the presence of his Isabelle," he replied, smiling sweetly at her.

"Rogue," she said.

"Shrew," he replied, throwing her a kiss just like her daughter always did before going to bed.

Without thinking, Isabelle caught it, the deed causing the earl's mouth to drop open. Embarrassed, Isabelle called her butler into the room and ordered refreshments.

When the butler had gone, he said, "You are full of

surprises, aren't you?" He chuckled as she turned a warm shade of pink. "You know, Isabelle—"

"Mama! Mama!" called Beth, coming to a halt and continuing into the room more sedately. "I didn't know you were here, my lord. Did you ride over on Bee today?"

"Yes, I did, and later, when you have had some tea with us, I will take you out and let you ride him again," said the earl.

"Oh, thank you, my lord," said the child, bouncing up and down on her chair.

"It is very good of you, my lord. Thank you," said her mother.

"No, my lady. I thank you," said Alex, winking at her.

Isabelle ignored him completely and turned to her daughter, asking her about her day at school.

"It was so funny, Mama. We were learning to do the backstroke at one end of the pool while the older girls were at the other end, playing about. All of a sudden we heard one of them screaming at the top of her lungs."

"Oh, dear. No one drowned, did they?" asked her anxious mother.

The girl giggled. "Oh, no, it was nothing like that. It seems Abigail Heart was angry over something her sister said, and she pushed her in and held her under for the longest time. When she finally let Amanda up, Amanda punched Abigail in the eye!"

"How awful! Beth, you should not be laughing at the misfortunes of others," chided her mother.

Benton entered with the tea tray, placing it on the table. Taking a napkin, he tucked it into the neckline of Beth's round gown.

"I asked Cook to put some of her apricot tarts on the tray, miss," said the old butler.

"Oh, thank you, Benton. That was very kind of you,"

said the little girl, her tone and manner quite grown-up.

When the butler had left, and they had all been served, the earl asked, "Tell me, how does Abigail's eye look?"

"It's all swollen and black and blue. One of the girls said she wished Amanda had held Abigail under until—"

"Beth, please," said Isabelle. "This is hardly a suitable topic for the drawing room, my lord. Please do not encourage the child."

"Oh, sorry," he said, winking at the little girl. After a moment, he added, "I understand Abigail can be a bit irksome."

"How do you know, my lord?" asked Beth.

"They are my wards. I am related to them as some sort of distant cousin. As a matter of fact, they are one of the reasons I am giving this party, but I begin to think I have misjudged that part of the scheme," said the earl, looking at Isabelle.

"I wouldn't hold it against them," she said. "Here they are, almost out of the schoolroom. I'm sure they are just suffering from an overabundance of nerves."

Beth looked from one adult to the other and then shrugged her shoulders.

"I suppose. Besides, it is good to know that Amanda is not the doormat I had supposed. I'm glad to know she'll stand up for herself."

"Oh, she stood up for herself. After she hit Abigail, Amanda grabbed Abigail's bathing costume and tore it half off her."

"Really, Beth! That is quite enough about the incident. Please wipe your mouth and excuse yourself. Go upstairs and wash your face. When you come back down, perhaps Lord Foxworth will be ready to take you outside to ride his horse."

"Yes, Mama," said the girl, doing as she was instructed.

"Sometimes I think she is entirely too observant," said Isabelle.

"She is delightful, and such a little beauty. A carbon copy of you, I might add."

She opened her mouth to protest, but the compliment to both herself and her daughter had been so prettily said, she didn't wish to belittle it . . . or the man who offered it.

"Thank you, my lord."

He made a point of looking around the room before saying softly, "Alex. Remember your promise."

"I remember, Alex."

"So we have finished the guest list. Foxworth Manor hasn't seen this sort of gathering since my father's day. Every bedchamber will be filled."

"And the nursery will be too."

Alex counted the infant brigade on his hand and shook his head. "There are only three girls by my calculations."

"And your boys, though you may deem them too old for the nursery."

"I have decided they will stay with my brother at the vicarage. They'll be happier there."

Lady Isabelle worried her lower lip, a sure sign something was bothering her.

"What is it? You may speak your mind, Isabelle."

"It is none of my affair, my lord . . ."

"Alex."

"Very well, it is none of my affair, Alex, but would you not enjoy Christmas more with your sons by your side? I know many members of the *ton* have little or nothing to do with their children, but somehow, I envisioned you taking your sons riding, showing them how to shoot, and so on. It will be rather difficult when they are staying elsewhere."

"I'm afraid I'm not that sort of father at all, Isabelle," he said. "I hope you'll not think less of me. The way you are with your daughter, how close the two of you are, that is an unusual situation among our class. Admirable, to be sure, but most of us are content to leave the rearing of our children to the tutors and governesses. I daresay my boys would find it odd if I did take them out riding."

"You do not have to explain yourself to me, Alex. I shouldn't have said anything."

He took her hand and gave it a squeeze, the gesture not the least loverlike.

"You may say anything you wish to me, my dear. I promise."

She swallowed hard, his tone and touch affecting her more than she cared to admit. She gave him a little smile, and he released her hand.

The awkwardness past, Alex said, "Let me see if I have everything. I will take this guest list back to my mother. She and Grace will write the invitations tomorrow, and I will put them in the post the next day. While we are waiting for the guests to arrive, you can help me settle on the proper entertainments for my guests."

"And help you practice being a proper sort of gentleman."

"A dull stick," he said in her ear as he rose. Then to Beth, who had suddenly appeared at his side again, he said, "You're a quick study, Beth. Come along. Bee has been wondering where his carrots are."

"I already fetched some from the larder. Cook doesn't mind."

"Good girl," he said, turning and smiling at Isabelle

before he took Beth's hand and followed her out the door.

Isabelle replaced the cups on the tray and retrieved a bit of pastry from the floor. She reached for her book, but stopped, a smile lighting her eyes as she thought about how easily Beth's tiny hand fit into the earl's large one.

Her breath caught in her throat, and she touched her cheek, wondering if the shiver running up her spine might be caused by a bit of the ague. Her skin was cool to the touch. It was not a fever, but something else, something she didn't wish to question. Not yet.

Isabelle rose, crossed the room, and strolled down the hallway to the dining room, which overlooked the gardens, and beyond that, the stable yard. She could see them in the distance. The earl, Alex, was lifting Beth onto the big horse's broad back. The little girl's eyes were shining; she could tell even from a distance. Beth was chattering about something while Alex looked up at her, listening attentively. He laughed and patted her leg. He nodded to the groom who stood at the giant's head, and they started off. With the groom leading, the horse moved slowly around the yard while Alex walked alongside, and Beth on top, happily chatting to the rake—her rake.

Isabelle dashed aside a tear and turned away from the idyllic picture outside. She was being foolish beyond permission. It was understandable, of course. Alex was the first man to pay her any sort of attention in six years. There had been that farmer, of course, but she had never taken his courtship seriously.

Courtship? Isabelle shook her head. The Earl of Foxworth didn't know what a courtship was. If he had any designs on her, they were meant for seduction, pure and simple.

She might enjoy his attentions for a while, but she

wasn't suited to such a role. She had guarded her own reputation too carefully to destroy it now. She had Beth to consider. All her sacrifices would be worth it then. With the money she had set aside, Beth would have the chance of a happy marriage with the man of her choice.

Yes, that thought helped her see the earl more clearly. She would have to keep her attention placed squarely on the future, Beth's future. That was the only way she would be able to manage the next few weeks.

It shouldn't prove too difficult. Alex was only a man after all was said and done.

But her eyes strayed to the window again. Alex was playing hopscotch with Beth, teetering precariously on one foot as he tried to make it from one end to the other without falling. Beth stood to one side, cheering him on.

Isabelle felt her heart swell with a long-forgotten feeling. It was as if the tiny spark that remained of her love for her husband had burst into flame anew.

"You're too old for such nonsense. It is mere infatuation," she whispered.

But as she watched, Alex lost his balance and pitched forward, disappearing from view while Beth rushed to his side. Isabelle held her breath, waiting for him to rise. He did so, but was feigning injury and leaning heavily on the little girl. Beth stumbled and down they both went, coming up a moment later, laughing uproariously. Unless she was very careful, thought Isabelle, that flame would burst into a wildfire.

Four

"Thank heavens we are here!" announced Lady Amelia, collapsing onto the nearest sofa as if she had traveled across the country instead of five miles.

"Whatever is the matter, my dear?" asked the dowager countess, lifting her silver lorgnette and staring down her nose at her cousin.

"No, no, I promised myself I would not complain," said Amelia, following this pronouncement with a loud sigh. "Where are you, girls? Come and make your curtsies to your cousin, Lady Foxworth."

The twins came forward obediently, sinking into perfect curtsies and replying to the countess's greeting with their best manners.

"How delightful," said Lady Foxworth, smiling on the identical twins. "Do you always dress in the same styles?"

"No, but I ordered a number of gowns for them like that. Abigail will always be the one in blue and Amanda the one in pink," said their mother. "It makes it so much easier to tell them apart."

"How clever of you," said the countess.

"Now, do go and find something to occupy yourselves, girls. Lady Foxworth and I wish to have a comfortable coze and cannot do so with you around."

The twins made good their escape, walking sedately

from the room before capering up the stairs to their shared quarters to change.

"I hate pink," said Amanda, the quieter of the two girls.

"And this blue accentuates my black eye," said Abigail, glaring at her sister. She flopped onto the bed beside her sister, staring at the ceiling.

Amanda giggled, but she reassured her twin, saying, "It is hardly noticeable anymore with that powder Mama put on it."

Abigail turned on her side, propping her head on her hand so she could look at her sister. "I was afraid Lady Foxworth was going to say something. She has a way of staring that gives me the shivers."

"I know what you mean. Do you suppose we will ever be that old and proper?"

"You may," said Abigail, "but I have no intention of becoming that sort of ogress."

Amanda expelled a little sigh. "I wonder when we will see Lord Foxworth."

"I should think he will have to put in an appearance at dinner. I mean, he cannot go about wenching all day and all night."

"Abigail!"

"Well, the man will have to stop and eat sometime."

"Surely he is not out . . . having his way with women at this hour. And not in the same house with his mother!" breathed the scandalized girl. Neither one was certain what a rake did with women, but they knew it was wicked.

Abigail tossed her head, sending her dark curls bobbing. "I daresay a rake like our guardian might do any number of shocking things."

"And this is a prime example of why young ladies should not gossip."

The twins bounced off the bed and whirled to face Lady Isabelle.

She smiled at them and said, "Of course, a lady also should not eavesdrop on others." Extending her hand, she walked forward and shook theirs. The twins didn't speak, but continued to watch her with suspicion written plainly on their faces.

"I am Lady Isabelle. I believe your mother has told you about me?"

Amanda recovered first and curtsied. "How do you do, my lady?"

"Very well, thank you. And you are?"

"I am Amanda. This is Abigail," she added, prodding her sister with an elbow. Abigail thrust her chin out stubbornly and refused to engage in the polite rhetoric.

Isabelle dropped her hand and smiled again.

"Your mother told me where I might find you. My room is to be right next door. Actually, that door connects to my sitting room."

"So you have been relegated to the same wing as the young people," said Abigail, favoring Lady Isabelle with a superior smile.

Isabelle's laugh caught her off guard. "I would not put it that way, my dear. I asked to be placed next to you so that we could become better acquainted. We will be spending a great deal of time together in London. Your mother has asked me to take you the last week of February to begin having your gowns made for the Season."

"Really?" asked Amanda, completely won over.

Abigail, however, was more skeptical. "That is only because Mama doesn't wish to be burdened with us. That is why we have to have a hired chaperone."

The words were a slap in the face, and all three occupants of the room knew it. Isabelle realized that her reaction to it would set the tone for the Season to come.

"Mama, did you see the size of your bed? And it's so soft!"

Isabelle's attention wavered, but she continued to stare at Abigail, waiting for the spoiled girl's next assault. It came, but was directed at Beth, who bounded through the door. The little girl glanced from the twins, whom she knew from school, to her mother.

"Mama?" she whispered.

"Pray do not tell us we must endure having a baby in the room next to ours."

"I am not a baby, Abigail Heart!"

"Beth, please go into my sitting room and close the door."

She disappeared through the connecting door just as someone knocked on the door to the hallway.

It opened just a crack, and a deep voice called, "Amanda, Abigail, are you in there?"

"Yes, Cousin Foxworth."

The door opened farther, and Alex stepped inside, his smile frozen as he regarded the tense tableau before him.

"Am I interrupting?"

"No," said Abigail.

"Yes," replied Lady Isabelle.

Alex hesitated. Some disputes were best left to the opponents, but he felt responsible for getting Isabelle into this mess, and he didn't wish to abandon her to the twin demons.

Crossing the room, he passed his wards and stopped in front of Lady Isabelle, giving a slight bow as he lifted her hand for a chaste salute. His back to his wards, he couldn't gauge their reaction to this, but he saw the sparks of outrage flashing in Lady Isabelle's eyes.

Straightening, he turned to the girls and smiled. "I

know the three of you will get along famously. You know, don't you, that your old schoolmate Pamela Baxter also spent her Season with Lady Isabelle. You could not ask for a better mentor."

"I'm sure it will be delightful," said Abigail dryly.

"May I have a word with you in the hallway, my lord?" asked Isabelle, not bothering to wait for his compliance as she marched to the door.

"Certainly. I shall see you lovely ladies at dinner tonight." With a nod to the twins, he followed Lady Isabelle, expelling a whoosh of air as he closed the door.

"What the devil was going on in there?"

"A power struggle, and I hope you have not undermined my authority with your rakish bow."

"My . . . there was nothing rakish about that bow or the kiss on your hand. Devil take you, what was I supposed to do? Leave you to the not so tender mercies of that hellcat?"

"Shh!" she breathed, taking his hand and pulling him farther along the corridor. "They are no doubt listening at the keyhole."

"Then let them," said Alex, his voice booming. She tilted her head and raised her brows, and he moderated his voice immediately. "Let them listen. They need to know that you are the one in charge and that they should thank their lucky stars that you agreed to squire them about London during their Season because their lazy mother certainly wasn't going to do it properly."

He was arrested by her smile, and he sheepishly returned it.

"I appreciate your knight errantry, Sir Galahad, but I fear you have only made matters worse. I was watching Abigail's face when you bowed over my hand, and I fear she has formed a most improper idea of our relationship."

"Improper? There's nothing improper . . . oh, I see," he said, following it with a soft "Damn!"

"Precisely. I only hope we may convince her otherwise during this house party. Otherwise, I shan't be able to serve as their chaperone in London. Their mother told me we would all be staying at your town house, and you can imagine the conclusions Abigail would draw from that fact. My reputation would be as black as yours, and I have no doubt she would spread the story far and wide."

"Unless, of course, I should happen to become betrothed before the Season," he said, missing the look of shock in his listener's eyes.

"Yes, unless that happens," she said faintly.

"Very well, Isabelle."

"Lady Isabelle," she said, again giving him that warning look.

"We are alone," he said, looking up and down the long hallway.

"Nonsense. You never know who may be listening at doors, and we must remember to behave circumspectly—now more than ever."

"You're right. I stand corrected, and I shall try to speak to you only in the most formal tones from now on."

"Good."

"Unless, of course, I know we are truly alone," he whispered for her ears only.

"Rogue," she said softly.

"Shrew," he replied.

"Lady Isabelle, I do hope you will not mind being placed in the middle of the table at dinner," said her hostess, lifting her silver lorgnette to peer at her guest.

"Certainly not, Lady Foxworth."

"Good, because dear Alex told me that you prefer not to reveal your family name, so I was unsure if you would be considered of lower or higher rank than our Amelia. Her father, of course, was a marquess."

"I am perfectly happy seated in the middle," said Isabelle, smiling at the dowager countess as she thwarted her inquiry.

From the end of the table, Alex silently applauded his mother's efforts to discover more about Isabelle's antecedents. He found he was quite curious himself as to her family background. Her husband had been a plain mister, the younger son of some minor baron. Her title, therefore, had to come from having been born Lady Isabelle. Her father had to have been either a marquess or a duke, and the latter was highly unlikely. The daughter of a duke, even one whose marriage had displeased the family, could not long keep her secret.

When the Marquess and Marchioness of Dunham arrived, he would ask Amy about Lady Isabelle. And if she didn't know, surely her grandmother would recall every scandal in the *ton*, whether recent or old news.

"Alex tells me you often go to London for the Season," said the dowager countess.

"In the past six years, I have spent five Seasons in London. I am surprised you do not attend, my lady."

"Oh, I could not possibly manage to undergo such a strenuous activity. My health is much too delicate, rather like our Amelia's health."

"I didn't realize; please know that I would be happy to help shoulder the burden of entertaining your guests. Anything I can do . . ." said Lady Isabelle.

"Entertain your son," muttered Abigail under her breath.

"What was that, Abigail?" asked the earl.

"Nothing," she said, ducking her head.

"You must know that a young lady does not mumble, nor should you put yourself forward by speaking unless someone addresses you first," said the countess.

"Yes, my lady," said the girl.

"Now, what were we discussing? Oh, yes, your offer to help me with this wearing house party. I shall keep it in mind, you may be sure."

"I shall be an interested observer too, Lady Isabelle, since you will be staying with us for the Season," Amelia said grandly.

"Well, we must enjoy our quiet time together before the rest of the guests arrive on Wednesday," said the earl.

"That reminds me. I received a very kind acceptance from the Duchess of Charlton today. She begs leave to bring her other granddaughter, Lady Anne. You know her, don't you, Amelia? She comes from Wiltshire like you."

"Oh, yes, I have met her from time to time. Let me see, she married that Plimpton fellow, the one with all the money and estates."

"Yes, but he died a few months ago, you know. A carriage accident, or something."

"Oh, dear," said Lady Amelia. "Any heirs?"

"The last I heard, she was—" the countess lowered her voice and said—"in a delicate way."

Alex had heard enough. "She was increasing, but she had the baby over a month ago. And no, it wasn't a boy. It was a girl, which means that fool Nigel Baines has inherited all the money and the estates and will probably run them into the ground. It also means Lady Anne will no longer have a home."

"Foxworth! That is not at all suitable for the dining table!" said his mother.

Isabelle held her napkin to her mouth to cover her smile, but her eyes gave her away. Glancing her way,

Alex swallowed his tart rejoinder. Instead, he nodded, indicating that he had received her silent message.

It would do no good to enrage his mother further, so he said humbly, "Forgive me, Mother. And I hope my speech has not shocked the rest of you ladies. The Lady Anne is an old friend of mine, and I find it distressing that she has been left in such an uncomfortable position by her husband's passing."

"We understand, my dear. But I think it is time we ladies left you to your brandy and cigars. Come along, ladies," said the dowager countess, leading the ladies away. Alex rose and watched them go, willing Isabelle to look his way, but she was behaving with the utmost propriety.

He would corner her later in the drawing room. Abigail and Amanda would no doubt be butchering some song on the pianoforte. His mother and Amelia would be doing the same to some acquaintance's reputation, leaving Isabelle ready for the diversion of a conversation with him.

Alex poured a small glass of brandy. He pushed away the box of cigars the footman had brought. Five minutes and then he could go to her, he thought as he sipped the amber liquid.

She had looked even more beautiful by candlelight. Her dark hair shimmered with each movement. And her skin had been positively translucent against the deep crimson gown. And her figure? She had the figure of a girl. Well, he amended, closing his eyes to recall her image all the better, she was certainly petite, but she had the curves of a woman.

Alex licked his lips. Draining his glass in a single gulp, he pushed away from the table. He rose and made his way to the drawing room, forcing himself to keep his pace slow as he passed the servants.

A footman threw open the door, and the sounds of

the pianoforte assaulted his ears—just as he had predicted. One glance at the first sofa revealed his mother and cousin deep in conversation, ignoring . . . His eyes swept the room. Alex frowned. His gaze searched the room again, peering carefully into any and all darkened corners.

He could not prevent himself from demanding, "Where is Lady Isabelle?"

He ignored Abigail's titter of laughter and turned to his mother, who spun around as if to find his quarry sitting on her shoulder.

"She said something about her daughter," supplied his cousin Amelia.

"But she will come down again?"

"As to that, she didn't say. I imagine she is too tired, and it is not as if the girls need chaperoning tonight."

"What? Oh, no, of course not."

He turned to go, but his mother called, "Well, surely you will not be so rude as to abandon us, Foxworth. It is Amelia's and the twins' first night with us after all."

"No, no, I wouldn't do that," he muttered, returning to sit down in the chair nearest the door.

"Tell us, Foxworth, what plans do you have for your guests' entertainment?" asked his cousin.

"I don't know. A fox hunt, a scavenger hunt, some sort of ball, a picnic."

"Oh, hardly a picnic, my dear. Not in December!"

"Lady Isabelle suggested moving some of the plants out of the conservatory and holding it in there. I don't really know how it would work. You will have to ask her."

The noise coming from the pianoforte stopped abruptly, and Abigail joined the others. A smirk on her face, she asked, "And when did you discuss the entertainments with her, Cousin Foxworth?"

Alex knew he had put his foot in it, and he turned on

the charm to cover his faux pas. It probably wouldn't convince the suspicious Abigail, but he didn't want his mother finding out about his visits to Isabelle's house. He wouldn't be able to forgive himself if her reputation was called into question.

"I thought perhaps it was when you visited her at her house," said Abigail. When he scowled at her, she added sweetly, "Dear little Beth mentioned it at school."

"As a matter of fact," he said, thinking fast, "I spoke to her about it when I was arranging for her to come and help with the twins. She has spent more time at *ton* gatherings than I have, and I thought she might have some novel idea for our little party. And she did. I think the idea of a picnic in December is quite unique."

"It might be just the thing," said Amelia. "Something to make everyone remember my girls."

"As to that, I daresay your girls will long be remembered by everyone they meet." He grinned at Abigail, and she glared at him in return. Returning his attention to Amelia, he added, "Being twins will make them doubly easy to recall."

Alex sat in silence while the older ladies discussed past balls and routs they had attended, both of them throwing out names and titles in their efforts to outdo each other.

Growing weary of their chatter, Alex mentioned the dinner he had attended at Carlton House, and he found himself the center of attention. He related the menu as best he could remember it, and the lavish decorations. Carlton House, he told them, was a showpiece without any further decorating, but it shone like a diamond that night.

When they had posed every question and sighed over every detail, Alex yawned and excused himself, saying wearily that he would seek his bed and advising them to do the same.

They bade him good night and began the all-important discussion of gowns and fripperies, a discussion that would last several hours.

At the top of the stairs, Alex paused. He was not tired, not sleepy in the least. He wanted to see Isabelle, to tell her . . . He wasn't sure, but he knew something would come to him. He turned left and walked a few paces before stopping again.

No, he couldn't go to her room, not even to the small sitting room that adjoined it. It wouldn't be at all proper, and with the twins next to Isabelle, he wouldn't be able to escape undetected.

Perhaps she was still in the nursery with Beth! With this happy thought, Alex climbed the next flight of stairs and hurried down the cold corridor to the nursery. A candle burned in one of the rooms, and he opened the door, hoping to find Isabelle sitting by her daughter's side.

Instead, he discovered a sleeping child, her nurse, Lucy, just lying down in the cot next to hers. She looked startled and started to rise. Alex put a finger to his lips and shook his head, closing the door behind him.

His shoulders sagging, Alex made his way to his own room for a restless night of tossing and turning.

Foxworth Manor was usually a quiet household until after noon. There was never a call for breakfast from the dowager countess, but the earl's arrival had changed all that. In London, Alex was often making his way home from a night of revelry at eight in the morning; in the country, he was on his way out the door for an invigorating ride.

Tompkins, Alex's valet, informed Finley, the butler, when his lordship would return. Finley told the housekeeper, Mrs. Teasley, and she told Cook so that the kidney pie and coffee would be piping hot and waiting in the breakfast room. They did not, however, anticipate the early arrival of the young masters, Viscount Granby and the Honorable Phillip Havenhurst.

Boys of eleven and thirteen, they headed for the small dining room, where breakfast was waiting on the sideboard. Within minutes, the earl's piping hot breakfast had disappeared, down to the last bite of toast and rasher of bacon, just as his lordship entered the back door.

"My lord, I must apologize," said Finley.

"I take full responsibility, my lord," said Mrs. Teasley, wringing her hands.

"What has happened?" he exclaimed, his consternation growing as Cook's frantic orders to her underlings reached his ears.

"In there," said the butler, flinging his arm out and pointing toward the breakfast room.

His heart thumping, Alex hurried down the hall and threw open the door.

"Good morning, Father," mumbled his sons, jumping to their feet while wiping their mouths on their sleeves and struggling to down the food they were chewing.

Alex surveyed the empty sideboard and their smiling faces and shook his head. "I might have known you two would be at the bottom of this," he said, smiling at them and holding out his hands.

The boys hurried to shake his hand, exchanging surprised glances when he pulled each of them close for a hearty hug. Tousling the dark hair of his heir, Alex observed, "I think you've grown six inches since I saw you in October. And, Phillip, you are almost as tall as he is. Do not tell me they don't feed you well at that school."

"No, sir," said the boys.

"Well, sit down. Finish your breakfasts and tell me how you are doing." He breathed a sigh of relief that they had chosen ale over the coffee, and poured himself a cup of the strong brew before sitting down and giving them an encouraging smile. Their youthful chatter made Alex forget his growling stomach.

When the footmen entered to replenish the sideboard, Robert said, "I'm sorry, Father. I guess we ate your breakfast."

"Think nothing of it," he said. "Just let me fill my plate before you go back for seconds," he added, shaking a finger at Phillip, who was favoring the bacon with a wolfish expression.

When they were seated again, Alex said, "I meant to write and congratulate you, Phillip, for being first in your class this term. We shall have to think of some reward for you."

"Thank you, Father," said the younger boy. Nodding at his older brother, he added, "Robert is the best at fencing. He beat every boy through the age of sixteen."

"Really? Well, I am impressed. Perhaps you would like to spar with me one afternoon. I used to be counted quite handy with a foil."

"I didn't know that, Fa—"

A footman opened the door, and Lady Isabelle entered, holding her daughter's hand.

"Excuse us, gentlemen. Are we interrupting?"

With a scraping of chairs, Alex and his sons were on their feet again.

"Certainly not. Do come join us," said Alex. "Beth, you sit here beside me, and your mother may sit on your other side. May I present Lady Isabelle Fanshaw and her daughter, Beth? And these are my sons:

Robert, who sometimes goes by Viscount Granby, and the Honorable Phillip Havenhurst."

The introductions complete, Alex led Beth to the sideboard to investigate what remained of the breakfast offerings. He poured a cup of coffee for Lady Isabelle and encouraged her to take more than the two pieces of toast she had on her plate. He glanced back at the two boys and caught them exchanging significant glances. He would have to correct their speculations immediately.

"Lady Isabelle has agreed to chaperone the Heart twins in London next Season," he said when they were all seated again.

"Abigail and Amanda?" said Robert, his expression revealing his opinion of these young ladies more than words could.

"Yes, and they are here for your grandmother's house party too, so I was invited in order to become better acquainted with them," said Isabelle.

"*Bonne chance,*" murmured Robert.

"Good luck? Now, why would you say that, Lord Granby?" she asked, spearing him with a look of polite inquiry.

Alex judged it was time to step in and said, "You know, Robert, just because you make an insulting remark in French, it is still rag-mannered."

"Yes, Father. I apologize."

Phillip changed the subject by asking Beth if she wanted to ride a pony.

"Oh, yes!" she breathed, squirming in her seat. "Do you have one?"

"I have a horse now," he replied, "but Father sent our old ponies to the Manor when we outgrew them. They're still here, aren't they, Father?"

"I think so. You'll have to ask Bottles or James about them."

"When can we go?" asked Beth.

"Not until you have finished your breakfast," said her mother, smiling down at Beth and then turning this sunshine on Phillip, who blushed a fiery red. "It is very kind of you to offer, Phillip."

"Oh, I'm happy to. I want to see Molly again anyway," said the boy.

"You two had better go upstairs and change. I instructed Finley to put you in the small bedroom at the end of my hall. You'll have to share, but I thought you would prefer that to being in the nursery," said Alex.

"Ripping!" said Robert, rising and clapping his brother on the back.

"Just a moment. Beth, are you finished now?"

"Yes, my lord."

"Young gentlemen, I charge you with seeing Miss Beth to the nursery and telling her nurse what she is about to do so that she may be dressed accordingly."

"Wear your woolen cloak, my dear," said Lady Isabelle.

"Yes, Mama," she said, taking Phillip's hand and skipping from the room.

Isabelle fixed the earl with a warm, somewhat smug smile that soon had him squirming in his chair.

"Why are you staring so?" he demanded finally.

"So you decided your sons should stay at Foxworth Manor after all," she observed.

"I decided I didn't wish to impose on Adam and Grace."

"Of course not," she murmured.

"It had nothing to do with our conversation last week. It is just that the boys need a firm hand. Adam is too busy with his parish duties, and Grace has Allie to tend to."

"Whatever your reasons, my lord," she said, her tone becoming formal as a servant entered the room, "I applaud your decision. And Beth will be head over heels about both of them before the morning is over."

"You are not worried about her, are you? They are very responsible boys. I am certain they will look after her well."

"I am not worried at all. Like father, like sons."

"Oh, I do hope not," said Alex.

"To ape their father would not be such a bad thing," she commented, "as long as they grow up and leave their youthful high jinks with the ladies behind."

Alex frowned and looked down at his plate. "Is that what you think? You think I simply never grew up?"

"Perhaps I could have expressed it better, but I believe that men who have earned the name of rake simply haven't outgrown their youth. They are more interested in the quantity of women they can conquer rather than being true to only one."

His appetite suddenly gone, Alex placed his fork on the table. His jaw clenched, and he fidgeted with the fork, his anger mounting.

"Alex," she said.

His head jerked up, and he said softly, "I'm surprised you agreed to help me, since you have such a low opinion of me."

"But I don't," said Lady Isabelle.

"Odd, then, that you would—"

"No, Alex, I . . . I spoke without thinking," she protested, rising and moving to the chair Beth had recently vacated. She placed her hand over his, stilling his nervous fingers.

He took her small hand in his, turning it over and staring at the wedding ring she still wore.

"Was your marriage a love match?"

Isabelle withdrew her hand, hiding it in her lap.

"Yes, I loved my husband. My father was not pleased, however, and he disowned me."

"I am sorry. I didn't know."

"Oh, Papa was very discreet about it. He had a solicitor come to our house after I was wed, and he gave me an official paper. You cannot imagine how alone I felt."

"I might have done," said Alex, his voice as desolate as hers had been bitter. "The morning Phillip was born and my wife died, I would gladly have taken my own life, but I had the boys to consider."

"Oh, Alex, I am so sorry," she whispered, her green eyes filling with tears. "I shouldn't have spoke so precipitously."

The dining room door crashed against the wall, and Abigail sailed into the room, ignoring Isabelle completely and saying an airy, "Good morning, Cousin Foxworth."

The footman who was stationed outside the door stepped into the room, murmured a quick "Sorry, m'lord," and hastened to close it again—quietly.

"Do you always enter rooms so noisily?" asked Alex while Isabelle bowed her head and dabbed her eyes discreetly.

"Certainly not. The door was lighter than I expected," Abigail said, looking pointedly at Isabelle's plate one seat down from the chair she now occupied.

"Some fresh toast and tea," she said to another footman, who hurried away. "You two are certainly up early."

"Some of us have more to do than others, Abigail." Alex watched the girl for a moment before rising. She nibbled at the cold toast, remaining silent. Not a polite word for Isabelle, he thought, his temper rising. He glanced at this lady, who had regained her composure, and was sipping her coffee as if his rude ward had not just given her the cut direct.

Isabelle glanced his way and then looked down. He could tell she was smiling by the way her cheek, in profile, became rounded like a small plum. She must have read his thoughts because she shook her head imperceptibly. Very well, he would not give the girl the set-down she so richly deserved.

Alex pushed away from the table and stood up. "If you ladies will excuse me. I'm going out to the stables to check on those ponies."

"You needn't leave just because I have arrived, Foxworth," said Abigail, her tone haughty.

"No, but I have finished my breakfast, and I still have things to do. Good morning, ladies."

"Oh, I cannot sit idle all morning either," said Isabelle, following him to the door. "Your mother wanted me to inspect the guest chambers with the housekeeper, Mrs. Teasley. Do you know where I might find her at this hour of the morning, my lord?"

"Certainly, my lady. Just follow me."

When they were well away from the breakfast room, Alex pulled Isabelle to one side and whispered, "If that young lady continues to behave in that insulting manner to you, I will send both her and her sister home."

"She is being difficult, but we must work harder to convince her there is nothing havey-cavey going on between us."

"And how can we do that? Will one of us have to remain in her sight at all times? I promise you, Isabelle, I shan't put up with it for long. My patience is not as limitless as yours."

"Perhaps we should take her into our confidence, tell her about your plan to reform."

"Have you gone mad?" he spat out. "She would have a heyday with that bit of information.

"I suppose you are right," she said wearily. "For now we'll just have to be very careful. If there is nothing untoward for her to discover, then she will soon tire of this game. Now, I really do wish to find your mother's housekeeper."

"Down this hallway and turn left at the last door. I'm going out to the stables, and I'll keep an eye on Beth," he said, lifting her hand to his lips before striding away in the opposite direction.

Lady Isabelle Fanshaw found it impossible to drag her eyes away until he was out of sight. Then a movement caught her eye as Abigail slipped back inside the small dining room.

Thank heavens the other guests would begin arriving the next day. With all the other young people about, especially the young men, Abigail would find other things to occupy her time.

Five

That afternoon, they were joined by Adam and Grace, who were staying for dinner, swelling their family gathering to ten at the table and two in the nursery. Beth, who was accustomed to being the youngest at school, was thrilled to act the big sister to little Allie. Robert and Phillip were flattered to be included at the adult table, but they looked longingly at the dinner Cook had sent up for the nursery crew, fully two hours before their dinner would be served.

Lady Isabelle, who had come up to chat with Beth while she ate her supper, said, "Why don't you sit down and keep the girls company?"

"We don't wish to intrude," said Robert, grabbing his younger brother's arm before he could sit down.

"Intrude? It is no such thing. The girls would love you to stay, wouldn't you?"

"Oh, yes, please stay," said Beth, smiling up at her two new heroes.

"Stay," echoed Allie with a giggle.

They made room for two more chairs around the little table, and Lady Isabelle poured them each a cup of milk.

To their weak protest, she said, "Nonsense, you are growing boys. You'll starve if you have to wait until seven o'clock. Help yourselves to some of this stewed chicken. The girls cannot possibly eat all of this food."

She pushed a couple of small saucers closer so they could help themselves.

"If you're certain, my lady."

"Quite certain. And have some of the potatoes too. Judging from the quantity of food, I can only assume that Cook heard you two were up here entertaining the girls and thought you might need a little something before dinner."

"I hadn't thought of that," said Phillip, tucking into the chicken.

"What is your favorite class at school, Robert?" she asked the quieter brother.

"He's the best fencer in the upper division," said Phillip proudly.

"Are you? Well, that is wonderful. I suppose being so tall for your age is an advantage. You have a greater reach," she said.

Robert stopped eating and smiled at Lady Isabelle. She was struck by the resemblance to his father, something she hadn't noticed before since he tended to keep his head bowed, his introversion ruling his manners. At thirteen, he was all feet and legs, and his face was losing its childish roundness. She could already see the beginnings of that strong jaw and those chiseled cheekbones.

"I didn't think ladies knew about fencing," he said.

"I don't know very much, only what I have read in books."

"I like to read too," he admitted.

"What do you like to read?"

"Mostly about knights and such, but they don't let us read about them very much. We're studying Plato's *Republic* right now."

"A rather dull tome, although there are some fascinating ideas in it."

"You've read it?" asked Phillip, much impressed.

"Parts of it that my teacher had translated for us. I'm afraid I attended a very traditional girls' school, nothing like your aunt Grace's academy. I never learned Latin or Greek."

"You didn't miss much," said Robert glumly.

"That's too bad," said Phillip. "I love the classical languages, but I like mathematics the best."

"Mathematics," said Robert with a shudder.

"I like mathematics too," said Beth, gazing worshipfully at Phillip, who winked at her.

"I know what you mean," said Lady Isabelle. "I vow, sometimes I can add two and two and come up with five!"

"Then I pray you do not teach mathematics if you decide to work at Grace's school," said a deep voice from the doorsill.

The boys jumped to their feet as their father stepped inside, his size seeming to dwarf the room.

"Keep your seats, gentlemen," he said with a wave of one hand. "I'm glad to see that you are taking to heart your role as hosts, and looking after our young guests."

"Yes, Father," said Robert.

"Lady Isabelle told us we should help ourselves," said Phillip, pushing away the saucer.

"Capital idea. I should have thought of that myself. I know you're not accustomed to eating so late. Tomorrow night, you'll be glad to be included with the younger people. I've had the schoolroom next door cleared. The footmen are going to bring down a larger table from the attics, one big enough for all of you, as well as Lord and Lady Dunham's daughters, who are arriving tomorrow."

"But we don't have to sleep up here, do we, Father?"

"No, no. That's why I put you in the bedchamber near mine. You'll just take your meals up here when the other guests begin to arrive. And I don't expect you to spend all your time with the infantry."

Beth frowned and announced indignantly, "I am not an infant."

"Of course not, dear. The term means children, not babies," said her mother.

"And you are definitely not a baby," said Alex, smiling at her. "I mean, a baby wouldn't be big enough or bold enough to ride Behemoth."

"You have ridden Behemoth?" exclaimed the boys, causing Beth to toss her curls and preen.

"Haven't you?" she asked.

"No, we . . . that is, not yet," said Robert, looking up at his father.

"Yes, well, I can see I've stirred things up quite enough for one afternoon. May I accompany you downstairs, Lady Isabelle?" said Alex.

"Yes, I suppose I should go and dress for dinner." She patted Allie on the top of the head and kissed Beth's cheek. "Good night, my love."

"Won't you come up to tuck me in, Mama?"

"Yes, my sweet, but it will not be as easy to slip away after dinner tonight, and you will probably be asleep by the time I come up."

"We'll come back and tuck you in, Beth. And you too, Allie," said Robert. "If that's all right with you, my lady?"

"Why, thank you, Robert. That's very thoughtful of you."

"We don't mind, do we, Phillip?"

"No, we don't mind."

"Good. That's settled, and here is Lucy to look after the girls. Good night, ladies," said the earl, herding his sons and Lady Isabelle out of the nursery. Wrinkling his nose, he said, "You boys need to go to your room and ring for a bath. Your grandmother will kick up a dust if you come to her dining table smelling of the stables."

"Yes, Father," they said.

Isabelle and Alex were soon left alone as the boys capered ahead.

"I don't believe I have seen you all day," he said, taking her hand and placing it on his arm as they strolled leisurely toward the stairs. Leering down at her, he added, "I would remember if I had, because you look particularly delectable in that shade of lavender."

"And you, my lord, look positively delicious in that tweed coat," she replied with what she hoped was a comparable leer.

He stopped and stared down at her a moment before breaking into a grin. "Touché, my lady. And you told Robert you didn't know how to fence."

Turning to face him, she said, "Didn't know . . . just how long were you listening outside the door?"

"Long enough to know that you have a knack for getting my older son to speak up."

"He's a little shy, but quite intelligent."

"I know. I don't expect others to realize it though."

"Still, didn't anyone ever tell you that it is impolite to eavesdrop?" she asked.

He placed one hand on the wall, leaning toward her until his face was only inches from hers, his gaze warm as he held her captive. If this was a test of her self-possession, it was straining it to the very limits. Isabelle struggled to keep her breath even, but it was so shallow, she felt almost faint.

"Your perfume is very tantalizing," he whispered.

She wrinkled her nose and smiled sweetly. "And your cologne, my lord, is faintly . . . horsey."

She twisted away from him, and he laughed, catching up with her in two long strides and taking her hand again.

"Is that an example of your rakish technique, my lord?" she asked as they started down the stairs.

"My . . . I . . ."

"I ask only because, if it is, I must say, I am not quite certain how you earned such a scandalous reputation. I mean, do the ladies truly succumb to that sort of heavy-handed thing?"

They had reached the next landing, where her room lay in one direction and his, the other. She released his arm.

"Now you are being a saucy shrew," he said quietly, dipping his head as if to steal a kiss.

Stepping out of reach, Isabelle cocked her head to one side and said audaciously, "Oh, I beg your pardon, my lord. I said ladies, and I believe ladies have more sense than that. I should have said . . . what? Females? Women?" With this, she tripped lightly down the corridor, disappearing as she turned the corner.

When Alex saw Isabelle at the far end of the room an hour later, his eyes lit up in anticipation of their next exchange. It was all he could do to make himself calmly greet the others, who were mere obstacles between the two of them. She wore a silk gown of the darkest blue; its cut was slender and unadorned by lace or ruffles. In her dark hair she wore a small Spanish comb of silver filigree, and around her neck she wore a matching necklace inlaid with small sapphires that twinkled in the candlelight. When she saw him, she smiled.

Alex would have flown to her side, but he was too well mannered to completely ignore his other guests.

Giving his sister-in-law's cheek a quick kiss, he said, "Good evening, Grace. You are looking as lovely as ever. I really do not understand how you can be content to

remain hidden in the country, when you would positively shine in London."

"Perhaps it is because my husband and daughter are
here," she replied with a smile.

He then shook hands with his brother, who was chatting with Robert and Phillip. He clapped Robert on the
back and shook Phillip's hand as if he hadn't just left
them an hour before.

The dowager countess, he noticed, was sitting in her
usual spot on the sofa, holding a glass of sherry in her
hand. He smiled at the near-empty decanter on the
table in front of her. His mother rarely drank anything
stronger than ratafia before her wine with her evening
meal. Amelia must be boring her silly for her to imbibe
sherry on an empty stomach.

His mother called to him, waving her glass to attract
his attention. He went to her side, picking up the decanter and moving it out of reach.

He glanced up to make certain Isabelle was still
there, waiting for him, before returning his attention
to his mother.

"Good evening, Mother. Good evening, Amelia. That
is a very fetching gown, cousin. You should wear that
shade of blue all the time."

"Why, thank you, Foxworth," said the dame.

"My dear boy," said Lady Foxworth, "I'm so happy
you could come."

Alex wasn't certain if his mother knew which son she
was addressing. Adam was the usual recipient of "my
dear son's." But he smiled and said, "Of course I am
here, Mother. Where else would I be?"

"Pay her no heed, Foxworth. She needs her dinner,"
said Amelia, who could put away an entire decanter and
never feel the effects.

"I should have stayed upstairs with my granddaughter," came the tart reply, showing that drink had not

made the countess completely mellow. "I do not see why the child could not eat dinner with me."

"I told you, my lady, we are trying to create a properly formal atmosphere to give my girls an idea of what Society is really like. Having your grandsons at the table is concession enough," said Amelia, ignoring the look of anger her hostess flashed her way.

Really, thought Alex, Amelia was completely self-absorbed. He couldn't blame his mother for her state. If he had been sitting for any length of time with Amelia bending his ear, he would want to be blinding drunk.

With a polite smile and nod, he moved on. Deciding to greet his wards with a mere nod, Alex made his way to Isabelle's side.

He had bathed and dressed with care, choosing black evening clothes with a snowy shirt and cravat, which was tied in the mathematical. The only touch of color on his ensemble was a red ruby shining from his cravat. His dark, cropped hair was dressed à la Titus, carefully arranged to appear windswept. He knew he was the epitome of fashion and elegance, but would she notice?

"Good evening, my lady," he said, sketching a brief bow.

She nodded, her green eyes dancing as she said quietly, "Have you resigned yourself to behaving as elegantly as you look tonight, my lord?"

"I am only following your lead," he said softly, his gaze admiring.

"Very eloquent," she murmured. "And very proper."

"I am delighted to have my tutor's approval," he replied, keeping his expression impassive for the sake of the others in the room. He had never before exercised such self-control when speaking to a lady whose appearance fairly screamed at him to be seductive. By the very propriety of her dress, she was tantalizing him.

"You know, Isabelle," he said, his voice so soft she had to lean closer to hear—a fact that afforded him a very pleasant view. "If I didn't know any better, I would say you are trying to tempt me into speaking some outrageous compliment. Otherwise, you would not be looking so beautiful this evening."

"Be careful, Foxworth, that you do not fall into that trap. Good manners must always demand propriety and restraint," she replied, but her eyes were twinkling. "What's more, I noticed you could not cross the room without flattering every female you encountered. That, my lord, is the sure sign of a rogue."

"Devil a bit! I spoke to my brother and sons too, so you cannot say I singled out the ladies. And I practically ignored my wards."

She laughed and shook her head. "You're right. I was only teasing you, my lord."

"A very naughty thing to do," he said, gazing into her green eyes and suddenly understanding the poet's metaphor of a man drowning in someone's eyes.

"Foxworth, come and settle an argument for me," called his mother, her words slightly slurred.

With a little grunt of reluctance, he turned and retraced his steps to his mother's side, all the while aware that Isabelle was following at a slower rate. When he glanced over his shoulder, she smiled at him before stopping beside his sister-in-law and engaging her in conversation.

"You must settle a wager, Foxworth, between Amelia and me," said the dowager countess, her voice carrying throughout the room and causing all heads to turn.

"If I can, Mother."

"I know you won that wager with Miles Parker last year, but how many did it take you?"

"What wager was that, Mother? Parker and I make

any number of foolish wagers when we are together. That is the basis of our friendship," said Alex.

"You know, the one where you said you could wrangle more kisses in a twenty-four-hour period than he could. He followed you around and counted, and then the next day, you followed him around."

"I don't remember, Mother, and the drawing room is not the place for such a topic," came the repressive reply.

Alex hardly knew where to look. He was aware of Grace moving toward Abigail and Amanda, complimenting them on their choice of gowns even though Abigail still wore the same insipid shade of blue and Amanda the pink. His sons were gaping, while his brother tried unsuccessfully to hold their attention.

"Of course you remember," said his mother, her voice rising. "What was it? Eighteen? Nineteen?"

"I don't think anyone could find that many willing ladies, not even a rake like Foxworth," said Amelia with a titter. "Confess, it was more like five or six, right?"

"If you must know, Amelia, it was twenty, and Miles Parker found only twelve willing participants. Now, is there anything else you wish to ask me about? Perhaps how many times I—"

"My lord and ladies, gentlemen, dinner is served," boomed the butler's voice as if making his announcement in a filled ballroom.

Isabelle, who was standing behind the servant, entered the room and took Alex's arm, tugging gently until he led her out of the room and down the corridor to the dining hall.

"Thank you," he said quietly, trying to regain his temper.

"You're welcome," she replied as he saw her to her seat.

The rest of the family filtered into the room. The

dowager countess, led by her other son, the vicar, looked properly chastened. Grace had enlisted the help of the two boys, delegating Robert to walk with Amelia, while she took Phillip's arm. The twins brought up the rear, giggling and whispering until Grace, their former teacher, quelled their merriment with a raised brow.

Conversation around the table was disjointed and awkward at first, but soon everyone had put the uncomfortable scene behind them, and the dinner proceeded smoothly, the conversation remaining polite and formal. The dowager countess, who refused to touch a drop of wine throughout the meal, was quite sober by the time she rose to lead the ladies back to the drawing room.

Alex sent the boys upstairs and said, "We won't linger too long over our port."

"A good thing, since tomorrow is going to be such a long day with our guests beginning to arrive," said his mother.

When they reached the drawing room, Isabelle sent Amanda and Abigail to the pianoforte, cautioning them to play pianissimo. Lady Foxworth and Amelia were soon dozing on the sofa, undisturbed by the girls' occasional discords. Grace led Isabelle to a sofa near the windows, where they happily discussed their daughters.

Alex and Adam entered the room a mere quarter of an hour later. Amelia slept on, but the countess sat up, blinking her eyes and massaging her forehead.

"I believe I will go upstairs early tonight," she said, rising.

"Shall I send for your maid, Mother?" asked Alex.

"No, no, I am fine," she said, pausing by his side and touching his sleeve. Giving his arm a little squeeze, she added, "Thank you, my dear boy."

He smiled, not sure how to respond to this. His mother rarely had a kind word for him, and to call him "her dear boy" twice in one evening was unheard of.

He watched her progress across the hall and up the stairs.

"You're welcome, Mother," he murmured quietly.

"Not such a bad evening," said his brother, who had witnessed the remarkable exchange. "Perhaps she will begin to try to smother you with motherly concern the way she did me all those years."

Alex shook his head and strolled into the drawing room with an acerbic "If she does, I'm sending her to live with you and Grace at the vicarage."

He meandered toward the sofa where Isabelle and Grace visited, wondering how he could get rid of his sister-in-law and take her place.

Adam followed on his heels, saying, "Oh, no, you don't. I already have two ladies at home telling me how to go on. I refuse to take in another."

"If I were in the habit of heeding the silly things you say, my dear husband, I would take exception to that," commented his wife.

"Now you're in for it," said Alex. "Very well, Adam. I can see you have your hands full with this one. I shan't saddle you with another."

"How considerate of you," said the vicar. "I hate to break up this little gathering, but I am quite weary, my dear. Do you think we could go home?"

"If you insist," she said with a sigh, although she was smiling at her husband fondly. She turned to Isabelle and added, "I will be over here early tomorrow morning to fetch Allie and her nurse. I appreciate your letting her share Beth's room."

"Beth is enjoying playing the big sister to Allie. We'll expect you around nine or ten o'clock."

"Good night, everyone," said Adam, taking his wife's arm and leading her toward the front door.

Alex walked beside them, and Isabelle waited by the drawing room door. When his brother and sister-in-law had gone, Alex returned to her side.

"I want to talk to you. Will you meet me in the library in half an hour?" he asked.

She nodded before turning and announcing that she, too, was going to bed.

"Amanda and Abigail, why don't you wake your mother and help her to her room?" said Alex. "I don't think anyone is going to be interested in waiting up for the tea tray tonight."

The twins left the pianoforte and did as he suggested, one on each side of their sleepy mother as they made their way toward the stairs.

Abigail stopped on the first step and called, "Aren't you coming up too, Lady Isabelle?"

"Yes, I was just getting your mother's shawl," she said, grimacing at Alex and matching her deeds to her words before following them up the steps.

Isabelle had butterflies as she watched the delicate ormolu clock on the mantel, its hands moving ever so slowly toward the half hour. She knew she was taking a chance, meeting the earl in the library, and not just because of the suspicious Abigail.

Who was she to agree to a clandestine assignation in the middle of the night, alone with a notorious rake? She didn't know the earl that well. What if he tried to seduce her? Not that he had a prayer of succeeding, she told her image in the glass. The big clock at the end of the hall gonged the half hour, and she nearly jumped out of her skin.

Cautiously, she pulled her shawl around her shoulders and opened her chamber door, listening for a moment before making her way down the long corridor. As she passed the twins' room, she cupped her hand around her candle so that no light would shine under their door.

The candles in several wall sconces were still burning in the great hall below, so she had no difficulty navigating the stairs or finding her way to the library. When she entered, Alex was waiting, standing beside a small table that contained glasses and decanters, pouring himself another glass of brandy.

"Would you like something?" he asked matter-of-factly. She shook her head, and he asked, "Any trouble?"

"No, none. I think they are asleep."

"Good. Won't you sit down?" he asked, pointing toward the worn leather sofa. When she had arranged her skirts, he joined her there, sitting close by her side.

"What did you want to talk about, my lord?"

"Alex," he corrected her, grinning down at her.

"Given the situation, if you don't mind, I would prefer to keep our conversation on a more formal level," said Isabelle.

"What is this about? You're not upset about that wager my oh-so-diplomatic mother brought up, are you?"

She rolled her eyes, saying dryly, "I daresay that was mild compared to some wagers written in the books at your club. Besides, I am acquainted with Miles Parker, and I know he would use any excuse to accost the ladies."

"I didn't realize you knew Parker so well," he said, watching her carefully.

She shook a finger under his nose, her eyes narrowed, and she said tartly, "Did you ask me in here to insult me?"

"No, no, I was just wondering."

"If you must know, I had occasion last year to comfort my charge because she had been kissed most improperly by that lout—probably in his efforts to win that stupid wager. What a terrible thing to do to a young lady—stealing her very first kiss!"

"Don't look at me! I asked permission before kissing them. I'm not some kind of Bluebeard."

"Oh, very well, Alex. I'm too tired to wrangle with you," she said, covering a yawn.

"I'm sorry, Belle."

Belle! She almost gasped. That was what Howard called her when they were . . . Watching Alex's lips move, she struggled to focus on his words.

"I'm keeping you up, and you've got to be exhausted," he was saying.

She shook her head, clearing it and answering sensibly, "I'm fine, Alex. Now, what did you want to talk to me about?"

She studied him as he fidgeted with the large ring on his right hand. He really was a handsome man. If he had asked for permission to kiss all those ladies, she could see why they granted it. She wouldn't mind . . .

Isabelle dragged her mind back to the conversation at hand. Speculations such as that were how he had earned his reputation as a rake.

"I feel very foolish admitting this, but I'm nervous about tomorrow, when all those people arrive. I don't know if I can behave like a prudish old maid."

"Who said anything about being a prudish old maid?" she said with a giggle. Of all the absurd images!

"You know what I mean," he snapped. "I just don't know precisely where to draw the line. I mean, what I said to you tonight before dinner, was that too warm?"

Isabelle's mouth dropped open at the realization that earlier, when he had flattered her, he had merely been rehearsing for when the real guests arrived, thought Isabelle. So much for her vain worries about him trying to seduce her. She had never felt so foolish.

He was watching her, waiting for her answer. Knowing he was not out to seduce her, it meant she could relax a little. She forced a sympathetic smile to her lips and patted his arm.

"No, it was not too warm; you were just responding to my compliment. There can be nothing wrong with that. What's more, it was a very pretty turn of a phrase," she said, sighing inwardly that she wished the compliment had been sincerely meant for her and not just a dress rehearsal for some eligible young miss. She almost jumped when he covered her hand with his, smiling at her in a manner that made her heart beat faster.

"That's good to know, because if I couldn't even say that much, I think I would have to give up trying to reform."

"Oh, no, you mustn't give up, Alex," said Isabelle, hoping her hand was not trembling under his. Slowly, she removed it, hoping her breathing would return to normal if he was not touching her.

"But it is very difficult, Belle. I mean, we were exchanging pleasantries, compliments, and my natural instinct was to . . . well, let me say, it took all my effort not to empty the butter boat over your head."

"Really?" she whispered.

Isabelle felt her heart pounding in her ears. When had it become so warm? She wished she had thought to bring a fan.

"Yes, perhaps you don't know how beautiful you are in that gown," he said, his deep voice caressing her ears.

"Now you are dealing in Spanish coin," she said airily, sitting up straighter and looking away.

"No, I don't need to. Or perhaps you don't know, Belle. For all of its long sleeves and modest décolletage, that gown you have on is one of the most elegant, most alluring garments . . . or is it just you? I don't know, Belle, it has been years since anyone has made me—"

"Stop it!" she said, not sure if her sharp tone was meant for herself or him. Rising, she moved across the room, hoping the distance would afford her the return of good sense. "If you think to add me to your conquests, my lord, you are sadly mistaken. I have too much pride . . . to allow you . . . to . . . oh, dear," she breathed, holding her hand over her mouth.

She studied his handsome face. His wide-eyed expression made her pause. It was not the same leer he had given her before when he had been teasing her—but he had to be teasing. He had to be acting the outrageous rogue just to shock her! He couldn't be speaking the truth! If he weren't teasing, she would have to leave Foxworth Manor immediately. She couldn't . . .

"This is all a hoax, isn't it?" she said tentatively. "You are only teasing me, aren't you?"

Alex glanced away, and when he returned his gaze to her, his dark eyes were hooded. Suddenly, he grinned and nodded, his voice grave as he said, "You have me, I'm afraid."

"That was not well done of you, my lord."

"Perhaps I am already weary of playing the paragon, Isabelle. Tomorrow, it begins in earnest, and I wanted to be myself just one more time before I had to change my ways," he drawled.

Isabelle breathed a sigh of relief. She wasn't completely convinced, but if he were willing to continue as before, then she might allow herself to continue in this farce. Which one was worse, she couldn't decide—to know his rakish words were meant to shock her or to seduce her?

Taking a deep breath, she said, "It wasn't very gentlemanly of you to make game of me. I am only trying to help. If you have decided you don't wish to find a proper, amenable wife, then go back to your old ways."

Alex rose and walked to her side, taking her small hand in his. "I am properly contrite, my lady, and I promise I shall try to keep my natural rakish tendencies in check."

"Good," she murmured, her breathing shallow and her mouth dry. Isabelle gave him a quick smile and disengaged her hand, walking regally to the door. There, she turned and said, "I will strike a bargain with you, Alex. When we are in private, you may say anything you wish—scandalous, rakish, it makes no difference. I promise I shall neither take it to heart nor take offense. That way, when you are with your guests, you can behave as properly as you please."

"You don't think that's being deceitful?"

"Certainly not. Lord Foxworth, the gentleman, is as much a part of you as the other side, only you must try to keep your roguish side hidden until some young lady has caught your eye and you have captured her heart. Then she will not mind receiving your outrageous compliments."

"But until then you will be my sounding board. A capital scheme! Now I believe I shall be able to survive the house party without disgracing myself in front of Polite Society. Thank you, my lady, and good night."

"You're welcome, Alex. Good night," she said, slipping out the door and up the stairs to her room.

There, she changed into her night rail and climbed into the big bed, feeling very small and hollow.

She had told him he might flirt with her as outrageously as he wished, and she would not take offense. Nor would she take it to heart.

The trouble with her offer, as far as she could see, was how would she be able to listen to his admiring comments without falling irrevocably, indisputably, in love with the rake.

Or was it already too late? taunted a little voice from deep within her heart, a heart she had guarded so carefully for so long. And now she had betrayed it.

Isabelle raised herself up and punched her pillow. She would not allow it! She had more control over herself than that! She had spent many lonely years hiding her feelings, her guilt. She could certainly manage to keep company with one handsome rake without letting him touch her heart.

She had no choice. The last thing she wanted was to fall in love with another rake like . . .

Tears dampened her pillow, until she punched it again, willing herself to stop. It had been years since she had cried over that; she simply would not allow herself to wallow in past misfortunes. The sins of the past would remain in the past.

The wicked little voice chortled, taunting her again. No need to cry for the past, it said, for you are in grave danger of having something new to cry over.

Alex slept very little that night, waking early and going for a long ride before the rest of the household was up and about. His conversation with Isabelle in the library had disturbed him more than he realized. Each time he had closed his eyes, he had seen the relief on her face when she had thought he was only teasing. It had shocked him to know that she held him in such low esteem that the thought of his compliments caused her such distress.

"Your compliments!" he said with a sneer. Bee flicked his ears, and Alex addressed the horse, saying, "You needn't worry. I'll not compliment you, old man. You might run away with me. But tell me, Bee, when did it become an insult to compliment a lady? Or is it only some ladies? Obviously, Isabelle's opinion of me is so low, the idea that I might find her attractive is too appalling for her to accept."

"Bah! Women!" he muttered, lifting the reins and sending the big horse along the wooded path. "Well, it doesn't matter. I now have permission to be as scandalous as I please—when we are alone. So I shall pay her back for her insult by shocking her to the very core. That will show the most proper Lady Isabelle a thing or two!"

They had reached the meadow, and he could see Foxworth Manor again. In the drive was a huge black traveling coach just pulling away from the door, its load discharged. Alex turned his gelding toward the stable, determined before he entered to the house to discover who had arrived so early. He had a feeling he knew the answer.

The stable yard was a beehive of activity with all the grooms he had brought over from Foxworth Court unharnessing the four horses while others took charge of the carriage.

Bottles came running when the earl entered the yard, holding Behemoth's head while Alex dismounted.

"Who has arrived?" he asked.

"I don't know, my lord, but judging from the age of that coach, I'd say it was Methuselah himself."

"No need for your impudence. Where's the coachman?"

"The one with the red hair over there," said the groom.

Alex strolled over to the man and greeted him.

"Good morning, m'lord."

"Who is your master?"

"My mistress is the Duchess of Charlton, m'lord. And I also brought her granddaughter."

"Lady Sophia?" asked Alex, his stomach knotting.

"No, m'lord. The Lady Anne and her new little one."

"I see," he replied, turning to see if Bee was still saddled and ready to escape. No such luck. Bottles had already removed his tack and was cooling him off.

Nothing for it, he would have to face them sooner or later. He might as well get it over with. It had been at least eight years since he had had a conversation with Lady Anne Pagely—no, it was Plimpton now—but he still dreaded it. At least he would not be tempted to frighten her with outrageous compliments!

When Alex entered the house through the back hall, he was drawn to the kitchen, peering through the door and goggling at the chaos.

Stopping Finley as he skidded past with a bottle of the cellar's best Madeira, Alex demanded, "What the deuce is going on in here?"

"It's her grace, my lord. She has a very specific diet," said the butler.

"And does it include my best Madeira at eleven o'-clock in the morning?"

"I'm afraid so, my lord. I knew you wouldn't wish to stint on her grace's needs."

Alex chuckled. The old lady hadn't been in his house for an hour, and already she was turning it topsy-turvy.

"Where are they?" he asked.

"She is in the drawing room, my lord, but the Lady Anne has gone to her room."

"And the infant?"

"I'm not sure, my lord. Either with the Lady Anne or in the nursery with her nurse."

"Let me have that. I'll play servant to her grace."

"Very good, my lord," said the butler, taking out his handkerchief and wiping the dust off the bottle before handing it to the earl.

When Alex entered the room, the Duchess of Charlton glanced up from her book and grimaced.

"I hope you do not plan to stay in here and try to entertain me all morning, Foxworth. After traveling, I am as cross as crabs—not fit for polite conversation or company."

"Well, they tell me I am not polite company, so we should get along famously, your grace. Besides, I have brought the bottle you requested from my cellars."

"What? Oh, good. Pour me a glass like a good boy, and be generous," she said.

When he was seated in the chair nearest hers, he waited for her to sample the sweet wine before sipping his own.

"Quite good, that," she said, watching him over the rim of her glass.

"Yes, and rare too, but I have enough to last the length of your stay, Duchess."

"Good," she replied, setting the glass on the table at her elbow. "Well, aren't you going to ask about her?"

"Her?" he said, pretending ignorance.

"Yes, Anne. Do not gammon me that you do not know she is here."

Alex smiled and shook his head, saying, "Yes, I know she is here. How is your cantankerous granddaughter?"

"She is a little down pin, but that is to be expected when one has had a child and lost a husband. I didn't want her staying in that house of hers for Christmas, not with the new heir. He is such a fool."

"Oh, I agree heartily on that score. He would drive

the Lady Anne mad within the month, unless she is much changed."

"No, she is as much like me as ever," said the old lady, cackling into her wine. "That is why I like her so much, and perhaps why you like me."

Alex choked on his wine, managing to swallow but coughing for a moment before catching his breath. It gave him a chance to form a response.

"My dear duchess, I am happy you have brought your granddaughter, saving her from a drab and lifeless Christmas, but pray do not think—"

"Don't worry, Foxworth, I'm not posting the banns for you two. She may not have forgiven you for the last time."

"There was no announcement," he said, and she patted his hand and smiled. Lady Anne might have been expecting an offer from him, but she was the one who had made it plain, she wanted nothing to do with him. And a good thing too. He would have made her miserable at that time, for he had seen nothing wrong with keeping a mistress while courting Lady Anne—something he would never have done with his wife. In retrospect, he supposed he had never loved Anne the way he had his wife.

"But we knew, didn't we?" the duchess was saying. Alex dragged his attention back to the present, nodding and hoping he was not agreeing to something repugnant. "However, that is in the past. I have only one request of you, Foxworth. Do not tell Anne she was not on the invitation you sent me, because I told her she was."

Alex chuckled. "You mean, do not let her know that her headstrong grandmother has brought her here unannounced and uninvited, just so that she can stir things up a bit, for her own entertainment."

"Precisely, my boy!" she said, picking up her glass

and draining it before rising. "Now, take me to my room."

"I will get Mrs. Teasley or Mrs. Pratt," he said, offering her his arm.

As they strolled out of the drawing room and across the marble floor of the hall, Alex said, "I do hope you will enjoy your stay here at Foxworth Manor, Duchess."

"Oh, I shall. I asked your butler about the guest list. It is likely to be a most entertaining spectacle—most entertaining," she said with a knowing laugh.

Six

Alex had the opportunity to judge for himself how the Lady Anne was doing when he ran into her as she left his library. Seeing her after all those years, it was a shock to realize all he felt was polite curiosity.

"How do you do, Lord Foxworth? So kind of you to invite me to spend Christmas in your home. I suppose it was actually your mother who thought of me, but I do appreciate it. It is difficult for me, being in mourning and without a home."

"No, it was my idea," he lied without qualm, taking her arm and guiding her back into the library before those tears welling in her eyes could spill over. "Let me give you something to drink, Lady Anne. A glass of . . . ?"

"No, Foxworth, nothing for me. I was on my way back upstairs. I sent my maid to the kitchen for a light nuncheon, when I discovered I had left my book at home. I hope you don't mind. I borrowed one of yours," she said, holding out the leather-bound book for his inspection.

"My library is yours, my lady, only pray do not think that is one of my books. It is one of my mother's, I think," he said after turning the volume and reading the title.

"Of course. I didn't suppose you would have taken to

reading Mrs. Radcliffe." An awkward silence ensued, and Lady Anne cleared her throat.

"This is ridiculous, Anne. We are not enemies. Quite the contrary. I believe you were very happy in your choice. Plimpton is . . . was a fine man. There is no reason for us to feel ill at ease with each other."

She smiled, and said, "You are right, Foxworth. Really, that mistress of yours did me a great service, waving at you in the park that day."

"I knew you would not be polite and forget," he said.

"Of course I could not," she replied with a chuckle. "Oh, I was devastated at the time and as angry as a hornet, but I got over it. Now I realize we would never have suited."

"But we can be friends, can we not?"

"Certainly," she said, smiling at him and walking to the door.

"Anne, it's good to see you again," he said, waiting for her to face him. She smiled and he added, "I am glad you were able to come."

"So am I, Foxworth."

By dinner that evening, all the guests had arrived and settled into their rooms. Lady Brisbane had swept in with her daughter, Penelope, and the colonel, raising a fracas when she wasn't assigned the large corner bedchamber, but retreating when she learned it had been given to the Duchess of Charlton, her friend and sparring partner.

By the time everyone began to assemble in the drawing room before dinner, Lady Foxworth declared she was already exhausted by the ordeal, though she had remained in her room all afternoon. Isabelle, who had come down early to see if she might offer her assistance, hid her smile and offered her sympathy.

"Are the children coming down before dinner?" asked the countess. "I haven't even had a chance to see Allie today."

"No, I believe we decided they could come down for dessert, didn't we?" asked Isabelle.

"Yes, that's right," replied the doting grandmother with a sigh.

"I think it is wonderful how close you and your grandchildren are, my lady," said Isabelle. "I wish my daughter had someone like you."

"Yes, we are very close. Well, little Allie and I. The boys are away at school, and besides, one doesn't make a fuss over boys. I know no one did with my sons," said the countess.

"Oh, I should think boys would enjoy being cosseted as much as girls," said Isabelle.

"Really?" said Lady Foxworth, her brow creasing with a little frown.

Just then, their quiet conversation was interrupted by the entrance of Mr. and Mrs. Forbes-Smyth and Lady Amelia, with Abigail and Amanda in tow. After greeting the newcomers, Isabelle drifted away, finding a quiet corner.

As soon as the young and handsome Jonathan and Barclay Forbes-Smyth arrived, they set about charming Abigail and Amanda while their parents watched fondly. The Marquess and Marchioness of Dunham soon entered, along with the Ladies Anne and Sophia, who escorted their grandmother, the Duchess of Charlton. Adam and Grace came in a moment later and joined them. On the sofa, the duchess held court, her audience consisting of Everett Deal, Lady Foxworth's brother, and his friend, a fellow aging dandy named Harcourt Pennywhistle.

Miles Parker, who quickly gave up on charming the unattainable Grace, called for a bowl to mix up his special punch. The lethal brew was a legend at his club, and he insisted everyone try it. Only Lady Foxworth refused, preferring a glass of orgeat in its place. Her brother Everett, who had arrived just in time to change for dinner, announced that he had tasted Mr. Parker's punch several times and would be happy to have his sister's portion.

With so many people filling the large drawing room, Alex couldn't get around to greeting all of them. He spotted Isabelle and nodded to her, but he made no attempt to approach her.

Just as it ought to be, Isabelle told herself, taking a gulp of Mr. Parker's potent beverage and nearly choking. She put the cup down on a delicate little table next to her chair and tried to blend in with the wallpaper, as a good chaperone should. On her face she pasted a polite smile in case anyone should think to engage her in conversation. No one did.

She was amused as she watched Alex, playing the good host, greeting his guests, and spending a few minutes in conversation with each cluster of people. When he greeted the haughty Lady Brisbane and her daughter, they kept their noses in the air. Colonel Sutter, who was dancing attendance on Lady Brisbane, greeted his host cordially. She would have to discover some interest of Lady Brisbane's. Perhaps if he were armed with that information, Alex would be able to turn her up sweet. Convincing an inveterate gossip like Lady Brisbane of his miraculous reformation would go far in restoring his reputation in Polite Society.

After what seemed to Isabelle an interminable period of time, Finley announced dinner. Isabelle hung back, waiting to see if anyone would notice her. Alex was helping his mother pair up the guests according to rank. Speaking to each gentleman in turn, he paired his uncle Everett with Miss Brisbane before assigning his cousin Amelia to Colonel Sutter.

Isabelle grimaced when she saw Miles Parker break away and head in her direction. Then Alex called Parker back, clapping his friend on the back and sending him off with Abigail. Next came the Forbes-Smyth brothers and Mr. Pennywhistle.

Isabelle had resigned herself to entering the dining room last, and alone, when she spied Mr. Pennywhistle crossing the room to her side. With a polite bow, he offered her his arm.

"I didn't know you would be here, Lady Isabelle," he said quietly. "Are you chaperoning one of these children?"

She flashed him a grateful smile and took his arm. "Not officially," she said. "I may act as chaperone to the twins, Abigail and Amanda Heart, in the spring."

"Lucky girls," he replied gallantly. "Those in the know whisper that any girl fortunate enough to be sponsored by the charming Lady Isabelle is assured of a successful Season."

"You're very kind," she replied, "but I must point out that the girls I have chaperoned in the past have all been quite delightful, both in appearance and manners."

"Perhaps, but they have not all been blessed with papas possessing deep pockets. And yet they made some of the most advantageous matches, year after year."

"You're going to turn my head with your flattery, Mr. Pennywhistle," said Isabelle, feeling very much more the thing.

They entered the dining room, its table stretched to its longest length. Alex was seating the Duchess of Charlton on his right and the Marchioness of Dunham, on his left. At the other end of the room, Lady Foxworth took her seat with Alex's friend, the Marquess of Dunham on her right and Colonel Sutter on her left. The others arranged themselves accordingly, the highest-ranking members of the guests ranging themselves closest to the host or hostess, the untitled couples— never sitting together—came next, and then the rest, the youngest sitting at the dead center of the table. Isabelle allowed Mr. Pennywhistle to select her seat. Then he took the one to her left, while the countess's brother was on her right. When they had all settled in, Lady Foxworth signaled the footmen to begin serving.

They began with a mulligatawny soup, its serving supervised by the ever-vigilant Finley. Alex carved and served a roasted beef while the other footmen offered the guests fricassee of fowl, stewed tomatoes with artichokes, filet of sole with a white sauce, and a potato pudding.

Isabelle ate sparingly and drank very little wine. She had the advantage of being able to see almost half the company assembled, including both Abigail and Amanda, who were surrounded by the two Forbes-Smyth sons and had, in between them, the questionable company of Miles Parker.

"They are only children to him," said Mr. Pennywhistle when she had ignored him for several minutes.

"I do beg your pardon, sir. Here you have been so thoughtful, seeing to my every need, and I am ignoring you."

"Not at all. I know you are concerned about your charges. Parker may be a rake, but he does not trifle with the infantry. A few warm anecdotes, perhaps, but that will be all."

"Thank you, Mr. Pennywhistle, for setting my mind at ease. Now, I promise not to allow myself to think about them anymore. Tell me, how is your dear mother's health these days?"

"She is much the same. I fear it is only a matter of time."

"I am so sorry. She has always been such a kind woman. It is easy to see why your manners are just as they ought to be."

"Thank you, my lady."

"Here now, Harcourt, pray do not monopolize this charming lady all evening," said Mr. Deal, leaning forward to peer at his friend.

"Very well, I will let you have your chance, Everett," said the shy Mr. Pennywhistle. "I really should speak to Miss Brisbane, just to be polite."

"Good, now you can tell me why we have such an illustrious group around this table. And I warn you, my dear Lady Isabelle, I will not be fobbed off by some tale about my sister wanting to invite all these mushrooms."

Isabelle said quietly, "I am quite as much at sea as you are, Mr. Deal."

"But Evelyn told me you arrived last week at the same time as that Amelia creature."

"And so I did," she responded, "but as I was telling Mr. Pennywhistle earlier, I am thinking of chaperoning the twins during the Season, and this was the perfect opportunity to get to know them better."

"Hmm, I don't know if I fully believe you, my lady, but I suppose it will do for now." He made a face and pushed the buttered prawns away. "Pray do not bring those things near me; the smell alone is enough to make me break out in welts."

The first course was removed, replaced by the second, and another round of delectable dishes made their appearance. From the end of the table, the decorous hum of conversation was broken by a sudden loud crack of laughter, and all heads turned.

"Oh, go about your business," ordered the Duchess of Charlton, pointing her fork down the table. "Cannot a man entertain an old woman without everyone staring?"

The other guests immediately resumed their conversations, except for Isabelle, who leaned in slightly, to watch Alex. His head was bowed as he leaned toward the duchess, his hand covering his mouth, obviously telling her some lewd tale.

Suddenly he looked up, caught her eye, and raised his glass to her. Isabelle had no choice but to follow suit. One couldn't refuse to take wine with one's host.

When they had each taken a sip, the earl returned his attention to the duchess, and Isabelle put down her glass, feeling the evening had gone quite flat all of a sudden.

At the end of the table, Alex was very much astounded by the Duchess of Charlton's conversation. He shook his head, thinking he had misheard.

"Would you please say that again, your grace?" he said.

"Are you hard of hearing, my boy? I said I didn't realize my niece would be here. Well, to be more exact, my great-niece, since she is my late husband's brother's granddaughter."

"Lady Isabelle Fanshaw is your great-niece?" he said quietly, once again staring at Isabelle, though she didn't look up this time. "On the side of your late husband, who was the Duke of Charlton?"

"Yes, quite, but most people don't realize it. When my son passed away, not long after Sophia was born, the title went to his father's brother—very briefly, because he died, too, shortly afterward. His son Rupert, my boy's cousin and Lady Isabelle's father, then inherited the title. There was little money to go with it, which is why people don't really miss having the Duke of Charlton about. Not to mention that he's a spiteful sort, and dull too."

"That explains why Lady Isabelle doesn't speak of him," murmured Alex, his eyes and sympathy going out to her.

"That's not why," said the duchess, speaking as if he were a thick headed schoolboy. "She doesn't mention him because he disowned her for marrying Fanshaw against his wishes, or so the story goes. He wanted her to marry some cit with buckets of money and no breeding. She refused to mend the family fortunes, and he never forgave her. Disinherited her, though there would never have been much of an inheritance. Cut himself and Isabelle's mother off from his own daughter . . . and granddaughter. A stupid man, and I can't abide stupid men," she added.

"Quite," said Alex, returning his attention to his plate while the duchess continued to recall other families and their checkered pasts.

The earl couldn't wait to speak to Isabelle to ask her why she felt she had to keep it a secret. It wasn't as if their family history was so unusual.

Suddenly, Alex noticed his cousin Amelia, who had taken a seat of honor, closer to his mother than Isabelle. He grinned. The ones he really wanted to tell were her and his mother, who set such store by rank and fortune. This would put a damper on Amelia's pretensions to superiority. Isabelle was the daughter of the Duke of Charlton. Never mind that she didn't socialize with the man; her place in society was assured because of her heritage, whether her father accepted her or not.

The second course was removed and the final course of desserts was brought in. The older children, dressed in their finest, were brought in to make their curtsies and bows to the new guests. Allie ran to her grandmother, who took her onto her lap and plied her with the fresh fruits, tidbits of apples and oranges, sweetmeats, and the pear trifle that Isabelle had suggested as a grand finale. Beth stood beside Isabelle, who helped her fill a plate, while the other two Dunham girls went to their mother's side.

The countess motioned to Robert and Phillip, saying, "Come and fill your plates, boys."

They hung back, looking to their father for permission. Alex nodded, smiling at the unusual tableau his mother and her three grandchildren presented at the end of the table. Her grandsons were on either side, and she was urging them to help themselves.

When the children had been served, they said their good nights and marched out of the dining room, the girls' maids bringing up the rear.

"Delightful children," pronounced Mr. Pennywhistle to the table at large. "And what a fine display this is."

Leaning forward to better see his friend, Mr. Deal said, "A pear trifle. Now, who would have thought of such a thing? In the summer, I have had all sorts of berries made into a trifle, but I would not have thought of pears."

"I do hope you like it," said the countess.

"Oh, we shall certainly like it, dear sister," said her brother, Mr. Deal, rubbing his hands together in childish expectation.

Ten minutes later, the entire table was talking about the trifle, begging the countess to share the receipt.

"You will have to ask Lady Isabelle," said the older woman. "I must confess that it was her idea. Wherever did you get the receipt, Lady Isabelle?"

"From my mother's cook. It was one of my favorites as a child," she said, unaware of the mortification she was about to suffer.

"So it originally came from the Tottenham?" said the earl.

Isabelle's head spun around, her eyes wide as she

looked from him to the Duchess of Charlton, who had suddenly lost her tongue.

"That is correct," she said tightly.

"But where in Tottenham?" asked the bubbly Lady Sophia. "That is where my late father's family seat is. I have never been there, but I'm sure my grandmother would be acquainted with your family."

"Shh!" hissed Lady Anne to her younger sister. "Cannot you see Lady Isabelle doesn't wish to speak of it?"

Isabelle took a deep breath. "There is no great secret about my family history, Lady Anne. I choose not to trade on it, but it is hardly shocking. And you are right, Lady Sophia, your grandmother is well acquainted with my family since she is my great-aunt."

"Isabelle, you needn't explain yourself," said Alex. "I should not have spoken."

"Perhaps not, but you did," she said, keeping her emotions under a tight rein. "Furthermore, unless I wish most of the table to expire from curiosity, I should tell them that my father is the current Duke of Charlton."

A ripple of quiet exclamations went around the table, but no one spoke. Alex pushed away from the table to go to her, to lead her away.

Then his uncle Everett began to tap his wineglass with his knife, saying loudly, "Jolly good, my dear. Jolly good for you!"

Everyone took their lead from this, and the noisy exchange that followed made Isabelle wonder why she had ever worried about keeping her past a secret.

"I always said she was well bred," declared the starchy Lady Brisbane as if she were speaking for the whole of Polite Society.

Not to be outdone, Lady Foxworth rose, a signal to the ladies to leave the gentlemen to their port. She circled the table and held out her hand to Isabelle, thereby putting her own stamp of approval on her guest. Together they walked back to the drawing room.

"Now that I know your family, I must confess that I remember the scandal when you married, my dear," said the countess.

"I prefer not to speak of it, my lady."

"But you have nothing to be embarrassed about, my dear girl. If my father had been the ogre yours is, I wouldn't wish to acknowledge him either. But the fault is his, not yours. Your Mr. Fanshaw was from the gentry and was a perfectly acceptable match. As I said, I remember when it happened, and everyone I knew sided with you, not your father."

"You're very kind, my lady, and I must apologize for the scene at your dinner table," said Isabelle.

"Scene? Nonsense! Only think of it this way; my dinner will be the talk of London when Lady Brisbane returns to town for the Season. It is also quite a feather in my cap to add another such prominent lady to my list of guests. Besides," she said, lowering her voice to a mere whisper, "I will enjoy reminding Amelia that she stems only from a marquess, while her daughters' chaperone is the daughter of a duke. Quite delicious! But here are your, let me see, your second cousins, and your great-aunt. I will leave you in their hands."

Isabelle gave a tentative smile to the dowager duchess, who dashed a sentimental tear from her withered cheek.

"I'm sorry I never sought you out before, my dear. I do hope you know, it was not because I wanted to sever the connection," she said, weaving back and forth from the stress of the evening. "You have more gumption than I ever gave you credit for."

"I didn't know you realized who I was, your grace."

"Of course I did. I have seen you any number of times in the past five or six years when you were leading some simpering girl about London. But I never spoke. You were always sitting in the corner, unobtrusive and quiet, so I assumed you wanted it that way," she said, clutching Isabelle's hand to steady herself.

"Please sit down, Duchess," said Isabelle, leading the frail old lady to the nearest chair. "May I get you something?"

"No, I shall be fine, I have these little spells. Don't hover over me so," she snapped at her three granddaughters.

They hastily found chairs and placed them close to the duchess, who continued. "I take leave to tell you, Lady Isabelle, that your father is a beef-witted cawker, always was. I never understood how your mother put up with him as long as she did, but we can't all be fortunate in our choices of husbands. Mine, for instance, should have had more stamina and lived longer," she added with her signature cackle.

Amy, Lady Dunham smiled, and said, "I have met you before, Lady Isabelle, but didn't know how to broach the topic of our relation."

Lady Anne spoke up, saying, "I always thought you were ashamed to claim the family, you see."

"Oh, no, not the entire family," said Isabelle, smiling at her newfound relations. "I was, and am, afraid to trade on my father's name, because he is quite capable of denouncing me publicly for doing so. I have never asked a solicitor, but when one has been officially disinherited, one simply doesn't exist. Or that is my understanding of the matter, and I didn't wish to cause a scandal. One day, I hope to bring my daughter out."

"I met her upstairs this afternoon. She is delightful," said Amy. "My girls are eight and nine. How old is Beth?"

"She is seven."

"Then we will have to bring her out with Maggie.

That is, if you think the cousins might become friends?" said Amy.

"I would like that," said Isabelle, almost overwhelmed by this unexpected kindness. An hour earlier, she had been alone in the world with Beth her only family. Now she had a great aunt and cousins too.

"And what about my little one?" asked Lady Anne, the newest mother.

The old duchess laughed and poked a finger at her youngest granddaughter, saying, "We will find a husband for Sophia very quickly, so she can produce another cousin for baby Caroline to come out with too."

Sophia turned bright red, but she was accustomed to her grandmother's outrageous discourse and knew better than to protest. To do so would mean only more teasing.

"You have all been so nice to me," said Isabelle. "I fear I will have to forgive Lord Foxworth for spilling the soup."

"I shouldn't if I were you, my girl," said the duchess. "It will do the rogue no harm to think that he is still in your black books." The ladies all laughed at this, and their conversation turned to the coming Season.

Abigail finished the piece she was playing with a resounding crash of ivory. The duchess turned to her granddaughter and commanded, "Anne, go at once and take over the pianoforte. I cannot bear another note from Miss Heart. Sophia, you run along and turn the pages for her."

As usual, the girls did as their grandmother ordered, and the drawing room became more pleasant as Lady Anne's expert fingers glided over the keys.

Lady Brisbane brought her daughter over to converse with the duchess and to glean information about Isabelle. She smiled, gave short replies, and then excused herself, moving away to sit on the sofa nearest the door, where she could intercept Alex and ring a peal over him for his indiscretion.

Isabelle's good humor was restored, and she smiled as she watched the other ladies, her thoughts on the earl. She was still not ready to forgive Alex for blurting out her private history, but it was not such a terrible thing after all. She had always supposed that Society would side with her father, the duke, on the matter of her marriage. It had never occurred to her that because he had alienated so many people in the *ton,* they would champion her instead.

The gentlemen entered rather quickly, and Alex headed straight for Isabelle. She ducked her head and waited, but he didn't appear, and she looked up to see that he had been caught by Lady Brisbane and his cousin Amelia.

A discreet cough commanded her attention, and she turned to find Miles Parker grinning at her as he took the empty spot beside her on the sofa.

"Quite the dark horse," he said, winking at her.

"I beg your pardon, Mr. Parker?" she replied.

"You, my lady. I never knew you were the daughter of a duke. Rather like thinking you've bought a hack at Tattersall's and discovering it's a purebred champion," he said.

Isabelle managed to not roll her eyes at the equestrian comparison, and she said sensibly, "Well, I wasn't the daughter of a duke until I reached the age of fourteen. My father never expected to inherit the title. And surely it is nothing to brag about, is it?"

"It's not?" he asked.

"Certainly not. If I cannot be judged on my own merits, then I would rather not be judged at all."

"Ah, we're back at Tattersall's again. Now that I can

understand. Good judge of horseflesh, that's Miles Parker. And of the ladies too," he added with a leer.

"I'm sure you are, Mr. Parker, or, at least, you think you are. Do you recall Miss Baxter from last Season?"

"Miss Baxter? No, I can't say that I do. A pretty filly?"

"A very pretty young lady, Mr. Parker, and one, moreover, whom you had the audacity to accost."

"Now, I never would, my lady," he said, beginning to look uncomfortable.

"Oh, but you did. You kissed her against her wishes. I didn't know the reason at the time, but I have since learned it was to win a bet with Lord Foxworth. Now do you recall?"

"Oh, the kissing bet," he said, grinning again. "Yes, I recall. I may have lost to Foxworth, but I had a wonderful time trying to win that one."

"You, Mr. Parker, are a callous reprobate, and I do not care to converse with you any further."

As she rose, he clambered to his feet and said, "Just wait until you get better acquainted with me, Lady Isabelle. You'll find I'm a very easy fellow to know."

Isabelle's temper was sizzling, but she walked away at a decorous gait, making her way toward the door by skirting the room to avoid conversation with anyone else. She had had enough excitement for one evening.

Reaching the door to the drawing room, she slipped into the hall, breathing a sigh of relief to escape all the well-intended comments. Her head was beginning to ache, and all she really wanted was the solitude and quiet of her room.

Then she spied Alex, who was speaking to the butler. Before she could escape this new pitfall, he turned and saw her.

Waving the butler away, Alex stayed where he was, his dark eyes solemn. As for Isabelle, it was as if she had been caught on a fisherman's line. She refused to swim toward the shore, but she could make no progress away from the angler, who had her well and truly caught.

Cocking his head to one side, he asked, "Am I forgiven?"

Or had he? She couldn't be sure he had spoken the words out loud. Perhaps she had read his mind. Perhaps it had been his heart speaking to hers. Isabelle stamped her foot at this bit of nonsense.

Alex grinned, glancing first at her foot and then into her eyes. He closed the short expanse between them and took her arm, leading her down the corridor to the library. Muffled voices within warned him away, and they continued on to the next room, the billiard room. More voices, clearly masculine this time, made them continue their quest.

Finally, they arrived at the breakfast room, and Alex pulled her inside, closing the latch firmly behind them.

"And what shall we tell the nosy Abigail if she comes looking for us?" said Isabelle, her eyes shining with amusement. Really, it was impossible to be angry, no matter how high-handed he acted.

"We shall tell Abigail to mind her own demmed business," he said, taking her hand in his. "Only tell me I am forgiven, and I'll slay a thousand dragons for you— or one puny, irritating ward of mine—whichever I should happen upon first."

"Absurd," she said.

"But am I forgiven?"

Recalling the duchess's advice, Isabelle ignored his question and strolled toward the windows, gazing outside, where the moon looked like a biscuit with a small bite missing.

"Pretty, isn't it?" he asked, his breath tickling the tendrils of hair on her neck.

"Very," she replied, very much on her dignity.

"And?" he asked, reaching up and tweaking a dark curl.

She turned and then wished she had not, for he was much too close. Still, she did not look away as she said, "Alex, I have only one question for you. You knew I preferred to keep my family history private. Why did you do it?" Her words sounded breathless even to her own ears.

He touched her cheek, gazing into her eyes. "I don't know, Belle. When the duchess told me, I was more than a little surprised." He dropped his hand and shook his head. "Perhaps I just wanted to punish you for not trusting me with the information."

Isabelle slipped away from him. It had been a difficult day, and she was weary. She was not fit for making coy, witty conversation.

"I suppose, since everyone is being so kind about it, I will have to forgive you."

"I am glad, I would hate to lose my tutor over such a trivial matter—not trivial exactly," he said, advancing again, taking her hand in his, and lifting it to his lips. He turned it over at the last minute and kissed her palm, sending shivers up and down her spine.

"Now we can be comfortable again," he said, smiling down at her.

"Yes, comfortable," she replied, all the while thinking that if he kept kissing her hand and breathing on her neck, she would never be comfortable again! She kept these thoughts to herself, of course, and returned his smile, allowing him to lead her back to the Great Hall. Here, Isabelle hung back.

"Would you think me a coward if I didn't go back inside?" she asked.

"Certainly not. You're a guest in my house, Isabelle. You may do exactly as you please."

"I thought I was more of an employee," she said.

"Employee? Now, wherever did you get that idea?" he said, chuckling as he bowed over her hand again, this time only grazing it with his lips. "If anyone asks me, I'll make your excuses."

"Thank you, Alex. Good night," she said, walking toward the staircase.

"Good night, Isabelle," he called, blowing her a kiss.

Isabelle had enough wits about her to ignore the intimate gesture this time, but she was smiling as she made her way upstairs.

The next day, Lady Isabelle Fanshaw sensed that her position in the household had changed subtly. The servants, who had been polite before, now bordered on being obsequious. The other guests sought her out rather than looking through her. Only Mr. Pennywhistle and Mr. Deal treated her as they always had, with the utmost respect.

Because of the number of guests, the breakfast room was not used the next morning. The dining hall, its table still extended, was pressed into use again, though many of the guests chose to stay abed until afternoon. So Isabelle and Beth found themselves breaking their fasts with the two old bachelors, Abigail, and Lady Sophia.

Mr. Deal and Mr. Pennywhistle plied Beth with jams and jellies, telling her an impromptu tale of a fairy princess locked in a tower, who ate strawberry preserves.

"Strawberry preserves have magic powers," said Mr. Deal.

"Really?" asked Beth.

"Cross my heart," said the old bachelor. "And when the princess ate the strawberry preserves, she discovered she could fly like a bird."

Gurgling with laughter, Beth asked, "So the princess flew out of her tower and lived happily ever after."

Dolefully shaking his head, Mr. Pennywhistle said, "I'm afraid not."

"But why not? That's what I would do," said Beth.

"Yes, if you remembered to open the window first. The princess, however, acted before she thought, and she flew straight into the glass and broke her pretty little nose."

"How dreadful," said Lady Sophia, her attention slipping from Abigail's aimless chatter about London.

"Oh, but it turned out all right," said Mr. Deal. "The princess found a frog and kissed it, thinking it would turn into her prince."

"And what happened to her then?" asked Beth.

"Oh, she turned into a frog too, and they lived happily ever after in the moat surrounding the tower."

"What nonsense," said Abigail, her nose in the air.

The gentlemen refrained from giving the impertinent miss a set-down. Wisely, they finished their meals and left the room. Beth followed after them, begging them to accompany her to the nursery to tell her new friends about the princess.

"I think I'll go with them," said Lady Sophia, leaving Abigail and Isabelle alone.

"That was quite rude of you, Abigail. You should really try to cultivate patience now, before your London Season begins. The *ton* looks down on young ladies with fresh tongues."

"I don't care. Those two old men are so irritating. Why on earth would they spend their time making up nonsensical stories for a child? Lady Sophia and I could not even hold a mature conversation. I swear, their prattle was worse than the child's."

Isabelle frowned and shook her head. "You know, Abigail, I begin to despair of you. Since they left the room, you have insulted not only two very kind, thoughtful gentlemen, but also a little girl—to the child's own mother no less. That is foolish beyond permission."

"Who are you to tell me how to go on?" she demanded.

"I am the person your guardian has engaged to be your chaperone in the spring, or have you forgotten?"

"I haven't forgotten, Lady Isabelle, but judging from your behavior with my guardian, both you and he have ulterior motives for your presence at Foxworth Court!" With this, Abigail flounced out of the room.

Isabelle had lost her appetite completely and went straight to the earl's library in search of a paper and pen. Suddenly, the idea of playing chaperone to the viperish Abigail was intolerable. She simply would not do it! If it meant leaving Foxworth Court—and Alex—then so be it.

"Lady Isabelle, may I have a word with you?"

Isabelle looked up from the note she was writing and stared at the girl standing in the doorway. Then she smiled as she recognized Amanda, the viper's twin.

"Of course, Amanda. Please come inside."

"Thank you, my lady," said the girl, walking to the desk and sitting down in the chair across from Isabelle's.

"My sister just came up to our room. She threw herself onto the bed, sobbing uncontrollably. It took me several minutes, but I finally had the tale from her."

"I am sorry, Amanda, but I cannot sympathize with your sister. She was unspeakably rude and disrespectful."

"Yes, that's Abigail," said the quiet twin, her own chin beginning to tremble. "The thing is, Abigail doesn't really mean half of what she says."

"Then I hope she learns not to say it, or her Season—and, therefore, yours—will be very uncomfortable."

"I know, and I dread it. But you see, this party that was meant to give us a chance to become more comfortable with Society has not gone as Abigail envisioned it."

"In what way, my dear?"

"It is foolish, of course, and comes of reading too many romance novels—something Abigail adores, I assure you. It is Lord Foxworth. He has paid almost no attention to us, preferring to keep company with you, instead. Abigail had the foolish idea . . ." The girl blushed a fiery red and wouldn't look up.

"Oh, my," breathed Isabelle. "She fancies herself in love with Lord Foxworth."

Amanda's head bobbed up and down, but she still couldn't bring herself to look up.

"Surely she knows it is just calf love?"

"I suppose," came the doubtful reply.

"No, I suppose not. When one is young . . ."

"She is so jealous of you, my lady. I suppose it is understandable," said Amanda, finally looking up, her eyes pleading for tolerance. "Here you are with your beautiful, sophisticated gowns, your self-assurance, and your elegance, and then there is Abigail, feeling . . . well, completely the opposite."

"I assure you, Amanda, there is nothing to be jealous about. Certainly the earl prefers my conversation to a girl . . . I don't wish to sound condescending, but . . . a girl not quite out of the schoolroom."

"And so I have told her. I have also told her that she would be bored to flinders if she wed our guardian."

"But she doesn't believe you, of course," said Isabelle.

"Oh, I think she is beginning to see it. Since the Forbes-Smyth brothers arrived and have obviously singled us out—preferring us even over Lady Sophia."

"Yes, I noticed that last night," said Isabelle. "And they are both quite handsome."

"And young," added Amanda before ducking her head again. "Not that Lord Foxworth is old!"

"But he is," laughed Isabelle. "He is twice your age, my dear. You might point that out to Abigail. And tell her from me that there is absolutely nothing between your guardian and me—not that I think she will believe you."

"She must believe me." Amanda looked from the note on the desk to Isabelle and added, "If she doesn't, I fear we will have to make do with our mother as a chaperone next spring, and neither of us wants that to happen."

Isabelle smiled and picked up the letter, tearing it into tiny pieces. "That makes three of us," she said, laughing when the timid girl jumped to her feet, circled the desk, and gave her a fierce hug.

"You will not regret it, my lady, and I promise you that Abigail will behave . . . even if I have to stuff a rag in her mouth!"

"I may hold you to that, my dear," said Isabelle, smiling at Amanda. "Now, you run along and tell Abigail that we will begin again."

"Thank you, my lady," said Amanda, hurrying out the door.

Isabelle shook her head and sighed. She knew Abigail's remorse was not going to cure her unruly tongue. She only hoped she did not come to regret her decision.

Seven

Deciding it would be best if she spoke to Abigail personally and set things straight with her, Isabelle crossed the Great Hall to go upstairs. Afterward, she would go to the nursery and see if Beth and her newfound cousins wished to go for a walk in the gardens. It was an extraordinarily fine day for December—cold, but bright and sunny.

"Psst, Lady Isabelle. May I have a word with you?" whispered Betty, the countess's maid.

"Of course," she said. "What is it, Betty?"

"Lady Foxworth is nowhere to be found."

One foot on the stairs, Isabelle hesitated. It wasn't her affair if the countess had gone off. Still, the possibility of the countess taking a solitary drive or ride without notifying her maid was highly unlikely.

"You must be mistaken, Betty. Her ladyship must be in the house somewhere."

"I have looked everywhere, my lady. I give you my word."

The maid's concern was genuine, but Isabelle still hesitated. If something had happened to the countess, then she should inform Alex, but how foolish she would feel if they discovered the countess dozing in some out of the way chamber while her guests were left to amuse themselves.

"Very well, Betty, I will help you look for her. Is there

another servant we can enlist to help in the search quietly?"

"Well, there's my niece Penny."

"Good, then bring her to my room, and I'll get my maid, Jane, to help too."

"Oh, thank you, my lady. I'll be back in a minute."

Isabelle went to her room, where Jane was straightening the bed and setting the room to rights.

"Jane, I need your help."

"Yes, my lady? Were you wanting to change to go shopping in Pixley with the other ladies?"

"They have gone shopping?" she asked. "Oh, that explains it. Lady Foxworth must have gone with them."

"No, my lady, they haven't gone yet. They are in their rooms, dressing. At least, I assume they are, since almost all the other abigails were summoned to their mistresses a few minutes ago. That's why I thought you were going with them."

"No, not now. There is something rather important I need you to do. It is probably all a hum, but Betty, the countess's maid, cannot find her mistress and is worried about her."

Just then Betty and her niece entered. Isabelle swore them to secrecy and they separated, each going in a different direction to search for the missing countess.

They searched the upper floors first, going to the nursery and finding it completely empty. They didn't dare start opening doors to the bedchambers, since a few of the guests had yet to make an appearance for the day and others were dressing for their outing.

On the ground floor, they tried every nook and cranny, meeting in the back hallway, to discuss their next move.

"I think we must tell Lord Foxworth," said Isabelle.

"Here now, what is this? Penny, get about your business, and you others, surely you have . . . oh, my lady, I didn't realize it was you," said Finley. The butler gaped at her disarray before recalling his lofty position and taking no notice of such matters.

"Never mind, Finley," she said, beckoning to him with her index finger. When he was quite close, she added, "We are looking for Lady Foxworth. We cannot find her anywhere in the house."

The butler listened solemnly, then allowed himself a glimmer of a smile. "Please step this way, my lady."

The three maids followed Isabelle, who followed the butler down the back hall that ran almost the width of the house. Before they reached the conservatory, they could hear the children singing and laughing. In a grand gesture, Finley threw open the double doors.

Isabelle peered inside. All she could see were plants, a veritable jungle of greenery.

"But I looked in here," said Betty. "Her ladyship wouldn't be in here, not with all those children."

"Yes, she is, I saw her go in there myself not more than a half hour ago," said the butler. "Mrs. Havenhurst came for an early visit."

"Oh, so Allie is visiting," said Betty as if that explained everything. "I am sorry to worry you, Lady Isabelle. I heard the other little girls squealing and the boys laughing earlier when I was searching for her ladyship, and so I thought she would never be in here."

Isabelle smiled. "That's all right, Betty. I'm just glad we found her. Now I had best go upstairs and change this gown. Thank you for your assistance, Finley."

"You're quite welcome, my lady."

"What's all this?" asked Alex, strolling out of the conservatory and looking Isabelle over with raised brows.

"I didn't know the entire household was in the conservatory," she quipped. "I'm afraid I didn't receive the summons."

The butler and maids slipped away, leaving her alone

with Alex, who was looking devilishly handsome in a bottle-green riding coat, snugly fitted doeskin breeches, and gleaming Hessians. If he had already gone for a ride, she thought, he had managed to keep his clothing pristine. She smoothed the skirt of her dusty gown and grimaced.

"Mama! Come and play hide-and-seek with us," said Beth, taking her mother's hand and tugging her forward a few steps.

"Not now, my sweet. I am not in a fit state for company." She waved as the child scampered away to hide.

"That brings me to my question, my dear. Just why are you looking rather, uh, disheveled?" he asked, again studying her from head to toe, a smile playing on his lips.

Isabelle blushed and explained, "I have spent the past twenty minutes searching for your mother."

"She has been in the conservatory the entire time with the children," he replied. "Come, I'll show you."

"Really, Alex, I should go and change."

"Nonsense," he said, taking out his handkerchief and wiping a smudge from her cheek. "There, now you are fine, and you really must see this," he said, offering his arm and leading her slowly toward the sound of the children.

"Betty didn't think . . . that is . . ."

"My mother's maid didn't know Allie was here, so she didn't expect her to be in the conservatory with her grandsons."

"Alex, I'm sure she didn't mean—"

"Do not bother to explain, Isabelle. You could have knocked me over with a feather, I was that surprised. When I arrived on the scene, she was having a profound discussion with Phillip about his studies and his aspirations. I took Robert to one side, and he told me she had already spent several minutes with him, asking about his studies and such."

"Well, she is their grandmother," said Isabelle.

"Yes, and has been for years, but she has never bothered to act like a grandparent, especially the doting grandmother she is to my niece."

"But that is my point. Perhaps she is learning how to be a doting grandmother from Allie," offered Isabelle.

"I suppose that is the only logical explanation," he said, lowering his voice as they arrived in the sitting area, which had several sturdy chairs and a small sofa, all made out of bamboo, painted in a natural yellow hue that complimented the cushions of brightly colored chintz.

"My dear Lady Isabelle," said the countess, waving her forward while she moved to one side of the sofa, making room for the newcomer.

"Good morning, Lady Foxworth, Grace," she said, nodding to both the countess and her friend. "I apologize for coming to you looking such a fright."

"Why, you look delightful, my dear," said the countess, making Isabelle think that the older woman's sight was not terribly good. "That is a very pretty gown. I do so love yellow, but I fear it is not pleasing with my complexion. It make me look positively sallow."

"Perhaps you just haven't found the right shade of yellow," replied Isabelle.

"Possibly, but I have no desire to go to London to find it," said the countess. "You know, when I first moved here to Pixley, I could not abide the thought of visiting the local shops and having a provincial like Mrs. Crane sewing for me. Now I cannot abide the thought of going to London. All that bother for a few gowns? It is hardly worth the trouble."

"You always look quite elegant, my lady," said her daughter-in-law. "She is Mrs. Crane's best customer."

"Oh, I have long used her for my gowns," said Isabelle. "It is well worth the drive over from Spursden. She always has the loveliest yard goods."

"That is what I was telling Lady Brisbane. I believe they are going into Pixley this morning," said the countess. "I told them to be sure and visit Miss Silverton's shop too. She is a distant cousin of ours," the countess informed Isabelle, adding in an aside, "Not from the right side of the blankets, but a charming lady all the same."

"Mother, why don't you go with our guests?" asked Alex.

"I would," she said, "but I don't wish to leave the children. Alex, did you know that Phillip was first in his class?"

"Yes, Mother, I did, and I believe I told you so."

"Oh, perhaps I did not hear you. And Robert, he has bested every boy at fencing, including the older boys," she said.

"Yes, that's right."

"Well, you must forgive a grandmother for bragging," said the countess, watching Robert as he rushed toward her chair with Allie in his arms.

"Bravo, Robert and Allie! Home free!" said the countess, taking Allie onto her lap and nuzzling her golden curls. Robert lounged over the back of the sofa, near his grandmother, grinning at his father as if sharing a joke. To his surprise, the countess turned and kissed his cheek, causing him to blush and jump back.

"Allie, you must thank your cousin for carrying you."

"Thank you, Robba," she said, giggling when he tickled her.

"You're welcome, Allie. I say, I am famished, Grandmother. Shall I ring for some refreshments?"

"Splendid idea, my boy. And tell Finley when he comes that we want some of those little cakes, the ones without the seeds. I'm sure you children would prefer to have them plain. Your father always did," she added, astounding her son so that he began to cough, requiring his son to beat him between the shoulders until he had recovered.

While they waited for the tea tray, Isabelle remarked, "This is a lovely room, my lady."

"Now you have done it," said Alex.

"What?" she asked, fearful that she had brought up a delicate subject. The countess hastened to reassure her.

"Do not pay any heed to Alex, my dear. He is teasing me because I insisted on having the room added to the manor house when I moved here three years ago. I invited the talented Mr. Nash to come out and look at the house. He was much too busy with the Regent's projects to take it on himself, but he sent one of his people to design the room and supervise the building."

"At an astronomical cost," muttered Alex before grinning and saying, "Well worth every penny, to be sure."

"Alex, do not tease your mother so," said Grace.

"Well, I have certainly enjoyed it," said the countess. "It is so lovely to sit here in the winter, inside, where it is warm and, yet with nature all around."

"Well, I must say, the hot-air heating does make it pleasant," said Alex. "I was worried that the marble floors would make it too cold for Mother or the plants, but they don't, thanks to the heating. It is so efficient, I'm thinking of having the entire house done."

"What, no more cozy fireplaces?" asked Isabelle.

"Oh, there will always be a need for that, but wouldn't it be wonderful to have the passageways and halls heated too?" said Alex.

"Warm corridors? I can't think of anything better," said his sister-in-law.

Finley entered, followed by a footman carrying a silver tray and another carrying a small table. The countess asked Isabelle to pour out while she made certain all the children had first choice of the sweets.

Grace took a sip of her tea and said, "You know, Alex, I wish you would speak to Adam about this heating business. He thinks it is just foolishness."

"Adam has never liked change, but there are so many new devices that will make our lives more pleasant," said Alex, shaking his head when his mother offered him tea.

"Such as?" asked Isabelle, intrigued by the passion in his voice as much as the information.

"I have been telling Mother about Donington Park, not too far from here. The Earl of Moira has installed water closets on two floors."

"Alex, that is hardly a fitting topic to discuss with ladies," said his mother, feeding a bite of biscuit to her granddaughter.

"I don't know why not. I wager you would not turn down having a water closet and a bathroom off your dressing room if I offered it," he teased.

"Nevertheless, we should change the subject to something more suitable. Tell me, Lady Isabelle, what do we need to do to make the conservatory a suitable setting for our winter *pique-nique?*"

"I am going to say good-bye on that note, ladies. I promised the gentlemen that we would attend a prize-fight in the next county," said Alex.

"In winter?" asked Grace with a delicate shudder.

"It's in someone's barn. It is hardly going to be the sort one can witness nearer London, but the crowd will be congenial and the sport powerful enough."

"Can Phillip and I come, Father?" asked Robert, leaping to his feet.

"Oh, Robert, surely you don't want to see such violence," said the countess with a shudder.

"Another year or two, Robert. When you are fifteen, perhaps."

"Very well," said the boy. "I think I'll go upstairs," he mumbled, shuffling out of the room with a hangdog look.

"Good morning, ladies," said Alex, following after his son and catching him up. "Robert, I'm sorry to disappoint you, but let this be a lesson. If your grandmother and aunt had not been sitting there, you might have had a chance of talking me into it."

"That's not fair, Father!" he protested.

Alex grinned and tousled his hair. "Not at all, but such is the power of the ladies. Never forget that. We gentlemen may hold the reins, but it is the fairer sex that tells us what is what."

"Yes, Father," said the youth.

The gentlemen did not return until early evening and had to scramble to dress for dinner. The young men were in high gig, having won their bets, and the older gentlemen were just weary. Most of the ladies had spent the afternoon in the shops and were also tired, so dinner was a quiet affair, without any momentous revelations.

After the gentlemen joined the ladies, cards were suggested, and more tables and chairs were sent for. The young people groaned at the prospect of such a dull diversion, until Mr. Parker suggested they do as the children had that morning and play hide-and-seek in the conservatory.

Lady Isabelle started to squelch the proposal, but Lady Amelia waved her daughters away with a hearty "Run along, my dears."

Isabelle turned to Alex for his support, but he had taken his brother aside for some sort of council, replete with head shaking and lively gesturing. She smiled at the brothers, so attuned to each other, and she wondered what they were talking about.

"I will be Mother's partner," said Alex.

Adam shook his head. "That won't work. The host and hostess cannot partner each other—especially since they will win almost every hand."

Then let Mr. Pennywhistle be Mother's partner," said Alex. "His manners are such that he will not reveal her secret. I shall ask Isabelle to be my partner, and shall explain the situation to her."

"Isabelle?" said his brother, cocking his head to one side in surprise.

"Yes, she's devilishly clever. She'll help us."

In the confusion of setting up tables and chairs, Alex pulled Isabelle to one side for a whispered conversation.

"Isabelle, I must ask for your help," he said.

"You know you may ask me anything, Alex."

"Yes, I know. I must ask you to play against my mother." He caught her hand in his when she would have spoken. "Let me explain. My mother is a terrible card player."

"So you want her to play against someone who will give back the pennies she loses?" asked Isabelle.

"No, I want someone to play against her who will not call the local magistrate and have her jailed for cheating at cards."

"I cannot credit it," she said.

"I know it is ludicrous. I have done everything I can think of to cure her of this aberration, but she continues to cheat. Short of warning people about it, what else can I do?"

"Yes, I see your dilemma," said Isabelle. "Very well, but who will be my partner?"

"I will, and Mr. Pennywhistle will partner my mother. Adam is speaking to him now."

"Good choice. He is the soul of discretion."

"Good Lord," breathed Alex, his eyes widening in horror. Sitting at the first table, across from each other, were his mother and Lady Brisbane.

"Oh, no, not Lady Brisbane," hissed Isabelle. "She is one of the biggest gossips in the *ton*. If she discovers that the countess cheats at cards, we are sunk indeed."

Alex grinned down at her with a conspiratorial wink. "Indeed we are," he said, giving her a little push toward the table.

Taking her cue, Isabelle said, "Mr. Pennywhistle, will you be my partner? I warn you, Lady Foxworth and Lady Brisbane are formidable players."

"So I understand, my lady," he said, patting Adam on the back and striding over to the table to seat Isabelle in the chair opposite his.

Adam shook his head and looked heavenward; Alex crossed his fingers.

The Duchess of Charlton passed by on her way to snag Alex as her partner and leaned close to Isabelle's ear, whispering, "Lady Brisbane is also the worst player you'll ever see. Good luck to you all," she added in normal tones, cackling as she latched on to the earl.

"We meet again, eh, Duchess?" he asked.

"Well, it was either you or my grandson-in-law, and since he invariably loses, I choose you. You don't mind, I trust?"

"Nor do I mind," called the lanky Marquess of Dunham. "I'll just read my paper," he added, placing this over his face and leaning back on the sofa for a snooze.

"I am delighted to be your partner again, your

grace," said Alex, taking her arm and escorting her to another table.

"Our opponents will not be such easy pigeons this time, but I think we will prevail," said the old woman, rubbing her gloved hands together.

"Grandmother, please remember that I cannot afford to lose my entire jointure," said her granddaughter, Lady Anne. "And I daresay Colonel Sutter doesn't wish to be reduced to debtor's prison either."

"Then play your best," chortled the old lady, taking her seat and shuffling the cards, her dexterity amazing considering the arthritic state of her hands.

The vicar, Alex's brother, leaned over from his chair at the next table and said, "Blessed are the merciful, for they shall receive mercy."

"I would rather have the colonel's pennies than his mercy," said the duchess. "As for you, my boy, you had best see to yourself. With Lady Amelia for your partner, you'll be the one needing mercy."

"Well!" exclaimed Amelia.

"She is only teasing, cousin," said Adam, returning his attention to his own table.

Stakes were set quite low, as befitted a friendly contest of whist with ladies involved, but Alex and Adam remained distracted, constantly looking over to their mother's table to be certain all was going smoothly. They needn't have worried. Isabelle and the amenable Mr. Pennywhistle managed to feign surprise each time the countess won a trump. As for Lady Brisbane, she was too happy to find herself on the winning side for once to remark upon her partner's extraordinary luck.

After an hour, several of the foursomes had called it quits. Mr. Forbes-Smyth and Lady Dunham wandered over to watch the play at the countess's table. Before long, Mr. Deal and Lord Dunham also joined the spectators, watching the cards with awe as the countess continued to win.

"Most devilish luck I've ever seen," said Lord Dunham, whose own skill was laughable. Turning to his old friend, he said, "Now I see where you get your talent, Foxworth. Your mother's got the devil's own luck with the cards. If I didn't know better, I would swear . . ."

Adam Havenhurst's chair caught on the rug as he pushed away from his table too hastily, sending it crashing over backward, and him with it. His foot caught the edge of the table and flipped it into Lady Amelia's lap with cards and coins flying everywhere. The ladies screamed, and Isabelle threw her cards in the air for good measure. Alex rose too, but managed not to turn the room topsy-turvy.

Helping his brother to his feet, he winked at him and whispered, "Quick wits, my dear brother, that's what you have."

"I'm so sorry," said the vicar when he was once again upright, blushing as he surveyed his shocked audience.

"Are you all right, my dear?" asked his wife, Grace.

"Fine, fine, but a little bruised. I don't quite know how it happened."

"It don't matter how it happened," grumbled the duchess, who was still holding her cards against her chest. "Foxworth, sit down and finish this hand."

"Of course, your grace," he replied, making a production of taking his seat again. Lady Anne and the colonel sat down too, and the play at their table continued.

At the countess's table, Mr. Pennywhistle gave a huge yawn, which he hastily covered with his handkerchief. Blinking several times, he said, "We should finish this hand and call it quits, my lady. I fear I am all done in."

"I don't understand these young people," said the duchess from the next table.

"Nor I," said the countess. "Perhaps you and I should have a game of piquet, your grace, and let the rest of them seek their beds."

"Now, Mother, that . . . what the devil!" exclaimed Alex, throwing his cards onto the table and rising again.

All eyes turned as Miles Parker staggered into the drawing room, clutching his face and howling. Blood ran between his fingers, and Isabelle grabbed Mr. Pennywhistle's handkerchief and hurried to the injured man's side, dabbing at the open wounds as she led him to the closest sofa.

"What happened?" demanded everyone at once.

Alex called for quiet, and Isabelle glanced up, looking relieved when her eyes found his in that sea of faces. He smiled and shouldered his way closer, kneeling beside her, but Isabelle was no longer looking at him or the bleeding man. Her attention had been diverted by someone in the doorway. Twisting around, Alex saw Amanda there, shaken and obviously frightened.

Then Isabelle leaned closer to Miles Parker, pretending to inspect his wounds.

"It was a cat, Mr. Parker, a hysterical cat," she whispered, meeting his teary gaze with a hard stare until Miles nodded.

Turning and thrusting the handkerchief into Grace's hands, Isabelle and Alex slipped away, listening as the rake began his tale about startling a sleeping cat while they were playing hide-and-seek in the conservatory. The countess insisted loudly that there were no cats in her conservatory, but Parker had everyone's attention.

Alex took Isabelle's arm and led her into the hall, where Amanda threw herself into Isabelle's arms, sobbing wildly. Isabelle took her handkerchief and dried

Amanda's tears while they led the girl to the library and listened to her tale.

"It was awful. We chose partners, at Mr. Parker's suggestion. I didn't know why he chose me, until . . ."

Alex left their side, poured a dose of brandy, and returned, ordering the girl to down it.

After her coughing subsided, he said ominously, "What did he do to you?"

"He . . . he . . . k-kissed me," she managed to say before dissolving into tears again.

"Is that all?" asked Alex, his frown lightening until Isabelle glared up at him. He shrugged.

"Yes," she said, shuddering before she added a whispered, "he put his . . . tongue . . ."

"There, there, my dear child," soothed Isabelle. "There, there."

"And what did you do about it?" asked Alex.

"I scratched his face as hard as I could," replied the usually shy girl with a touch of satisfaction. Then the horror of her own actions sent her into fresh paroxysms of guilty tears. Alex produced his own handkerchief and grimaced at Isabelle, cocking his head toward the door and moving away from the sobbing girl.

"There, there," said Isabelle, putting the earl's fresh handkerchief into Amanda's trembling hands. She then followed Alex to the door.

"I cannot call the fellow out for kissing her," he whispered.

"No, of course not, for both their sakes."

"This is what comes of sheltering girls too closely," he grumbled.

"And allowing them to be alone with rogues," she said.

He opened his mouth to protest but fell silent. What could he say? He couldn't very well defend his friend's rakish actions to Isabelle, who thought a rake was no better than the devil himself.

"What do you propose I do?" he asked finally.

"First, we must make certain any scandal is averted. I will calm Amanda and get her upstairs without her having to face anyone. You must take care of the rest."

"You want me to take care of everything else?" he complained. Isabelle chastised him with a look, and he glanced back at Amanda, who continued to sniffle and blow her nose. Alex grinned, deciding at a glance that the "rest" was infinitely preferable to dealing with Amanda. With a wink, he said, "Thank you, Isabelle."

"I'll lead her up the servants' stairs while you try to keep everyone in the drawing room for a few more minutes to give us time to reach her room. If you should see Abigail, send her up immediately," said Isabelle.

"Of course. Good luck," said Alex, leaning forward and giving her lips a light kiss.

Her eyes widened and her mouth flew open, but she offered no rebuke. Alex grinned and fled.

"I had to come see you," he whispered, slipping inside Isabelle's sitting room, his movements furtive.

"Alex, you should not be here. It has grown quiet next door only in the past fifteen minutes," she protested, frowning when he ignored her.

"Good, then the twins should be asleep," he said, walking to the single window and pushing it open to the cold, dark night. "Did you know it's snowing? The first snow of the season."

Isabelle heaved a sigh and pulled her flannel wrapper close, reflecting that at least she had blown out the candles, and there was only the light from the fireplace illuminating her state of undress. Her bare feet were silent as she padded across the soft carpet to the window. She peered past his broad shoulders at the silent snow that was coming down in fat, glistening flakes.

"It's beautiful," she said, shivering and looking away from the snow to the earl, who continued to peer out the window. His boyish excitement was captivating, and she smiled.

He turned to grin at her, seeming to really see her for the first time. "You must be freezing," he said, closing the window and putting an arm around her shoulder, rubbing up and down vigorously as he let her back to the fire.

Isabelle sat down on one side of the delicate settee and indicated that he should join her. She tucked her bare feet under her and waited until he was seated.

"You must be dying of curiosity to know what occurred after I left," he said.

"I own that I am curious," she replied. "First of all, did the card games end without anyone figuring out your mother's, uh, little problem?"

"Yes, yes, that was the least of our excitement," replied Alex, his dark eyes twinkling in the firelight.

"Please do not tell me another gentleman came in bleeding," she remarked.

"No, no, the ones in the conservatory came back, none the wiser about what had occurred between Miles and Amanda."

"Good," she said, "that's one worry behind us."

"Yes, and I soon sent Abigail upstairs, as you well know. Finley brought in the tea tray, and everyone sat around it—except Miles, whom I sent to bed. Anyway, the conversation was desultory, to say the least, and finally everyone went to bed. I decided I should speak to Miles tonight, so I went to his room."

"I hope you told him he would have to leave first thing in the morning," said Isabelle.

Alex shook his head, chuckling in the most infuriating manner. At last, resting his arm along the back of the small sofa so that his hand lay on her shoulder, he said, "I suggested that very thing to him, and you will never guess what he said to that."

"And I really don't intend to do so, Alex. Please just tell me what occurred," she grumbled, stifling a yawn.

"I am so sorry, my dear. You are exhausted and here I am, making a play out of my tale. But I promise you, it will be worth it. Very well," he said in response to her raised brow. "No more roundaboutation. Miles Parker, that rake about town, is head over heels in love with shy little Amanda Heart!"

"No! It can't be!"

"Oh, but it is. I promise you, Belle, it is the worst case of calf love I have ever seen. He sat beside her at dinner last night and tonight, and—"

"But Mr. Pennywhistle assured me that Mr. Parker did not tamper with the 'infantry,' or something like that," said Isabelle, sitting forward on her seat.

"Well, obviously, the old rogue does not consider my ward one of the infantry," said Alex.

"But why would he . . . maul the child if he fancies himself in love with her?"

"No, no, he didn't realize he was in love with her until she slapped him silly and scratched his face. You see, when he first kissed her, he didn't know she was quite as young and innocent as she is. It seems Abigail told him some wild tale about Amanda and the dancing master at school. . . ."

Their shared laughter bubbled up, and they had to cover their mouths with their hands.

Thinking she had herself under control, Isabelle whispered, "But the dancing master at their school is Grace's—"

"Uncle Rhodes!" supplied Alex, doubling up with

laughter and falling off the sofa, turning and burying his face in the cushion. He reached out and grasped Isabelle's hand, pulling her down to whisper in her ear.

"Round, short Uncle Rhodes," he managed to say before burying his face again, this time against her knees, but Isabelle was too wrapped up in his tale to notice. "I mean, can you visualize Rhodes Dodwell and Amanda together? It must have been a torrid affair," he added, his laughter starting anew.

Isabelle slipped to the floor too, and they held each other, burying their faces against each other's shoulders until their laughter finally subsided. Weak and teary-eyed, they leaned against the sofa's seat, staring at the fire and shaking their heads in disbelief.

Isabelle didn't dare turn and look at Alex for fear another wave of hilarity would sweep over them.

Instead, she whispered, "Oh, that felt ever so good, Alex. But now what do you do? I mean, you are Amanda's guardian."

"I told Miles he could stay if he can convince Amanda to accept his apologies. We will doubtless have to smooth things over before she will even agree to see the poor devil."

"And I will also have a few choice words with Abigail about her imagination," said Isabelle.

"Good. I told Miles I didn't hold out much hope for him, but he said he is suitably humbled and will abide by anything Amanda tells him to do."

"I hope he is being truthful," said Isabelle doubtfully.

Alex touched her arm, and she looked up at him, captured instantly by the warmth in his eyes. When she would have turned away, he cupped her chin in his hand, studying her for a moment before leaning forward and kissing her lips.

When he lifted his head to gauge her reaction, Isabelle surprised herself by smiling at him. She knew, at the very least, she should express indignation, but his kiss had been so very pleasurable, she would have felt a complete hypocrite to rail at him.

He smiled back, the corners of his eyes crinkling in the most endearing manner. "Shall I go?" he whispered.

Isabelle was not usually given to impulse, but this time she gave into it without hesitation, replying to Alex's question with a kiss, her arms going around his neck as naturally as if she had been doing this all her life. He pulled her onto his lap, holding her away from him and looking deep into her eyes. Then he kissed her again with agonizing thoroughness, the pressure of his lips soft and then demanding, tender and then passionate. Then it was over. Trembling in each other's arms, their foreheads touched while they regained their equilibrium.

It was Lord Foxworth, the rogue, who said it first, his voice so low, Isabelle strained to hear the words and then wished she had not.

"We both know that shouldn't have happened. I should go."

Isabelle bit her lower lip to keep from crying out, but she nodded, climbing off his lap and rising, straightening her wrapper—anything to keep from looking into those eyes again.

"When this house party is over . . ." He didn't finish.

He didn't have to, thought Isabelle. They both knew what he meant and why he had stopped. He was a rake and a rogue, looking to reform and get himself a proper wife. She was a chaperone for his wards, or would be in the spring. There was no way they could carry on, could perform their duties, if they let this sort of thing continue.

"Good night, Lord Foxworth," she whispered, looking up to watch his silent retreat in the gentle firelight.

He stopped at the door, and Isabelle steeled herself for his reply, but he surprised her, as he often did.

"Will you be going to services tomorrow?" he asked.

His tone was distant and polite, as if they were fully dressed and meeting in the drawing room before dinner. It hurt worse than if he had heaped curses on her.

"Services?" she managed to say.

"Yes, tomorrow is Sunday."

"Of course," she replied. "I am looking forward to hearing your brother's sermon."

"Good, then I'll see you in the morning. Good night," he said, opening the door and pausing a moment to make certain no one was in the hallway before slipping outside.

"Good night," whispered Isabelle. She took a deep breath, expelling it with staccato precision. Then she staggered into the bedroom and fell across the bed, muffling her sobs with her pillow.

When her tears were spent, she turned over and gazed at the dark canopy, forcing herself to be rational. She could no longer deny it. She had made the gravest of mistakes. She had fallen in love with a rogue . . . again. And if she was going to keep her position in Society and her reputation intact, she had to behave as if Lord Foxworth were nothing more to her than a friend.

It just wasn't fair! she wanted to wail.

But as she had told her daughter any number of times—life was not fair.

Giving the pillow a powerful punch, Isabelle whispered, "But it ought to be!"

Eight

Alex Havenhurst, the Earl of Foxworth, looked at his image in the glass and let fly with a string of expletives. His valet, the fussy Tompkins, "tsk-tsked" and removed the ruined cravat, carefully handing his master a fresh, crisp one. A moment later, the same ritual was performed.

"If you will allow me, my lord . . ."

Alex turned his glittery rage on the servant, then took a deep breath and nodded. It would do no good to rail at Tompkins, when his anger was directed only at himself.

What the devil had he been thinking? Just because Isabelle had told him he might compliment her and flatter her when they were in private, she had not given him permission to seduce her—which he very nearly had.

"Egads, Tompkins, are you trying to strangle me?" he snapped.

"No, my lord, but if you will insist on breathing like a bellows, it is going to seem too tight. There, now, that's . . . perfect!" said the valet, standing back to admire his handiwork.

"Thank you, Tompkins," said the earl, giving the impeccably tied cravat a cursory glance.

"My pleasure, my lord. I have laid out the brown—"

"I want the black one," said Alex. "It suits my mood."

"Very good, my lord," said Tompkins, his bandy little legs churning as he hurried to the adjoining room to fetch the coat his master requested.

Alex grimaced at his image. He wasn't usually so fussy. This was what guilt could do to a fellow when he was trying to be dull and decent. When he had been going about London with his rakehellish ways, he hadn't lost a minute's sleep. One night of guilt over the merest trifles—a little kiss, for heaven's sake—and he hadn't been able to sleep a wink.

"Here we are, my lord."

"Thank you, Tompkins. That's fine," said the earl, shrugging into the tight-fitting coat and waiting impatiently while his valet tugged it this way and that, standing back from time to time to inspect his master.

Tompkins reached out again, and the earl shook his head. "Never mind that, Tompkins. I'm going to be late," he lied, striding out of his bedchamber and colliding with his sons.

"Father, are you ill?" asked Phillip, peering up at his sire with concern.

"No, I am not ill," replied Alex.

"Oh, well, good. We're going to ride over to the vicarage early, if that's all right," said Robert, studying his father closely and frowning.

"The vicarage, huh?" said Alex. "I think I'll go with you," he added, his step lighter. He would speak to Adam about . . . no, he couldn't very well do that. His brother was the vicar, after all, and he had a tendency to cut up stiff about matters of morality. No, Grace was the better choice; she was much more sensible and would be more sympathetic to his plight.

After informing Finley that he and the boys were going to church early, Alex led the way to the stables and ordered their horses saddled. His groom, who was usually quite talkative, led Bee out of his stall without saying a word.

"What's the matter with you, Bottles?" asked the earl—anything to take his mind off his own troubles.

"Nothing, m'lord. It's just that . . . well, you warned me."

"I warned you? What did I warn you about?"

"You remember when we first got here. Three weeks ago it was," said the groom with a huge sigh.

"Yes?" said Alex, looking around to make certain the boys were not close enough to overhear the groom's conversation. Bottles was a very earthy sort, and one never knew where his latest exploits might have led him.

"You warned me about those three brothers then. I shoulda listened t' you, m'lord."

"Three bro—oh, now I remember," said Alex, grimacing in sympathy. "Don't tell me they caught you and Penny in . . . ?"

"Oh, they caught us. I don't know how they knew we were meeting in the . . . well, never mind where. It was almost as if . . ."

"You think Penny told them where you would be?" asked Alex.

"Oh, no, m'lord. She wouldn't do . . . well, no, of course she wouldn't. She was that embarrassed, she was," said the groom. "Anyway, the upshot of it is, we're reading the banns today."

"Indeed, well, I'm sure things will be all right, Bottles. I mean, she is a pretty girl, and probably very nice too."

"Well, I'd like t' think so, m'lord, but I mean, a fellow has to ask himself if she is willing with him, you know, might she be . . . still, 'twill do no good to dwell on it. By next month, I'll be a husband, and she'll be my wife—for better or worse, as they say. Complaining won't make it any better," he added glumly.

"That's the spirit, Bottles. Chin up and all."

"I'll try, m'lord. I'll try."

Alex clapped his groom on the back and made a note to find the happy couple a little cottage close by.

When Alex and the boys were mounted and away from the house, he found he was feeling much improved as they trotted out of the stable yard, despite the blustery wind that had blown up overnight.

The snow had all melted when the sun rose, but the thought of it made Alex smile. How beautiful Isabelle had looked in the soft light of the fire. There on the carpet, it would have made for a cozy . . .

"Do you think we might stay at the vicarage for luncheon, Father?" asked Phillip.

"What, you and Robert?" he asked slowly, leaving his daydream reluctantly. Phillip nodded, and he looked from one boy to the other. Oh, to be their age again, and have not a care in the world. "If your aunt Grace asks you."

"Thank you, Father," they replied in unison. "Uncle Adam has promised to show us the graves where the witches are buried, just outside the churchyard."

"How interesting," said Alex, not really paying them any heed. He had thought her beautiful in every setting, but by firelight, no other could compare.

"Uncle Adam says the villagers burned them at the stake, but that because they had been holy sisters, their bodies didn't burn, even though they died in the flames," added Phillip.

"I think he's telling us a Banbury tale," said the elder boy. "Don't you agree, Father?"

"Well, there are things in this world we cannot fathom," murmured Alex, his mind centering on Isabelle once again.

They rode in silence through the quiet village, the street deserted so early on a Sunday morning. Passing the blacksmith's house, they waved at the big man who was just coming out of his shop, dressed in his Sunday best.

"Mr. Gray says I have outgrown Star," said Robert hopefully. "Bottles said the same thing as he was letting the stirrups out all the way the other day."

Alex glanced at his son and noticed how his long legs were drawn up as he rode his small horse.

"Well, you're not ready for Bee yet, but I would agree with Mr. Gray. When we go home this afternoon, I will speak to James about finding you another mount for the duration of our visit at the Manor."

"Thank you, Father!"

"What about me?" asked Phillip.

"You have almost outgrown your horse too. I'll tell you what we'll do, boys. After Christmas, we'll go to London together and look over the offerings at Tattersall's. How does that sound?"

Their excitement and gratitude was worth the trouble such a journey would be, thought Alex, responding to their enthusiasm with a fond smile. And to think, if it hadn't been for Isabelle, he would have sent his sons to the vicarage for Christmas. Another reason to treat her respectfully, he thought, his gloom settling on his shoulders again.

They were greeted at the vicarage by Grace's plump housekeeper, Mrs. Brown, who took the boys to the kitchens for a little something. Alex remained in the small, neat drawing room, standing at the window and staring into the yard. Not a flower blooming, he thought with a grunt. How fitting that it should be winter; it suited his mood right down to the ground.

"Alex, how good to see you. I wasn't expecting you to

come by so early. I'm afraid I haven't any refreshments
to—"

"Do not trouble yourself on my account, Grace," he
said miserably. "I came because I needed to talk to
someone."

He crossed the room and took her hand, leading her
to the comfortable sofa and sitting down beside her.

"What is it?" she asked.

"It's . . . uh . . . I don't know where to begin."

"Try the beginning," she said, her manner motherly.

"Yes, the beginning. Well, you know the beginning.
You were the one who put the notion in my head," he
said, frowning at her suddenly. "As a matter of fact, if
you hadn't done so, I might not be feeling so deucedly
uncomfortable right now."

"That's all well and good, Alex, but if you do not explain what has happened or what I have supposedly
done, then I cannot help you."

"Yes, yes, you're right, of course. Well, it is Isabelle. It
was you who suggested I might hire her as a sort of
tutor to teach me how to be respectable again. I mean,
I know I am out of practice, doing the polite, by Polite
Society's standards." He knew he was rambling, but he
didn't know how to stop. The lack of sleep was taking
its toll on his mind, and he shook his head to keep his
eyes from closing.

"Alex, did you get any sleep last night?" she asked,
standing up when he shook his head.

Though he protested, Grace refused to listen. Lifting
his feet, she placed them on the sofa, and then pushed
his shoulders against the soft cushions.

"Now, I want you to lie down and close your eyes, just
for a few minutes," she added when he tried to rise.

Pushing him back down, Grace gave him her stern
schoolmistress look, shaking her finger at him in warn-

ing. Alex lay back on the sofa and closed his eyes while his sister-in-law tiptoed out of the room.

Meeting her husband on the stairs, she cautioned, "Be quiet when you go downstairs, my love. Your brother is asleep on our sofa in the drawing room."

"Alex? Asleep on our sofa? Whatever for?"

"For some six or eight hours, unless I miss my guess," she quipped. "The poor man did not sleep at all last night."

"Hmm, I wonder what could be troubling my big brother. He is usually the one causing others to lose sleep," commented the vicar, giving his wife a quick kiss before proceeding down the steps and heading to the kitchen. Greeting his nephews cordially, he joined them in their second breakfast of the day.

Isabelle took the coward's way out the next morning and pleaded the headache so that she would not have to go to church with all the others. With so many guests, the manor house normally hummed with activity, but when almost everyone had gone to church, it was as silent as a tomb—an analogy suiting Isabelle's green melancholy.

Still clad in her nightrail and flannel wrapper, she pushed away the tray Jane had brought up and wandered to the window, opening it to look outside. The beautiful snow had melted, leaving behind patches here and there in the shadows. The trees were bare, the grass was dead. How appropriate, she thought with a sigh. Pulling the window closed, Isabelle left the small sitting room and returned to her bedroom, climbing into bed and pulling the covers up to her chin.

She closed her eyes and tried to sleep, but she was too agitated. She wanted to talk to someone, anyone, about her troubles, but she couldn't. To do so would be to betray her feelings . . . and worst of all, her daughter.

She had kept the terrible secret so long because she had had no one to trust. Perhaps if she could find someone about to expire, she might be able to unburden herself, thought Isabelle, a smile forming on her lips in spite of her troubled spirit.

"A priest, that is what you need," she whispered.

Suddenly, Isabelle sat up, her mind crystal clear, her dilemma all but solved. She would speak to Alex's brother. He was a vicar and a man of integrity too. He would listen to her problem and tell her if there was a solution. Perhaps he would tell her that her fears about Alex were groundless, that she should follow her heart and to the devil with Society!

As these thoughts flew through her mind, Isabelle leapt from the bed and began dressing, her plan continuing to form as her fingers fumbled with tapes and buttons.

With a coal-shuttle bonnet covering her head and her gray wool cloak covering her gown, she headed out of the room and down the long corridor. If she timed it right, she should be able to make it to the church before the vicar finished his sermon. Then she would remain hidden until she could speak to him in private.

"Amanda!"

Isabelle froze, bowing her head for a moment before looking up to see Miles Parker, his injured cheek covered with a plaster. His countenance fell when he recognized her.

"Oh, I thought you were Miss Heart."

"No, Mr. Parker, I am not," she replied with a frosty stare.

Tears sprang to his eyes, and he rubbed his nose.

Completely undone, Isabelle said, "Please, Mr. Parker, you mustn't."

"I . . . I know, my lady. I know I don't deserve to speak to her again—ever," he added dramatically, "but I must apologize for frightening her. When I realized what a pure, innocent child . . ."

"Mr. Parker, you mustn't speak of this in the hall, where anyone might overhear. Come into my sitting room," she said, pulling him along the hallway and into her room, leading him to the small settee where the previous night . . .

"I have some rather tepid tea in the pot, if you . . . no? Now, Mr. Parker, you must try to get hold of yourself."

"I know, you are right, my lady." He pulled out a spotted handkerchief, mopped his eyes, and blew his nose. "I wish I knew how to go on, but . . . I have been a rake so long . . . a here-and- therian . . . I am not worthy of Miss Heart."

"As to that, Mr. Parker, only Amanda can decide."

"Yes, yes, but how does one go about courting an angel?" he asked, turning his tear-stained face to hers.

"First, you must change your ways, and then you must convince her that you have done so," said Isabelle, smiling as she recalled saying almost the exact same thing to Alex. He hadn't managed to change, of course. If he had, he would never have kissed her like he had.

"Lady Isabelle? I asked you, how I can do that?" said Mr. Parker, dragging her attention back to the present. "I don't know if I can change. I mean, it would entail altering my entire way of life. I don't know if that is possible."

Isabelle felt her breath catch in her throat. What had she been thinking? She had been ready to reveal her darkest secret to the vicar, Alex's own brother, just in the hope that he had changed his ways and might wish to make her his. What a fool she was! Once a rake and a rogue, always a rake and a rogue.

"Thank you, Mr. Parker," she said, receiving a startled

look from the poor man. She rose and smiled down at him. "I, uh, appreciate your honesty. I do not have an answer for you. I can tell you only this. Amanda is not an angel, but she deserves someone who will love her and remain faithful to her. If you truly love her, you cannot wish anything less for her, can you?"

"No, my lady," came his miserable reply. Mr. Parker stood up and trudged to the door, his shoulders sagging. "You will tell her for me, won't you, that if I could change, I would. And tell her that I shall always love her. I cannot **stay** here any longer. I must leave. Please tell the countess for me . . ."

When he was gone, Isabelle removed her cloak and bonnet. She would not be going out after all. It was a good thing that she had happened upon Mr. Parker. He had shown her the truth. A true rogue could never change his ways, and Alex was even more of a rogue than Miles Parker. Hadn't he proven it when he had won that kissing wager?

Resolve settled over Isabelle like a shroud, and her heart withdrew to the farthest regions of her breast. Nothing Alex said would ever touch her again, she vowed. He might heap compliments on her from morning to night, and she would be polite, but she would not believe a word he said. He might kiss her, but she . . . she would do her best to resist him.

She wiped away a tear and gritted her teeth in determination. She would not, could not, weaken. She must always remember: Once a rogue, always a rogue.

"Nonsense, you will stay here with your sons for an early dinner, Alex," said his sister-in-law, folding the blanket that had fallen on the floor when he sat up.

Yawning and stretching, Alex didn't have the strength to put up an argument. Besides, he recalled as his mind began to shake off the cobwebs of sleep, he had yet to consult with Grace about Isabelle.

"Very well, Grace. I accept your invitation. Thank you. Now, if I can borrow a bedroom to straighten myself up?"

"Of course, Alex. Come with me."

Fifteen minutes later, his face washed and his crumpled cravat somewhat repaired, Alex went downstairs to the drawing room, where his sister-in-law was quietly stitching a sampler.

"Adam and the boys have gone to look at the witches' graves," she said, patting the sofa in invitation.

"Unka Alex," said Allie, toddling toward him and squealing when he swept her up and kissed her neck. Putting her back down, she wandered off to resume playing with her doll, and Alex sat down beside Grace.

He touched the cloth she held and commented, "Very pretty."

"Thank you, Alex, but I don't think you came over here to compliment me on my stitching. You were saying something about Lady Isabelle when you arrived, though you were making very little sense."

He grinned and sat back, very much at his ease in the comfortable vicarage. Grace and his brother had taken the tiny cottage and made it into a cozy home, adding on until it would easily accommodate their growing family. Adam had always had the knack of making himself comfortable with whatever he possessed. That was his secret to happiness and why being a vicar was the perfect choice for him.

"Do you ever regret wedding a vicar?" he asked his sister-in-law suddenly.

Grace stabbed herself with the needle and sucked on the bleeding finger a moment while she frowned at her brother-in-law.

"I thought you wanted to talk about you." To his

shrug, she said, "Very well, then, no. I have no regrets. Oh, I sometimes wish Adam would not be so . . . preachy. He has a tendency to be priggish at times," she whispered, glancing toward her daughter.

"Yes, but he was always like that," said Alex.

"Then, what do you mean? Do you mean, am I sorry I chose to be his wife instead of your mistress?"

"Shh!" he hissed. "The baby!"

Grace chuckled and said, "She does not know the meaning of those words. Sometimes, Alex, you are more like your brother than you realize. But what were you babbling about my friend Isabelle?"

"It's just that . . . Isabelle, Lady Isabelle, that is . . . she's . . . the most maddening, beautiful woman I have ever met. I don't know what to think about her."

"Really? What does it matter what you think of her as long as she helps you regain your respectability. And from what I have seen since she arrived, you are as polite as the veriest dragon of the *ton*. Even Lady Brisbane commented to me on your transformation!"

"Did she indeed?" asked Alex, preening at this measure of his success. Then he scowled. "That's all well and good, Grace, but what you don't know is that I have an agreement with Isabelle that I can be as disreputable as I please with her, just so I can stand being the perfect host, the perfect gentleman, with everyone else."

Grace giggled and said, "I wonder if that is how she has managed to successfully launch so many young ladies?"

"Pray, do not be absurd."

"Well, Alex, you must see the humor in the situation."

"Really? Must I?" he intoned, rising and pacing back and forth twice, stepping carefully around his niece, who watched his progress with great interest. Deciding it must be a game, she followed behind him, falling down with a thud when he turned too sharply and ran into her.

Alex leaned down and picked her up, dusting her off and gently setting her down by her doll again.

Gritting his teeth, he returned to sit on the sofa.

"I kissed her," he said, burying his face in his hands.

"Well, um, a little kiss . . ." Grace's eyes widened when Alex lifted his head momentarily and rolled his eyes.

"Oh," she breathed. "Well, that is, uh . . . I recall the very comprehensive kiss you once gave me . . ."

"Grace!" he said, pointing at his niece to remind her mother to watch her tongue. She fell silent, and he straightened up, leaning back and staring at the ceiling.

"Did she hit you too?"

Alex shook his head, staring at his sister-in-law in disbelief. "For pity's sake, Grace, must you bring up history like that? Haven't I paid enough for my past sins with you? I mean, I would think having my daylights darkened would have been sufficient in itself."

She bit her lip to stifle her amusement, then she asked, "So what did Isabelle do?"

"She . . . it will go no further?" he demanded, glancing around to be sure they were alone before continuing. "She kissed me back."

"Oh," breathed Grace, using the linen needlework she held as a fan to cool her face.

"Precisely," said Alex, his expression changing as he recalled Isabelle's passionate response, the way she had adapted to his every variation.

His sister-in-law was watching him closely, and suddenly she gasped. Alex came to attention, looking around the room, expecting to discover some eavesdropper or other intruder.

Frowning down at her, he asked, "What the deuce was that for, Grace?"

"You!" she exclaimed, her eyes wide and her mouth open in amazement. "You are in love with Isabelle!"

"I most certainly am not! Of all the addlepated notions! If I were in love, I would know it. I am not some green lad! I have been in love—really in love—before! I absolutely adored my wife!"

"But, Alex, that was, what . . . eleven years ago that your wife passed away? Since then, you have done everything you could to distance yourself from any such emotional attachments. Why, you haven't even shown your own sons very much love until now, and why have you changed your ways with them all of a sudden? I'll tell you why, Alex. Isabelle has opened your heart."

"What a deal of rubbish, feminine rubbish! I am not . . . in love . . . with . . ." He expelled a ragged breath, as if someone had punched him in the stomach. Slowly, he began to shake his head, a feeling of wonder coming over him, and a smile forming that reached all the way to his eyes and into his heart.

"By Jove, Grace! I think you are right! I *am* in love with Isabelle! I just didn't recognize it. I thought I was just, you know, attracted to her. I thought I had lost the last fiber of decency because I wanted her more than I have ever wanted any woman, and—"

"Um, Alex, I think you should reserve that speech for Isabelle," said his sister-in-law, fanning herself more vigorously, her face a bright crimson.

"Yes, yes, you're right," he said, leaping to his feet. "I've got to tell Isabelle. She'll laugh when I tell her," he said, his own laugh giddy. "She'll . . . she'll . . ."

He could feel the blood draining from his face, and he sat down so abruptly, the sofa creaked in protest.

Horror had replaced the joy in his eyes and wiped the smile off his face.

"What am I talking about? She'll never believe me. She . . . she has this extraordinary aversion to rakes. I had the devil's own time of it convincing her that she should even take on my reformation."

"Alex, you're selling yourself short. After all, Isabelle is a woman. I daresay, if the devil were a woman, you could convince him to become an angel."

"No, no, I can't. She listens to my silly compliments and feels nothing because she thinks they are all lies, the lies of a rake and a rogue. That's why she told me I might flatter her outrageously, because she knew I could not hide my true self completely. When I had convinced some poor, silly chit that I was a perfect gentleman, only then, Isabelle said, could I let her see the true Lord Foxworth."

"But surely, Alex, Isabelle has some regard for you. I have seen the way she looks at you."

"It wouldn't matter if she loved me from tip to toe, Grace. Isabelle will never trust me, never believe that I love her with all my heart," he said, again burying his face in his hands while she patted his back.

"We must apologize for intruding," said his brother.

Alex looked up to find his brother and his two wide-eyed sons staring at him.

Pride made him straighten and say politely, "I am sorry to expose you to my problems. I trust what you have heard will go no further."

"Of course not," said Adam, placing his hand on Robert's shoulder to guide him outside again.

"No, no, you might as well stay," said Alex, motioning them forward. His sons looked like they would much prefer to vanish, but they entered the room and sat down on the carpet beside their little cousin. Adam took the chair beside Grace and patted her knee, exchanging a glance with her that spoke volumes.

An uncomfortable silence reigned until Alex said, "Well, I don't wish to spoil your dinner, and I do have a houseful of guests to entertain." He got to his feet reluctantly.

"We'll ride back with you, Father," said Robert, rising and pulling his brother to his feet.

"No, no, you should stay for dinner. We have put your aunt Grace and Mrs. Brown to a great deal of trouble, preparing a big meal . . ."

"Nonsense, you will all three stay for dinner," said the vicar. "But first, I am going upstairs to remove these boots. I told you they are too tight, my dear."

Grace stood up and called her daughter to her side. Adam picked Allie up, and the trio went out of the room, leaving Alex alone with his two sons.

"I am sorry if I shocked you, boys," he said. "You're not accustomed to seeing me behave like . . ." He couldn't complete the sentence. His thoughts were too jumbled.

"But, Father, we like Lady Isabelle. We wouldn't mind having her for a stepmama," said Robert.

"Yes, and little Beth is a real trooper," said Phillip.

"Yes, Beth is a little sweetheart, not afraid of anything or anyone. I would be happy to call her my daughter, but the problem is her mother. Lady Isabelle has a rather low opinion of me, I fear."

"Because you are a regular out-and-outer," said Phillip, slapping his brother's hand away when Robert punched his arm. "Well, he is. We know about his reputation. Everyone does. Even at school, the other fellows know he's a rake."

"I'm sorry, Father, he is such a child," said Robert, the brothers nearly coming to blows.

"Here, stop that. There's no need for you to argue

over the truth, boys. I am afraid Phillip is right. What is more to the point, Lady Isabelle knows my reputation and does not believe I can mend my ways."

"But, Father," said Robert, his young face searching his father's, "doesn't being a rake mean that you can get the ladies to do as you please?"

Alex chuckled and said, "Something like that."

"Then surely you can do that with Lady Isabelle. I mean, not only do you know the right words to say from practice, but you should be doubly successful, because you will be sincere this time!"

A thoughtful frown showed his sons that he was digesting this bit of information. They watched and waited breathlessly.

"You know, Robert, you might just have something there." Alex grinned as hope began to fill his heart.

"You can do it, Father. You can do anything!" exclaimed Phillip, striking a pose, one arm in the air as if raising a sword.

"Don't be a looby," said his older brother, hitting the floor as Phillip used his pretend sword to knock Robert off his feet.

A wrestling match ensued until their aunt entered and separated them with a word.

"You may not mind your home being reduced to rubble by two unruly boys," said Grace, "but I would appreciate it if you would not allow them to wreck mine, Alex."

"Sorry, Grace," came his reply as he stared up at her, his face wreathed in smiles.

She sat down abruptly and clapped her hands in glee.

"So you have decided to try to win her over," she breathed, squeezing his hand in excitement.

The boys moved closer, and his brother listened from the doorway.

"Yes, but I will need all of you to help," said Alex, his tone conspiratorial.

"You can count on us, Father."

"We will sing your praises at every opportunity," said Grace. "Oh, it will be wonderful having Isabelle as a sister!"

"Pray, do not count your chickens . . ."

"Yes, yes, I know," she said.

"But this remains just between us," he said, his dark eyes traveling to each member of his audience and resting there until he had their silent pledges.

"Good," he said. "We haven't much time. Isabelle is leaving on Christmas Day, which is this coming Friday."

"Just tell us what to do," said Grace.

"You can help by mentioning to Isabelle how changed I seem," he said.

"Are you changed?" asked his brother, entering the room and sitting down beside his wife. "I mean, this is not just a plot to . . ." He glanced at his nephews and then looked down his nose at his older brother.

Alex crossed his heart and said solemnly, "Word of a Fox."

Adam nodded and said, "Very well, Alex."

"So everyone will help?"

Their heads bobbed up and down.

"Dinner is ready, madam," called Mrs. Brown from the doorway. They rose reluctantly and made their way toward the dining room.

Alex laid his hand on his brother's sleeve, holding him back to speak a word in private. When the others were out of sight, he said, "I will probably need your help most of all, little brother."

"Mine?"

"Yes, if I am to succeed in convincing Isabelle of my sincerity, I shall most certainly need divine intervention."

Adam chuckled and clapped his brother on the back. "You will most definitely be in my prayers, Alex."

"Thank you, Adam," replied the earl.

His brother put a restraining had on his arm and added firmly, "And so will the Lady Isabelle."

Nine

"I have not sealed it, my lady. I wanted you to read it first, and if you approve, perhaps you will give it to Miss Heart," said Miles Parker, his hat in his hand as he stood outside Isabelle's door.

"Very well, Mr. Parker, if you insist," said Isabelle, taking the letter from him.

"I have asked if I may call on her when she comes to London for the Season. I know you do not approve, but perhaps you will find it in your heart to relent."

"Perhaps, sir."

"That is all I can ask, my lady. Good-bye."

He picked up his portmanteau and proceeded down the back stairs.

Isabelle watched him go, a frown on her face. She hoped she had not misjudged the man. Shaking her head, she shut the door to her sitting room and opened the envelope. The handwriting was appalling, and she fished her spectacles out of her pocket before trying to interpret the dreadful scrawl.

Her eyes widened as she read Mr. Parker's humble apology.

Dear Miss Heart,
I know you have no reason to forgive me for the treatment you received at my hands. I can only plead insanity, for why else would I have destroyed every hope for my own

*happiness? I know you cannot forget, but you may man-
age to forgive a poor, weak man for his mistake. If you feel
any pity for me, I hope you will allow me the great privilege of calling on you when you arrive in London this
spring. Until then, I remain your faithful servant,*

Parker

Isabelle reread the note again before going to the adjoining room and knocking on the door. She waited for
Amanda's weak response before entering.

Amanda was sitting up in bed, the covers pulled up
to her chin and a cup of hot chocolate on the tray beside her. Abigail perched on the side of the bed, fully
dressed.

"I have a note for you, Amanda, though you must tell
me if you do not feel up to reading it just yet. It is from
Mr. Parker," said Isabelle.

"I don't think you should read it, Manda," said her
sister.

"I don't know," came the faded response.

"Amanda should make her own decision on this,
Abigail, without any further help from you," said Isabelle, making the girl look away, her lips pursed in a
tight "O."

"Well, surely it cannot hurt to read it," said the girl
under the coverlet. Isabelle crossed the room and
handed it to Amanda. "It's open," said the girl.

"Yes, he left it open and asked me to read it first, to
make certain it would not upset you. I read it, and
found nothing objectionable about it," said Isabelle.

"Oh," she said, pulling out the letter and smoothing
it in her lap.

Amanda started sniffling the moment she began to
read. Isabelle frowned, surprised by the girl's reaction.

"What does he say?" demanded her twin.

Amanda tossed it to her sister with an airy, "You may

read it, Abigail. There is nothing personal in it at all. It is perfectly dull."

"Amanda, I don't understand your attitude. You seem to be disappointed that Mr. Parker's letter is un-exceptionable. What did you expect him to say?" asked Isabelle.

"It's not that bad," said Abigail, clambering onto the bed and thrusting the note under her sister's nose again.

The twins had forgotten Isabelle was even in the room, and she listened with growing understanding and impatience.

"He does want to see you in London, you see?"

"I know, but I wish he had not felt it necessary to leave, Abigail. It will be such a dull house party without him here," said Amanda. "If only I hadn't acted like such a ninny."

"Well, perhaps I should not have painted you as being quite so experienced," said Abigail.

Isabelle stepped forward, looking from one twin to the other for a moment, shocked and angry.

"Do you mean to tell me, Amanda, that you were a party to that deception about you and your dancing master?"

"Abigail said it wouldn't hurt."

"But this is appalling!" exclaimed Isabelle.

"No, not at all, my lady," said Amanda, coming to life and throwing off the covers. "That first evening, he sat between us at dinner and treated us like children."

"And so you are, by his standards," said Isabelle.

"Exactly," said Abigail. "In order for him to see us as grown-up ladies, we had to pretend we knew more about . . . well, about life, than we really did."

"Hence, the tale about your dancing master. For shame to slander the good name of a kind man like Mr. Dodwell."

"Oh, pish tush," said Abigail. "He will never know, and it did turn the trick. Mr. Parker immediately began to treat us like he had you and Mrs. Havenhurst."

"And every other lady under the age of fifty and over the age of eighteen," said Amanda. "It was so exciting, and we were having such a wonderful time together! When we decided to choose partners for hide-and-seek in the conservatory, Mr. Parker chose me," she said proudly.

"And it would have turned out fine if you had not lost your head!" said Abigail. "I was with Mr. Forbes-Smyth, and he was just about to kiss me, when you screamed. That put an end to my fun!"

Isabelle shook her head. "I must say, girls, I am not only amazed at your foolishness, I am astounded that you don't mind confessing the whole, as if you were relating the events of a . . . a child's tea party. Have you no finer feelings?"

"Oh, please do not scold us," said Amanda, tears welling in her eyes again. "I really didn't think what we were doing was so very bad."

"Not bad? It was conniving, dishonest, libelous . . ."

"But, you see, what started it was, I could not bear to have Mr. Parker treat me like a child. There he was, so handsome and sophisticated, a confirmed rogue, and he . . . he just looked right through me."

Amanda tossed her dark curls and buried her face in the pillow. Isabelle was torn between sympathizing with and rebuking the girl.

Finally, she threw up her hands and said, "If Mr. Parker is the sort of man you wish to wed, Amanda Heart, then you are welcome to him. If you knew what I know about rakes, you would not be so hasty to throw your bonnet over the windmill for such a poor specimen. When we arrive in London in the spring, you are welcome to him . . . and he is welcome to you," said Isabelle.

Amanda looked up, her face shining with tears, and said, "Oh, thank you, my lady!"

With an unladylike snort of derision, Isabelle turned on her heel and fled, closing the door that connected her sitting room and their bedchamber and turning the key.

Isabelle took her dinner in the nursery that evening, enjoying the company of the children much more than she would have the other guests. Beth, and her two new cousins, Maggie and Dillie, were quiet in Robert's and Phillip's presence. The boys were oblivious to the little girls' adoration as they bent Isabelle's ear about a thousand things, usually something involving their father—a man who could do no wrong, in their young eyes.

"Do you know what is the best thing of all, my lady?" asked Phillip.

"No, I doubt that I do," she said, smiling at the boy.

"Father is going to take us to Tattersall's and let us choose new horses."

"Really? That is exciting news," she said. "Both of you?"

"Yes, we have outgrown our smaller horses," said Robert. "Father says that since we are very likely going to be as tall as he is, we might as well find a mount that suits us now and keep it for several years."

"That makes sense," said Isabelle, pretending an interest she didn't really feel. Horses, to her, were best when harnessed to a carriage and driven by a competent coachman.

"Now, boys, do not bore her ladyship about your horses," said a deep voice from the doorway.

Isabelle's hair on the back of her neck stood out, and she shivered, knowing he had entered the room and was standing behind her chair.

"Most ladies care only about the soundness of the horse harnessed to their carriages," he said, reading her thoughts in the most uncanny manner.

"Not me," ventured Beth. "I like big, giant horses, like Bee."

"Yes, you and Bee have a special bond," said the earl, pulling up a chair beside the child and chucking her under the chin. "How are all of you this evening?" he asked, directing his question to the other little girls too.

"Fine," they replied in unison.

"And how is the Lady Isabelle tonight?" he asked, watching her over the top of Beth's dark curls.

"I am fine too, my lord."

"Good, then we are all fine. Your parents would like you to come down to the drawing room, Lady Margaret and Lady Dehlia. We had an early dinner too, and the gentlemen have already joined the ladies."

"Oh, come along girls," said their nurse, getting out of her chair in the corner and herding her charges toward the door.

"I think your grandmother would like you two to come down too," he said to the boys. "Have you finished your dinner?"

"We're finished. Can Beth come with us, my lady?" asked Robert, grinning at his father.

"Well, I suppose she could, but there is no one for her to see," said her mother.

"But there'll be treats, and she won't want to miss out on those," said Phillip.

Starting to rise, Isabelle said, "Well, I suppose I could change and—"

"You are hardly dressed for the drawing room," observed the earl, smiling at her. "Why don't you children run along? We'll wait for you here."

When they were alone, Isabelle said, "You always get your way, don't you, my lord?"

"I don't know what you mean, Belle."

"Don't call me Belle," she said, rising halfway out of her chair before he caught her hand and pulled her back down, letting his hand travel up her bare arm.

"I hope we are not going to spend the rest of the week avoiding each other," he said. "I did apologize for my behavior."

"Yes, I know," she said.

"Well, do you think you can be civil to me until next Friday?" he asked, his thumb rubbing up and down on the inside of her arm, making her tremble.

Isabelle turned to face him and demanded harshly, "That depends, my lord, on whether or not you will call me by my proper name and"—she paused and removed his hand from her arm before finishing—"and you will stop handling me in the most improper manner."

Alex sat back, nodding at her. "I think that can be arranged, Isabelle. But does that mean our agreement that I can be myself in your company is still in force?"

"I don't see why not, my lord, but remember, it had nothing to do with the physical, only with our conversation," said Isabelle, glowering at him.

He chuckled in the face of her annoyance and said, "I don't remember it like that. I don't think we covered the physical aspect of our encounters, but I am willing to be big about it and not kick up a fuss."

"How chivalrous of you, my lord," said Isabelle, a glimmer of a smile sparkling in her green eyes.

"Alex, remember?" he amended. "We are alone, after all."

"Alex," she said, rising this time without any impediment. Isabelle walked regally to the door, pausing a moment to see if he would make another outrageous comment. She felt a twinge of disappointment, but shook it off, and was feeling quite smug by the time she reached her room, congratulating herself that she had held her own with the silver-tongued earl.

She frowned when she entered her bedroom. On her pillow was a perfect red rose. Of all the aggravating things to do! Where on earth had he found a rose in the dead of winter? She picked it up to throw it down and trample it beneath her feet, but the subtle fragrance made her pause. She looked at the soft, velvety petals and could not resist stroking them against her cheek. Why destroy something so beautiful?

Then she noticed the calling card with the handwritten message. Once again, he had read her thoughts.

"Can we afford to cast aside something so beautiful?" It was signed simply "A."

"Oh, my lady, I didn't know you were in here. I was going to turn down the bed, but I see you have already done so," said her maid.

Isabelle whirled and asked, "You didn't turn down the bed, Jane?"

"No, my lady. Oh, where did that come from? How beautiful," said the maid.

"From the devil," she murmured, giving a false laugh when the maid's eyes flew open.

"Beg pardon, my lady?"

"Nothing, Jane. I'm going to go to bed early tonight. Would you mind staying in the sitting room until the house is quiet so no one will disturb me?"

"I would be happy to, my lady," said the maid, a puzzled expression on her face, but she was too well trained to question her mistress. "Let me fetch your nightrail."

When the maid had disappeared into the dressing room, Isabelle took the card to the fireplace and pitched it into the flames. How dare he enter her bed-chamber and turn down her bed! That he would perform such an intimate errand, she told herself, was proof that he had not reformed in the least.

She picked up the rose, and it pricked her finger. She wanted to crush it. It only reminded her that he was still the same rogue he had always been.

Still, she couldn't bring herself to destroy the velvety flower. With a stamp of her foot, she stuck it in the pitcher on the dressing table and sat down, planning to ignore it completely. But with every movement the fragrance surrounded her, and she finally gave in, taking the rose and holding it to her nose.

The delicate scent would always remind her of her wicked rogue, she thought, closing her eyes and breathing deeply.

When the maid returned, Isabelle had already taken the pins out of her hair, and it fell around her shoulders like dark clouds. Ten minutes later, Jane closed the door to the sitting room, and Isabelle drifted off to sleep, her dreams filled with her handsome earl on a huge horse, the scent of roses in the air as he leaned down and pulled her onto the saddle, his arms encircling her, warming her, loving her.

"How did it go when we left, Father?" asked Robert when no one else in the drawing room was looking their way.

"All right. I managed to spend five minutes with her without . . . well, without any problems cropping up."

"Good for you," said Phillip, rolling his eyes.

"Don't pay any attention to him, Father. He is disap-

pointed because Grandmother didn't have any bonbons for him."

"I am not," said Phillip.

"Enough of that, or you'll be sent upstairs," said their
father. "I happen to know where your grandmother
keeps the bonbons, and I will tell you if you promise to
ride into Pixley tomorrow and replace them with some
more at Miss Silverton's store."

"We will," said Phillip.

"Good, then go to the breakfast room and open the
bottom left door to the sideboard. She keeps all sorts
of goodies in there."

"Thank you, Father," said Phillip, grabbing Beth's
hand and hurrying out the door with his brother following at a more decorous speed.

"Those boys of yours are quite the young gentlemen," said his friend Thomas, the Marquess of
Dunham.

"They are a handful but very well mannered. I must
own, I am very proud of them."

"My girls are being quite the little ladies too," said
Lord Dunham. "I have actually enjoyed—"

Just then, a squeal pierced the polite hum of conversation, followed by a loud crash. The marquess
ducked his head and covered his ears.

"So much for polite children," he said gloomily.

Alex jabbed his elbow into the marquess's side and
pointed to the source of the noise.

"It wasn't your girls, Dunham. Look. It's those silly
young people playing blindman's buff. Young Barclay
backed into the suit of armor in the corner and—"
Alex gave a shout of laughter as the young man began
inching out of the drawing room, his back to the wall
and his face crimson. Everyone was laughing by then,
including Barclay Forbes-Smyth, whose stockingknit

pants had been pierced by the sword and split down the length of one leg.

"If you will excuse me," he said, ducking out the door. Miss Brisbane and Lady Sophia started after him, but their progress was stopped by the older ladies.

"If Amanda and Abigail had been here," said Sophia, her speech cut short by Alex's raised brows.

"Even the grown ones can be more trouble than they're worth at times," said the marquess, shaking his finger at his wife's sister.

Lady Sophia giggled and stuck out her tongue at him before linking arms with Miss Brisbane and scampering away.

"Speaking of the twins, where are the other young ladies tonight? And Lady Isabelle too? I have missed her sensible conversation today," said Dunham.

"They were indisposed," said Alex.

"Indisposed? All three of them? I hope it is nothing catching," said the marquess.

"Don't worry your hypochondriacal self about it, Thomas. I told my wards to stay in their rooms because of a little indiscretion, and Lady Isabelle is fine. She had a headache earlier, but when I spoke to her in the nursery not half an hour since, she was fine."

"Well then, that's good. I understand we are to have a picnic tomorrow, an unlikely thing to do at Christmastime, don't you think? I certainly don't think it would be wise if one were sick already."

Alex shook his head and heaved an exasperated sigh at his old friend. "Let me explain once more, Thomas. Lady Isabelle is not sick. The twins are not sick. And the picnic is going to be held in the conservatory."

"Capital, capital. I will look forward to it. The usual fare, I suppose. Quail eggs, wine, cheese, and such," said the marquess, rubbing his round little stomach in anticipation.

"I wouldn't know, Thomas. I have left all that to the ladies," said Alex, feeling a headache threatening his own health. Without Isabelle there, the evening and his guests had lost all pleasure.

Finley brought in the tea tray, and everyone began to assemble nearby, though the countess served the children first. Robert, Phillip, and Beth, who had followed the butler into the room, had chocolate at the corners of their mouths, and their pockets were bulging suspiciously. Still, they accepted their plates with enthusiasm and helped Beth carry hers to a nearby table.

They would make excellent big brothers, thought Alex. If only he could convince Isabelle that he would make Beth an excellent father.

He had four more days to accomplish it. A shiver of dread ran down his spine, and he chafed to go to her. But that, of course, was exactly what he couldn't do. Nothing would seal his doom faster than to act out of hand. He had to be the perfect gentleman.

He only hoped he was equal to the task!

In the morning, Isabelle helped the two housekeepers who directed the army of footmen on the rearrangement of the plants in the conservatory. The head gardener also assisted, though his insistence that certain plants could not be moved away from the windows proved more of a hindrance than a help. By the time they finished, there was a wide, winding pathway leading from the smaller drawing room to the far corner of the conservatory where the two walls of glass met, giving a perfect view of the garden beyond. There were no flowers outside, but the green shrubs were still beautiful. Inside, the blooming flowers had been arranged around the seating area, flanked by other tall, leafy plants.

Several tables and chairs had been arranged for the older members of the party, but the floor was strewn with blankets and pillows, inviting anyone who cared to do so to lounge on the ground just as they might at a summer picnic. The guests could remain comfortable since the heating system Alex had had installed kept the room warm and toasty.

The countess had invited the neighbors, all of whom had accepted the invitation and arrived promptly at the appointed hour, which meant most of the house party had not yet come downstairs.

"In London, only the gauche arrive on time," said Lady Brisbane to her colonel.

"Well, this isn't London," he replied, greeting Squire Lambert with a hearty handshake and bowing over Mrs. Lambert's hand.

Turning back to Lady Brisbane, he said, "The squire has one of the best packs of hounds in Leicestershire, and that is really an accomplishment."

"I see, how wonderful," said the lady, giving the squire a two-finger shake.

"I suppose Lord Foxworth told you about the hunt on Wednesday, colonel," said the squire, rocking on his heels as he pulled his waistcoat down to cover his round midriff.

"Indeed he did. I am looking forward to it immensely," said the hunting-mad colonel.

Isabelle felt the earl's presence before he spoke, his voice close to her ear as he said, "Lady Brisbane may be a snob, but she won't cross Sutter, not when it comes to his fox hunting."

"Ah, I wondered why she was so cordial," said Isabelle, causing Alex to choke. She whacked him on the back, until he moved out of reach.

"You are looking very virginal this morning," he said, taking in her white gown and gloves. "A reminder for me, perhaps?" he said, bowing over her hand and having his nose pinched.

Straightening, he rubbed the offended appendage and grinned when she said sweetly, "And your choice for black signifies . . . ?"

"Touché, my dear. But you notice I wear a white shirt and cravat to cover my pure heart," he added.

Isabelle giggled. She could not keep from it, he was so absurd. She ought to chide him for having entered her bedchamber and leaving that rose, but she couldn't find it in her heart to be angry with him. Such was the power of sweet dreams, she thought.

Glancing around, Alex asked, "Where are my two wards? I plan to keep an eye on them. I don't want any more deviltry."

"So you know what they did," she whispered, smiling and nodding to Grace and Adam.

"Yes, as you know, Parker said enough to make me suspicious, and I spoke to the girls yesterday when I discovered Parker had gone. That is why they remained in their rooms. I told them I wanted them to have time to think about what they had done to the poor chap."

"He is hardly a . . . oh, very well. I grant you, he was the victim of this tragedy," said Isabelle.

"Indeed, I believe he was ready to offer for her, but I told him he needed to wait, that she needed to spend some time in London before he approached her."

"Then you believe he really did fall in love with her?" asked Isabelle, completely amazed.

"Not only that, my dear lady, but I think Miles Parker will make her a fine, steady husband—if he doesn't come to his senses in time, that is," said Alex, moving away before she could recover enough to ring a peal over him.

Isabelle wanted to tell him that he was wrong, but she couldn't very well do so in the midst of all the

guests. Instead, she smiled and spoke politely to everyone she met, holding her head high and counting the
minutes until she could be away from Foxworth Manor
and its company of bedlamites.

"Mama, Maggie and Dillie and I want to play hopscotch, but there is not room with all these people,"
said Beth after tugging her mother's skirt to gain her
attention. "Can we go into the garden?"

"It is much too chilly today, sweeting. Why not wait
until tomorrow? It may be warmer then, or perhaps the
grooms can make room in the stable for your game."

"Devil a bit!"

"Beth! A lady never uses such an expression!" said Isabelle sternly, drawing her daughter away from the
others. "Who taught you to say that?"

"Nobody," said the girl, ducking her head and shuffling her feet.

"Well, you must have heard it someplace, probably in
the stable yard. Just for that, you may not go there for
two days," said Isabelle.

"But, Mama! That means I can't ride the pony or
Bee!"

"That is correct, and perhaps the lesson will make
you remember your tongue before speaking. Now, go
and play with your friends."

"Yes, Mama," said Beth, walking away with her lower
lip sticking out.

"So that is what I have to look forward to," said
Grace, smiling at her friend.

Amy, Lady Dunham, chimed in, "Oh, yes, and you
too, Anne," she said, nodding to her sister, Lady Anne.

"Well, I have a little time," said Lady Anne with a
chuckle.

"But time flies, and they become more strong-willed
with every year that passes. Maggie is a gentle little soul,
but my Dehlia has a will of iron."

"So does Beth," said Isabelle. "Usually, she is quite biddable and wants to please me, but there are times . . . 'twas so much easier when it was just the two of us at home. But there is nothing for it. She must go to school, and she needs to play with other girls."

"Oh, it is so difficult to let them go," said Lady Dunham. "Speaking of my girls, I think I shall go and see what they are doing."

"I'll help you look," said her sister, trailing along behind, leaving Isabelle and her friend Grace alone.

"At least Beth is a day student," said Grace. "When I was teaching at my uncle's school, it fairly broke my heart to see the girls who boarded with us arrive for the first time. They were so frightened," said Grace, keeping her eye on her own daughter, who was bouncing up and down on Alex's knee.

"Yes, at least the school is close enough that Beth can live at home," said Isabelle, her breath catching in her throat. "I suppose it is inevitable. She has to grow up, but it is difficult all the same."

She nodded at her friend's expanding stomach and smiled, saying, "You will have another little one when Allie takes that first step away from your side, but Beth is my only one."

"You talk as if your life is over, Isabelle. There is no reason you cannot have a dozen children if you want to," said her friend with a laugh.

"You forget, Grace, one must first have a husband, and I . . . I have decided not to marry again."

"Really? And when did you make this decision?"

"Oh, some time ago," she lied, unwilling to tell her perceptive friend that the resolution had been made only two nights before, when she realized she was in love with Alex.

"You know, Isabelle, in my experience, resolutions

like that are rarely kept. Love has a way of changing people's minds."

Isabelle shook her head and said, "Spoken like a wife who adores her husband."

"And so I do, but you may someday find someone who feels the same about you."

"Perhaps," said Isabelle, trying to humor her friend.

"I mean, look at Alex," said Grace. Isabelle nearly choked. "Who would have thought he would be looking for a wife? I guess those of us who know him well never noticed how much he has changed."

"I shall have to accept your word on that, not having known him previously to be able to compare," said Isabelle. "But enough of that. I'm going to find my little one and make certain she is behaving herself."

"And I am going to go to see what is on the buffet table. I am constantly hungry these days," said Grace, gliding away.

Isabelle strolled through the greenery, looking at the young couples lounging on the blankets. Barclay Forbes-Smyth was feeding Abigail sweetmeats by tossing them at her mouth. Lady Sophia was sitting much too close to Jonathan Forbes-Smyth, but no one seemed to care. Even Mr. Pennywhistle was seated on a blanket, reclining against a heavy pot, while the Duchess of Charlton, seated in a comfortable chair she ordered moved from the drawing room, bent his ear with gossip.

"Everyone is enjoying themselves, Lady Isabelle. Isn't it time for you to relax and do the same?" asked Everett Deal, offering her a plate piled with all sorts of delicacies.

"How kind you are, Mr. Deal," she said, accepting the plate and his arm.

When they were seated at one of the tables, he commented, "My sister tells me this picnic was your idea."

"I had read about one similar to this in the spring when the rains refused to let up. This conservatory is so large and beautiful, it seemed the perfect thing to do."

"Oh, I quite agree. As a matter of fact, I much prefer this to a picnic outside, where one becomes wind-blown, hot, or chilled, depending on the whims of the weather."

Their conversation was interrupted by a round, squat man, smiling and bowing to Isabelle. "Good afternoon, Lady Isabelle. I don't know if you remember me?"

"Of course I do, Mr. Dodwell. I hear tales about you from my daughter, Beth, all the time. Allow me to introduce Mr. Deal, Lady Foxworth's brother. Mr. Deal, this is Rhodes Dodwell. He owns and runs Dodwell's Progressive Academy for Young Ladies, where my daughter, Beth, is a student."

"Delighted to meet you, sir," said Everett Deal. "Won't you join us?"

"Thank you, I would like that," replied the little man, placing a heaping plate on the table and pulling up a chair. "My wife will be so disappointed she missed this. She has a dreadful cold and didn't wish to get out."

"I am sorry to hear that. Is there anything I can do?"

"No, no, she is already on the mend, thanks to Mrs. Brown's restorative soup." Looking around, Mr. Dodwell lowered his voice and said, "I understand you are planning to chaperone the twins next Season, my lady."

"That is a possibility," she replied.

"You be very careful with those two," he said. "They can be quite the handful."

"So we have discovered," said Mr. Deal, who loved a good gossip. "Just the other night—"

"Gentlemen, let us remember where we are," said Isabelle.

Their efforts to appear contrite looked more sullen

than repentant, but Isabelle didn't comment on this. She refused to gossip about Abigail and Amanda when she might be their chaperone in a few short weeks.

After a moment's silence, Mr. Dodwell said, "So, Christmas is this Friday."

"Indeed it is. I hope I will have the opportunity to meet your wife at the ball my sister is giving on Christmas Eve," said Mr. Deal.

"Oh, yes, I think she will be sufficiently recovered to attend that. I believe that is one reason Margaret stayed home today. She wanted to save her strength for the ball. If you don't attend something like that in Pixley, your reputation might be nonexistent by morning."

"Surely it is not as bad as all that," said Isabelle.

"But you come from Spursden, my lady. Pixley is different and always has been. But I shouldn't worry about it. A pretty young thing like you will have no one telling tales," said Mr. Dodwell. "The people of Pixley do enjoy their gossip though. You should have heard the tales that were spun when that dandy—what was his name? Perkins? Parks?"

"Parker," supplied Mr. Deal.

"Yes, that was it. He left Sunday, riding past the church just as everyone was leaving. I vow, I thought Leticia Lambert was going to tackle the man and demand to know what had caused him to leave the house party early."

"Oh, that, it was as good as the play," said Mr. Deal with a wink. "My valet told me—"

"If you gentlemen will excuse me. I really must check on my daughter," said Isabelle, not wanting to know what the two old hens were going to say about Miles Parker's early departure.

As she looked around the cozy room for Beth, she heard snippets of conversation that sent shivers up and down her spine. It seemed the countess's neighbors had nothing better to do with their time than gossip.

"Why the scowl?" asked Alex, taking her arm to stroll through the greenery.

"I cannot wander about trading witty repartee with you, my lord. I am looking for Beth," said Isabelle, wishing her tone didn't sound quite so shrewish to her own ear.

"I saw the girls skipping down the back hall ten minutes ago. I didn't think to ask where they were going—probably to the kitchens."

"Thank you," she said, disengaging her hand and speeding away.

"Wait a minute, Isabelle. I'll go with you."

They quickly reached the kitchen, which was a hotbed of activity, but there were no little girls begging sweets from the cook.

"Have you seen the girls?" asked Alex.

The tall, broad-shouldered cook shook her head. "Not since early this mornin', m'lord."

Alex pulled Isabelle back into the hall and spied the housekeeper, Mrs. Pratt, in conversation with her sister, Mrs. Teasley.

"Ladies, have either of you seen the little girls?"

"I haven't, my lord," said Mrs. Pratt, turning to her sister, who shook her head too. "Well, they're such little dears. They can't have gone far. We will keep a lookout for them and tell them you are asking for them."

"Thank you, Mrs. Pratt. Oh, and Mrs. Teasley, would you ask Finley to bring up some more iced champagne? I noticed some of the guests had empty glasses."

"Certainly, my lord."

As he led Isabelle away, she asked anxiously, "Where could they be? I cannot shake the feeling that something has happened to them."

Putting an arm around her shoulders and giving her a reassuring squeeze, Alex said, "I'll get Robert and Phillip, and we'll have a proper look."

"While you get the boys, Alex, I'll go up to the nurseries."

They split up, Isabelle climbing the back stairs while Alex retraced his steps to the conservatory. By the time he had rounded up the boys and returned to the back hall, Isabelle was flying down the stairs, practically throwing herself into Alex's arms.

"Phillip here thinks they may have gone outside."

"Surely not. I told her it is too cold to play hopscotch outside," said Isabelle, turning the knob on the back door as she spoke.

"You'll freeze to death," declared Alex, following her outside when she ignored him completely. He shrugged out of his coat and threw it around her shoulders, but she took no notice.

"Look, Lady Isabelle, there's the outline for their hopscotch game," said Phillip.

"Perhaps it is an old one," said Alex.

"No, it wasn't here earlier," said Robert ruefully.

"But where are they?" demanded Isabelle, biting her lip to keep from crying.

Robert tugged on his brother's sleeve and said, "Come on, Phillip. We'll run ahead to the stables and see if they've gone down there."

"Come inside," said Alex, pulling her along after him.

"Alex, the last time I spoke to her," began Isabelle. Then she buried her face against his chest, and he pulled her close, keeping his arms around her.

"Now, now, my love, Beth will be found. Everything will be all right," he said, hoping his words would prove true.

"Father! We have them!" shouted Phillip, scampering up the path while Robert kept pace with the three bedraggled little girls.

Isabelle turned and rushed to meet her daughter, picking her up and hugging her tight.

"Where are your shoes?" she demanded, holding Beth away from her and looking down at her muddy, shoeless feet before hugging her neck again.

"Let's save our questions until we are all inside and upstairs," said Alex, shepherding his small troop through the door and up the stairs to the nursery. With a word to his sons, he sent them back down to the picnic.

Beth's maid, Lucy, and the sisters' maid, Sukey, exclaimed in horror when they saw the state of the girls' clothing. Isabelle turned the girls over to the servants before entering the old schoolroom and sitting down at the children's dining table. Alex joined her, placing his large hand over hers and giving it a squeeze.

"I must look as bedraggled as the girls," she said with a weary smile.

"Not at all," said Alex, reaching out and pulling a twig from her hair. "What you look like is a very relieved mother."

"I suppose you think I am being silly."

"Not at all, only . . ."

"Only what?" she asked.

"It occurs to me that as Beth gets older, you will have more scares like the one today. She's stretching her wings."

"I know." Isabelle gave him a watery smile, her expression becoming stern when the door opened and the girls entered the schoolroom.

The trio had removed their damp clothes and were dressed in pristine white nightgowns, their faces scrubbed and their hands clean.

"Come and sit by the fire," said Isabelle, waiting until

they were seated before she asked, "Now, tell us what happened, and no varnishing the truth."

"Well, we wanted to play hopscotch, so we went outside and drew the figure," said Beth.

"Except that the pathway was too hard to draw on. Our stick kept breaking," said Dillie, the eldest of the three.

"So we decided to get some water to soften it up."

The girls looked at each other and giggled.

"And then what?" asked the earl, his unsmiling question quelling their good humor.

"We went down to the stable and filled a bucket," said Maggie, her blond head bobbing as if she were agreeing with herself.

"But it was ever so heavy," said her sister.

"And it sloshed all over the place," said Beth. "Then I lost my balance and down I went, and the bucket too, all over me and Maggie."

"Our maid, Sukey, has a fit if we muss up our clothes, so we decided to go back to the stable and dry off by the fire," said Maggie.

"And you never considered that your disappearance and disobedience might upset your parents?" asked the earl.

Dillie and Maggie looked around, but they did not point out that their parents were still ignorant of what they had done. Beth, however, had seen the look of relief in her mother's eyes, and she hung her head.

"I am sorry, Mama."

"And so you should be," she said, hugging her daughter to her again. "You will not return to the stables for the remainder of our stay, young lady. Understood?"

"I understand," said the child glumly.

"As for you girls, your maid will undoubtedly tell

your mother, and she will decide what your punishment should be."

"Yes, my lady."

"Now, I want all three of you to stay in the nursery for the rest of the day. Perhaps you should take a nap."

"But we're too old for naps, Mama!" said Beth, a fit of sneezing seizing her. When she had recovered, she said, "Yes, Mama."

Isabelle felt her daughter's forehead and breathed a sigh of relief to find it cool to the touch. She kissed her cheek, and stood up, taking Alex's arm and leaving the three miscreants to stew over their misdeeds. Their chatter erupted as soon as the door closed, making Alex shake his head.

"I don't think those three are very remorseful," he said.

"Not at bit," she said with a chuckle. "But if they manage to muddle through without catching a fever, I shan't make too much of it."

"They're healthy girls. I'm sure they'll not come to any lasting harm from a little foot wetting." He stopped and took her by the shoulders, turning her to face him. "You, however, may be another story. You are shivering."

Isabelle slipped out of the coat she still wore and handed it back to its proper owner. She could not tell him that her trembling had less to do with the temperature than with the appellation he had used earlier when she had been so worried about finding Beth. "My love," he had called her.

She put aside these treacherous thoughts and said sensibly, "Thank you, Alex. And thank you for helping me find Beth."

"My pleasure, my lady," he replied, slinging the coat over his shoulder and holding out his arm. She placed her hand on his shirtsleeve, and they continued downstairs.

"I am glad to know we are still friends, Belle," he said, looking down at her with a smile. "We are friends, are we not?"

Isabelle wished her heart were not beating so erratically. She wanted to sound unruffled and serene when she replied. His dark eyes were warm and open as he waited patiently for her reply. She could not even pretend to dislike him when he was being so obliging.

"Yes, Alex, we are friends."

"Good, I was afraid I had . . . but we'll start anew from this day, shall we?"

"Yes, I . . . I think that would be best."

"Good," he said, covering her hand with his as he escorted her back to the conservatory and her picnic.

Ten

Tuesday was a day of recovery for the party. Monday's picnic had lasted until late in the evening, changing to an impromptu musicale with almost all the guests being persuaded to perform in some capacity. Lady Anne and Grace's uncle Rhodes had stolen the show, playing a duet on the pianoforte that rivaled the best London had to offer. Lady Foxworth had accepted all the accolades, remembering from time to time to thank Isabelle for her contribution.

Tuesday was another cold day, and only the bravest of the guests ventured outside. The gentlemen passed the time playing billiards and cards, while the ladies preferred conversation while pretending to stitch or read. Isabelle tried to keep busy, avoiding the earl as much as possible. She found it much easier to remain calm and even-tempered when he was not within her sphere.

For his part, Alex spent the morning trying to corner Isabelle, his frustration growing when he seemed to continuously miss her as she flitted from one group to another. Mrs. Pratt said she had seen her go up to the nursery. Up he went, only to discover that she had just left, going down the back stairs.

Finally, he decided to forget his quest. His temper frayed, he went to his library for a glass of something soothing and a bit of peace and quiet. Unfortunately, he discovered the room was already occupied.

"Good afternoon, Lady Anne," he said politely, knowing he could not simply retreat without doing the polite.

"Good afternoon, Foxworth. I hope you don't mind my sitting in here and reading. If you have work to do, I can leave," she said, smiling at him.

Alex shook his head, suddenly happy for the distraction. "No, you needn't leave. I was only looking for a quiet place, but you won't disturb me." He poured a glass of brandy and sat down near the fire, picking up his newspaper that Finley had carefully dried and folded. A companionable silence fell over the room.

"This is nice," he said after a quarter of an hour had passed with Lady Anne reading her novel and him shuffling through the paper.

"Yes, it is," she replied. "It is much more pleasant now that we are mere friends."

"I'm sure I make a much better friend than a lover," he said, turning to face her, his arm resting on the back of the sofa. "For you, that is."

"Undoubtedly. You know, Foxworth, I would probably have run you through within the first year—if we had married, I mean," said Lady Anne, leaning forward and picking a piece of lint off his coat.

"Oh!"

The couple in the library turned as one to find Isabelle staring at them. Alex jumped to his feet, the very picture of guilt—though he had done nothing wrong.

"Lady Isabelle, do come in," said Lady Anne.

"No, I didn't mean to intrude. I was looking for . . . for this," she said, grabbing a riding crop that had been left on the table, and fleeing.

"You can sit down again," said Lady Anne, smiling up at the earl.

"Devil take the woman," he said, sitting down and picking up his newspaper again, opening it with a snap.

He could feel Lady Anne's eyes boring into him. Her book lay in her lap, completely forgotten.

With a grimace, he said, "Is there something you wished to say, my lady?"

She chuckled and said, "Oh, words are hardly necessary, my dear Foxworth. I can read you as easily as I read this book."

"I don't take your meaning," he said, regarding her without blinking.

"Yes, you do, but I shan't quiz you about it. Only, how long do you intend to let things go on as they are? I mean, shouldn't you make a push to, uh . . ."

"A *lady* would not even mention it, but then . . ." He let the unspoken accusation hang in the air, but his arrogant manner didn't quell her giggles.

Finally, Alex grinned. "You are still a perfect hoyden, Lady Anne," he said.

"And you are making a perfect cake of yourself, Foxworth, but I do wish you and your lady well."

"Thank you, but I fear your good wishes are premature. Lady Isabelle feels much the same about me as you did."

"Oh, judging from the expression on her face when she discovered the two of us in here, I have little doubt about her sentiments."

"Really?" said Alex.

"Really, Foxworth. Just give her time. Be patient."

"Not one of my strong suits," he murmured.

The entire house party was promised to Squire Lambert for dinner that night. He had invited the entire village, or everyone with any claim to gentility. Mrs. Crane, Pixley's dressmaker, was also Mrs. Lambert's sister, so she was there with her shopkeeper husband—a fact that had once appalled Lady Foxworth and now delighted her. Seeing the countess greet Mrs. Lambert and Mrs. Crane like her bosom friends, the other ladies and gentlemen of the house party followed suit. Miss Silverton had also been included, Mrs. Lambert feeling that she should not be blamed if her grandfather had been born on the wrong side of the Foxworth blankets. Lady Foxworth introduced her as a cousin, and her acceptance was insured.

"Colonel, Mrs. Forbes-Smyth, allow me to introduce you to the squire's son, Richard. I believe this young man is as mad about hunting as you are," said Alex, knowing they would soon be deep in conversation.

Thomas, Lord Dunham, sat on one side of the fire, happily chatting with Lord Briscoe, an old friend who also enjoyed discussing his various aches and pains. Adam and Grace arrived, and the vicar was pulled into conversation with Mr. Forbes-Smyth, who was more interested in books than horses, much to his wife's dismay.

The other ladies of the house party blended in with the local guests. The Duchess of Charlton, for some reason, had Isabelle stationed at her side, keeping her captive and preventing Alex from speaking to her in private. He had hoped to have an opportunity to casually mention to Isabelle that he and Lady Anne were just old friends, but he hadn't been able to pry her loose.

After an unexceptional dinner, Mrs. Lambert ordered the furniture moved back and the rugs taken up in the drawing room so that the young people might enjoy some informal dancing. Alex applauded this suggestion, then watched in dismay as Lady Isabelle offered to play the pianoforte, and Mr. Pennywhistle volunteered to turn the pages for her.

They continued in these roles for an hour. Mrs. Lambert finally halted the proceedings and begged someone else to take over.

"I wish Mr. Dodwell had been able to come," she said. "He doesn't mind playing for hours, and I needn't feel guilty since he is already wed. But both of you should be dancing," she said, smiling coyly at Isabelle and Mr. Pennywhistle.

Alex said, "Why don't you young ladies take it in turns?"

His suggestion was greeted with polite whining—by the young ladies and the young gentlemen.

"Really, Mrs. Lambert, I don't mind playing," said Isabelle.

"No, no, we will think of something," said their hostess.

"I'll play, Mrs. Lambert. I am not dancing anyway," said Lady Anne. "I am still in mourning."

"How kind of you to offer," said Mrs. Lambert, pulling Lady Isabelle to her feet and shooing her away.

"I'll turn the pages for you, Anne," said her brother-in-law, leaving his cozy chair.

Alex moved closer to the pianoforte and whispered, "Thank you, my lady."

"Just do not take no for an answer. I will be watching," she said with a wink.

Alex hurried away to secure Isabelle for the next dance. It would be a waltz, if Lady Anne was paying attention.

Perfect, he thought as the music began and he took her in his arms for the second time. No kisses this time, but it felt so right to hold her again.

The room was not like a ballroom, and though there were only a few couples, their movements were restricted. Alex wanted to twirl her until she would be forced to cling to him, but he could not, of course.

"I am glad you were set free," he said, attempting humor to draw her out.

Isabelle would have none of it, keeping her chin perfectly level and her lips perfectly straight.

"Are you angry with me?" he asked softly, knowing the answer but desperate to break down the barrier she had erected between them.

"Why should I be angry, my lord?" she said finally.

He sighed, frustrated by her aloofness. "I thought perhaps you had formed the wrong idea about me and Lady Anne."

"Let's see, would that erroneous opinion be that you and the merry widow were enjoying a private tête-à-tête behind closed doors?" she asked with a syrupy smile.

"Yes, that . . . no, I mean, it wasn't a tête-à-tête at all. Isabelle, you are being deliberately aggravating," said Alex, wishing he could move his hands a bit and give her a good shake.

"Well, even if what you say is true, my lord, you must know how it appeared, and it was not at all the proper thing for a man to do who is trying to restore his reputation. What if Lady Brisbane had come in? All your previous work would have flown out the window," she said.

"You are all abroad if you think I give a fig about Lady Brisbane!" he hissed.

"Oh, my mistake, my lord. I thought you were trying to reform. I see I must have been mistaken," she said, gazing up at him, her eyes wide and ingenuous.

"Isabelle, if you do not come down off your high horse . . ."

She giggled, and he stopped in the middle of the floor, causing Richard Lambert and Lady Sophia to plow into them. Alex immediately pulled Isabelle close and swept her away, while she pretended not to notice his improper hold.

"You were teasing all along," he whispered, his mouth near her ear.

"Nearly," she said, smiling up at him.

"My beautiful little shrew," he said.

"My tall, handsome rogue," she replied.

Another perfect red rose awaited her when Isabelle entered her bedchamber that night. She watched carefully as her maid exclaimed in surprise to find the rose, and the bed turned down again, but Isabelle wasn't fooled. Alex had managed to sweet-talk Jane into assisting him.

Was there a female anywhere who could resist the rogue?

Still, she thought as she placed the rose with the other one in the pitcher, she could not quibble at her maid's weakness. Wasn't she just as weak? All Alex had had to do was ask, and she had accepted his invitation to dance. He had held her close, much too close for propriety's sake, and she hadn't mustered up the willpower to protest.

Yes, she thought, eagerly climbing into bed and closing her eyes to the promise of another night of delights in her dreams, she was like a fish, well and truly caught. And the Earl of Foxworth was the master angler.

Wednesday morning dawned crisp and clear, with only the slightest breeze ruffling the dry grass underfoot—a perfect day for fox hunting, declared the colonel. With most of the gentlemen, including the hunting-mad Mrs. Forbes-Smyth, returning to Squire Lambert's estate for the hunt, the ladies decided to make another shopping foray into Pixley.

Both Lady Dunham and her sister, Lady Sophia, had

ordered gowns from Mrs. Crane on their last visit, and they were to have a fitting. Their grandmother chose to remain at the Manor with Lady Anne. Lady Brisbane and her daughter declared that they simply had to have some of that divine perfume from Miss Silverton's shop.

When her daughters begged to go, Lady Amelia asked Isabelle to go along to keep an eye on them, stating she had a raging headache. Isabelle was only too happy to comply, since she wanted to purchase some small tokens for her newfound cousins and the other children.

The countess announced that she was much too weary and would remain abed until dinner. In her stead, she sent Alex with a long list of the essentials she required.

"I don't see why I have to do all this just because I choose not to hunt," he grumbled, pocketing the list and slipping into his greatcoat.

"You see, Lord Foxworth, that is another reason to join us," said Mrs. Forbes-Smyth, who was dressed in a gray riding habit, booted and ready for the hunt.

"Oh, hunting has never interested Alex," said his uncle Everett. "Nearly drove his father mad, I can tell you."

"But you will not, Uncle, for fear of boring everyone to flinders and making them miss their day of hunting," said Alex, his remark eliciting chuckles from the gentlemen who were waiting for their horses to be brought round.

"Still and all, Foxworth," said Colonel Sutter, "there's something to be said for escorting the ladies, bless 'em."

"Yes, if they will ever come downstairs," he muttered, taking out his pocket watch and flipping it open.

"I tell you what, my boy, I'll go along too," said his

uncle Everett. "There is no reason you should be the only lucky gentleman among so many doves."

"Thank you, Uncle. I'll take you up in my curricle," said Alex.

"Heavens, my boy, I am much too old for such foolishness. I would be little more than an icicle by the time we left the drive. No, I will ride with the ladies in the closed carriage with a hot brick at my feet, if you please."

"Suit yourself," said Alex, wishing he had not come back from his morning ride quite so early. He might have spent a quiet day all on his own without a horde of guests expecting him to do the polite. Still, Isabelle was going into Pixley too. He was suddenly glad his uncle had turned down the ride in his curricle.

The old dandy held out his arm, staring at it as if he were looking at a maggot. "Tsk, tsk, this coat is quite odious. I must go upstairs and change. When I selected it this morning, I thought it was purple, but I believe the morning light has turned it absolutely puce."

"You might as well go up and change," said Alex. "The ladies are certainly in no hurry."

Just then, the well-modulated drone of adults was shattered as Robert and Phillip burst into the hall.

"They said to tell you they're almost ready," announced Robert.

"With your mounts, he means," explained his brother.

"Did you just come from the stables?" asked Alex.

"Yes, Father. It is as good as a circus down there, trying to get the carriage horses harnessed, all the hunters saddled, and then the grooms' ponies too, because they don't want to miss the hunt either," said Phillip.

"You see what you'll be missing, Foxworth," said Mrs. Forbes-Smyth. "Surely you boys will be going along with us. I'm sure between the colonel and myself, we could find a likely mount for you both."

"I think they're a bit young yet," said Alex. "If you would like to go with the grooms and watch, boys, you are welcome to do so," he added.

"No, thank you, Father. We would rather go with you. We have saved up some money and want to buy a present for Grandmother."

"Ah, you've a couple of good lads there, Foxworth," said Mrs. Forbes-Smyth.

"I think so too," he replied, smiling at the boys before lapsing back into his bored reverie.

Isabelle, who had breakfasted in the nursery with her daughter, entered the Great Hall after dressing hurriedly in her favorite green carriage dress and matching bonnet. Robert and Phillip rushed to greet her and ask about Beth, who had developed a slight case of the sniffles.

She felt her heart leap when she saw Alex, but she murmured a polite, "Good morning, my lord."

"Good morning, Lady Isabelle. So you are going into Pixley too?" he asked, feigning surprise.

"Yes, I have some shopping to do, and Lady Amelia asked if I might keep an eye on the twins."

"Oh, I see," he replied. A spark of deviltry flashed in his dark eyes, and he said, "My uncle thought it was too cold for a ride in my curricle. What about you, Lady Isabelle? Are you hearty enough for a little ride al fresco?"

The pleasure of snuggling against Alex's strong frame was too tantalizing to decline, and she replied, "Why not?" Besides, she told herself, it would keep her from being wedged into an overcrowded carriage with Amanda and Abigail.

"Just let me go upstairs for something warmer," she said, throwing him a cheery smile.

A few minutes later, Isabelle paused on the landing, her eyes immediately singling Alex out from the rest of the group milling around the Great Hall. Lounging against the long trestle table, Alex glanced up and promptly dropped his curly-brimmed beaver hat. In a few long strides, he crossed the hall and was there to take her hand when she reached the bottom step. His dark eyes sparkled in admiration, and he expelled a long, low whistle.

"You look wonderful," said the rake, his words for her alone. "I don't know when I have ever seen a great-coat filled out so beautifully."

"You are too kind, my lord," Isabelle replied primly, smoothing the top cape of her creamy wool coat. When her dressmaker had suggested adapting the men's style to fit her shapely figure, Isabelle had been skeptical. Now she was delighted she had agreed.

"I am only being truthful," said Alex, patting her hand, which rested on his sleeve, and leading her toward the front door. "We shall probably be finished with our shopping by the time the rest of the ladies finally come downstairs. And if I know my uncle, it will take him all morning to choose another coat."

"So we are going alone, just the two of us?" asked Isabelle, trying to keep her tone light as she allowed him to hand her into his curricle. Suddenly, she wished Beth had not developed a case of the sniffles. She would feel much more confident with her daughter sitting between them on the narrow seat.

"No, the boys wanted to come too, so they will ride their ponies alongside us," said Alex as they stepped outside, where his groom waited with the curricle and his sons waited on horseback. "Ready, boys?"

"We're ready, Father," called Robert, lifting his riding crop in salute.

Alex set the pace, and they soon left the drive behind

and entered the country lane, where the boys rode on either side of the carriage.

Over the sound of the horses' hooves, Alex said, "Shall we favor m'lady with a song, gentlemen?"

"A Christmas song, Father?" said Phillip.

"Yes, and you start us. You have the best voice," said Alex.

Phillip cleared his throat and sang out, his childlike voice pure and clear.

"'I saw three ships come sailing in, on Christmas day, on Christmas day . . .'" Alex and Robert joined in.

When they had finished, Isabelle applauded and said, "Thank you, gentlemen. That was lovely."

"Now it is your turn to lead us," said Phillip.

"Oh, I don't know," she replied. "I was not blessed with a very good singing voice."

"Now, now, no false modesty," said Alex.

"Very well, but what shall we sing?" she asked.

"How about The 'Twelve Days of Christmas'?" said Robert.

"I wager no one knows all the verses," said Alex.

"I will accept that wager," said Isabelle, offering her hand to shake on it. The earl pulled his team to a stop, took her hand in his, and gave it a single shake before releasing it.

"Very well, my lady. Boys, we will follow Lady Isabelle's lead. But wait, what shall we wager?" asked the earl, grinning down at her.

"If I win," she said, tilting her head to one side and smiling, "you will lead Abigail out for the first dance of the Christmas Eve ball."

"High stakes," said the earl, winking at the boys. "And if I win, my lady, I will lead out the first dance with you."

"Agreed," said Isabelle, taking a deep breath and beginning. "'On the first day of Christmas, my true love gave to me . . . a partridge in a pear tree.'"

The others joined in for the beginning of each verse, pausing to allow her to name the gift her true love gave. Isabelle never hesitated—five gold rings, six geese a-laying, seven swans a-swimming, nine ladies dancing, ten lords a-leaping, eleven pipers piping.

Only one verse remained, and Alex groaned when she hesitated, giving him a smug smile.

"I can see it all now," he moaned.

Isabelle glanced at his strong profile, and a sudden ache settled in her heart as she pictured him, Abigail in his arms, opening the ball with a waltz.

"She's going to win, Father," teased Robert.

"I fear you are right, my boy," came his father's glum response.

"'On the twelfth day of Christmas,'" she began, singing it slowly while her mind worked feverishly. The treat of another waltz in Alex's arms, in Alex's arms . . . "'My true love gave to me . . . twelve . . . twelve . . .'"

"You won, Father!" shouted Phillip.

"Never gloat in the presence of your opponent," said Alex, pulling back on the ribbons, transferring them to one hand, and lifting her gloved hand to his lips. "Especially one as beautiful as this one is."

"Your horses, my lord," said Isabelle.

He smiled and lifted the reins, sending his horses along the road at a sprightly clip.

"'On the twelfth day of Christmas, my true love gave to me,'" he sang at the top of his lungs.

"'Twelve drummers drumming,'" sang the boys and Isabelle together.

Alex's head jerked around, and his dark eyes narrowed suspiciously while the boys continued the song. Isabelle looked back at the earl, her brows raised in innocent query.

"Did you . . . ?"

She smiled and said sweetly, "You'll never know. Oh, look, here we are."

Alex stopped his team and set the brake before hopping to the ground. Isabelle accepted Robert's help, and had already alighted when the earl came around the curricle.

"Thank you, Robert."

"You're welcome, my lady," he said, executing an elegant bow worthy of a London beau. Then he spoiled the effect by saying, "Can we go off on our own, Father?"

"I suppose so," he replied, his words sending his sons scampering toward the blacksmith's shop. "Mind your manners!" called their father.

He then turned his attention to Isabelle, causing her to blush when he caught her scrutinizing him.

"Yes, my lady?" he teased.

"Oh, nothing. I was just thinking how proud of them you must be . . . the boys, I mean."

"No, you were not," he said audaciously while offering her his arm.

Isabelle fell into step by his side, relieved to take up this position, since she could pretend she was walking beside someone, anyone, else. She had been confident that she could assume the role of being the earl's friend. Then the rogue had had the temerity of acting the part of a perfect gentleman and devoted father. Such a combination was much too captivating, especially since she was already in love with him.

"I have to go in Miss Silverton's shop to get some things for my mother," he said.

"And I wanted to see if she had any more of the pretty fur muffs like I bought for Beth for Christmas. I thought I would get them for Maggie and Dillie. I would also like to get something for the boys. Do you have any ideas?" she asked, losing her train of thought when she glanced up and found he was staring at her.

"What was that?" he murmured.

"I . . . what?" she breathed.

"Come in, Lord Foxworth. Come in, my lady," said the tall, bony spinster, breaking the spell. "How wonderful to see you again."

"Good morning, Miss Silverton. How are you?" asked the earl, giving Isabelle a chance to recover.

"So good of you to ask," she gushed. "I am fine, just fine. I am so looking forward to the Christmas Eve ball tomorrow."

"I am glad you can attend," he said. "I have a list here, from my mother, which I hope you will be able to fill."

While he fished in his pocket for the list, Isabelle wandered away, deciding distance was needed if she was going to keep her head. She picked up one of the white fur muffs and held it to her cheek. Yes, they would be the perfect presents for Beth's new cousins.

She jumped when the earl said, "I have just the thing."

"Yes?" she said, her tone distant.

"For the boys," he said, frowning at her. "You said you wanted to get something for them?"

"Of course, Alex, I'm sorry. I was woolgathering," she fibbed. She couldn't very well tell him that it was taking all her self-control to keep from flinging herself into his arms and kissing him madly.

This ridiculous thread of nonsense made her smile. His eyes questioned her, but she only shook her head and said, "What is it?"

"Over here," he said, leading the way to a circular wooden board surrounded by a little ledge. "You set up the nine small wooden pins in the middle. Using this string, you send the peg-top in among them; whoever knocks down the most wins."

"Show me," said Isabelle, watching while he carefully wound the string and set the top loose. It wobbled precariously and stopped short of the pins.

"Well, it is supposed to spin into the pins," said the earl, picking up the top and beginning the entire procedure again. Isabelle shook her head and put her gloved hand over his.

"Never mind. I'm sure the boys will be able to make it work."

"Would you like to try?" he challenged, offering her the top.

"Oh, no, I wouldn't wish to show you up, my lord. Oh, Miss Silverton, I would like to purchase this game, please."

"Minx," growled the earl, putting the top down and knocking over all the pins.

With a gurgle of laughter, Isabelle asked, "What is the game called, by the bye?"

"It is a silly name, my lady, but it is called the devil among the tailors. Shall I wrap it for you?"

"Yes, but could you take it in back? I am buying it for Lord Foxworth's boys, and since they rode in with us, I'm afraid they will come in at any moment."

"You are buying it for Lord Foxworth's sons, my lady?"

"That's right," said Isabelle, watching Miss Silverton's eyes light up. "They have been very kind to my little girl during her stay at the Manor, so I wanted to get them something," she said.

"Oh, I understand, my lady," said the shopkeeper, taking the toy and disappearing into the back room.

Alex sidled up to her and whispered in her ear, "It will be all over Pixley by dinnertime that you and I are . . . you know."

"Nonsense," she said.

"Oh, well, as to that. You know what they say. Never a fire without smoke."

"Pray, try to be sensible, Alex," she said, her heart sinking when she looked up to find the spinster listening to her words.

Miss Silverton gave a titter of laughter and said, "Did you want me to wrap it in silver tissue, my lady?"

"Yes, Miss Silverton. That will be fine," said Isabelle, resigned to the fact that the entire countryside would know that she had called him by his given name . . . in public . . . while he hovered over her like a . . . vulture!

As if he could read her mind, Alex chuckled and said, "I think I have done all I can do here, my dear. I'll go over to Mr. Gray's blacksmith shop and see if he has finished engraving the knives my mother is giving the boys. I'll be back in a little while, Miss Silverton," he called before strolling toward the door, where he turned and blew her a kiss.

Isabelle stuck out her tongue at him, and turned, once again finding the eager Miss Silverton fairly drooling with anticipation over the tittle-tattle she would soon be repeating.

But her cup was not yet full, for Robert and Phillip came running in, their cheeks red from the cold. They headed straight for Isabelle, their manner with her both affectionate and familiar.

"Will you help us select something for Grandmother, my lady?" asked Robert, taking her hand and pulling her toward the array of delicate bottles containing all sorts of perfumes.

Isabelle was not about to allow one nosy shopkeeper prevent her from helping the earl's engaging sons. She smiled, turning to include Phillip in her affectionate expression.

"Does she like perfume?" asked Isabelle.

"I don't know," said Phillip, who was more interested in the set of tin soldiers on display behind the case. "Ow! What did you do that for?" he asked, glaring at his brother, who refused to explain.

"Robert, apologize," said Isabelle.

"I'm sorry, Phillip," he said, scowling at his younger sibling.

"Oh . . . I . . . yes, well. Don't worry, my lady. It was just a little joke," said Phillip.

"A painful joke to play," she said. "Shall I call Miss Silverton and see if she has any ideas for your grandmother?"

"No, that's all right. We want to look for ourselves first," said Robert.

The boys moved away from Isabelle and engaged in a whispered exchange before coming back to her side, smiling widely.

"Are you feeling quite the thing?" she asked.

"Yes, yes, we were just talking about Father," said Phillip, grunting when his brother elbowed him in the ribs. "We want to get him something too, you see."

"That's right," said Robert. "It's rather difficult though, because he has changed so much since we last saw him."

"Yes, we hardly know him," said Phillip.

Isabelle put an arm around Phillip and pulled him close, smiling over his head at his older brother.

"I know," she said. "I think it is wonderful that he has taken such an interest in you boys. He's a very good father."

The boys frowned at each other, and Robert gave his brother a little shove.

"It's not just that, my lady," said Phillip, the more loquacious of the two. "Father is changed in other ways too."

"Yes, perhaps you don't know about his reputation," said Robert.

"He's a rake, you know," said Phillip.

"But not anymore," added Robert.

"Boys, you shouldn't speak so about your father," said Isabelle, looking from one eager face to the other in alarm. She could see Miss Silverton drifting closer and closer. She had to get the boys to change the subject, but their eyes were bright with purpose—though she had no idea what that purpose might be.

"Oh, but Father said we should!" said Phillip.

"He said he needed our help," said Robert.

The shop bell rang, and Isabelle was faintly aware that their audience was growing, but she had no power to stem the tide of their youthful fervor.

"Yes, he said you would not believe that he had changed his ways, that you would not believe that he loves you, my lady," declared Phillip, his voice strong and clear.

"But he does, Lady Isabelle. You must believe us. Father loves you with all his heart!"

The silence was deafening.

Then the sound of Abigail's voice broke the stillness as she snarled, "I knew it! I told you she was his mistress!"

Another sound, a muffled thump, heralded Miss Silverton's limp body hitting the floor as she fainted, overcome by the sheer volume of juicy information at her fingertips.

The fire flashing in Isabelle's eyes silenced the boys, their eager faces turning ashen beneath her anger.

"Not another word," she said, her voice so soft, they leaned forward to hear her, jumping back when she sprang into action.

* * *

The blacksmith, Mr. Gray, and his wife had recently opened a public house that boasted a private parlor. Knowing his guests would be spending the morning in Pixley, Alex had engaged the parlor for their use, asking Mrs. Gray to have at the ready such treats and dishes that ladies might enjoy.

Smiling, he picked up a fluffy lemon meringue tart and popped it into his mouth, closing his eyes and savoring the tangy flavor.

"Absolutely wonderful, Mrs. Gray," he said, smiling at this lady. "I will find the ladies and be sure that they remember the delicacies that await them in here. They're so good, in fact, I believe I'll have another. Hmm."

The door to the private parlor crashed against the wall. Mrs. Gray took one look at the wild-eyed lady and threw her apron over her face before fleeing.

"Isa—oof!" The blow to his stomach caused the lemon tart to fly out of his mouth and into the fury's face, enraging her further. Alex lost his footing and fell onto the tray behind him, tarts and cakes flying everywhere as the table collapsed beneath him.

Coughing and spewing the remains of the tart, he grabbed her ankle, the only appendage at hand. Isabelle twisted to kick him with her other foot, but he anticipated this move and threw his other arm around her legs, bringing her crashing down on top of him, tarts and all!

"Devil take you, woman!" he finally managed to say.

Crawling off him and out of reach, Isabelle sat flat on the floor, glaring at him.

"The devil take you too, my lord rogue!" she growled. Clambering to her feet before he could grab her, Isabelle ran out the door, past Alex's sons, the twins, the countess's brother, Lady Brisbane, and Miss Brisbane.

They skidded into the private parlor, agog with curiosity and alive with the promise of scandal.

"You've made a right cock-up of the whole thing, haven't you, my boy?" said Alex's uncle, chuckling at the sight of his elegant nephew swimming in a sea of squishy pastry.

"We're sorry, Father. It's all our fault," said Robert.

"No, Robert. It's all my fault, I fear," said Alex. "My fault from start to finish."

Eleven

"Devil take you, Isabelle, a wager is a wager," whispered the earl through her closed and locked door. "I won and you lost, and you have to pay the piper."

Silence greeted this childish taunt, and Alex pounded on the door again.

"I will expect you downstairs at eight o'clock to lead out the dancing with me. Understood?"

More silence, the lack of sound nagging at him like an open wound.

"Bah!" he said, storming off down the hall to drown his sorrow as he had been doing for the past day and a half.

Isabelle finally removed the pillow from her ears and took a deep breath. She gave Beth a pathetic smile and continued packing. Her maid gave a sniff and shook her head as she folded another piece of clothing.

"Jane, if you cannot manage to do that without weeping, I will do it myself."

"Yes, m'lady. I mean, no, m'lady."

"Beth, why don't you go back to the nursery, my sweet? You should play with Maggie and Dillie while you can. We'll be leaving this afternoon."

"I don't want to. They told me that Lord Foxworth wants to marry you, Mama."

"Did they?" said Isabelle.

"Yes. Why don't you want to marry him? I like it here,

and then Robert and Phillip would be my brothers, and Allie would be my cousin too."

"It is not that easy, my love."

"But if the earl wants to marry you . . ."

"But I don't know that he wants to. He has not said any such thing to me, sweet. And even if he had, I wouldn't marry him. Lord Foxworth is not the sort of man I would ever marry," said Isabelle.

"Oh," sighed Beth. "It would have been nice to live here with Bee and Molly."

"Molly?"

"The pony. She is just the right size for me," said Beth solemnly.

"Perhaps we will purchase a pony for you when we get home to Spursden."

"It won't be the same as Molly," said Beth, sniffling.

Isabelle looked from her daughter to the maid and threw up her hands, retreating to the dressing room.

It wasn't as if she hadn't thought about what Robert and Phillip said. It wasn't as if she hadn't considered the possibility—remote though it might be—that Alex did love her. The problem was, would he love her in six months, or in a year?

In her experience, rakes and rogues never reformed. It was not in their makeup to change from libertine to steady husband.

And she could settle for nothing less than a steady, loving husband.

Isabelle dashed away the tears that trickled down her cheeks.

She looked at the emerald-green silk gown that she had been planning to wear to the ball. A good thing, she told herself, that she had not purchased something new for the occasion. This old gown she had worn several times. It would not be wasted when she gave it away. She certainly could never wear it again.

Isabelle jumped when a sharp object hit the door leading to the hallway. Now he was trying to come into her dressing room!

"Lady Isabelle, I can see you through the keyhole. I want to speak to you," called the Dowager Duchess of Charlton. "Open this door . . . please."

"Are you alone?"

"Of course I am!"

Isabelle crossed the room and unlocked the door, allowing the duchess to enter before she locked it back again.

"Don't trust him, eh? Did it occur to you, child, that all he would have to do is get the keys from the housekeeper?"

Isabelle shrugged, but the duchess's words had hit home. Oddly enough, she hadn't worried that Alex might do such an underhanded thing. She had trusted that his honor would prevent him from either breaking down her door or having Mrs. Teasley open it for him. A little voice inside whimpered that it might have been nice to have him break down the heavy door.

"Harumph!" muttered the dowager duchess. She took her silver-tipped cane and lifted the full skirt of the green silk gown away from the wall, letting it fall back in a swish of shimmering fabric.

"Pretty gown. Seems a shame not to wear it."

Isabelle licked her lips and asked, "Was there something you wanted, your grace?"

"Of course, I want you to come to your senses, girl."

When Isabelle didn't react, the old woman grumbled, "And I want you to get me a chair to sit down. I'm an old woman."

Isabelle narrowed her eyes suspiciously, but she went in the other room, where her maid and daughter were pretending to be busy. Carrying a straight-backed chair into the dressing room, she closed the door on them.

The duchess sat down and studied Isabelle for a moment before giving her head a sorrowful shake.

"I hadn't noticed the resemblance before."

"What resemblance?"

"To your father. I thought you were a perfect copy of your mother, but I was wrong. You've got more of your father in you than anyone would guess."

"What is your point, duchess? I have things to do here."

"Yes, I see that you do. I wonder why you waited almost two days before leaving. If my heart were broken . . ."

"I didn't say anything about my heart being broken. I am leaving because I have been disgraced, mortified . . ."

"Oh, yes, all those high-sounding words! They don't mean a thing, you know, when you climb into bed alone at night."

"Really, your grace, I don't want to speak about such personal matters."

"Why not? If there is anyone you can talk to, my dear, it's me. You see, I remember what happened eight years ago."

Isabelle stiffened, but she didn't throw the old woman out. She told herself she should, but she didn't.

"You think anyone cares now? Do you think anyone knows?" asked the duchess.

"I don't know what you are talking about," said Isabelle weakly, backing up to prop herself against the wall.

The duchess leaned closer, and her gravelly voice cracked as she whispered, "Yes, you do, but nobody else will know. Beth is the perfect copy of you, her mother. No one will ever guess who her father really is. They'll never guess that Fanshaw was paid to wed you."

"He wasn't! Howard loved me!"

"Of course he did, and that's what everyone remembers from that Season. You must have been four and twenty, and he had been hanging after you for years. Everyone was shocked when you agreed to wed him all of a sudden. And then the baby came, two months early, and everybody thought they understood."

"I loved my husband," whispered Isabelle, wiping the perspiration from her brow and sliding down to sit on the floor, her knees drawn up to her chest. "Howard was so good to me, so good to Beth."

"I don't doubt it. Howard Fanshaw loved you, and he was a good man, nothing like that scoundrel you . . ."

Isabelle buried her head in her chest and let out a keening wail, her breath ragged.

"Foxworth is a good man too, child. What's more, he loves you, loves both of you," said the duchess.

Isabelle shook her head, unwilling to agree to this statement. "He can't," she breathed.

"Can't?" said the old woman with a faraway look in her faded blue eyes. "You never knew your great-uncle, my husband. By Jove! He was a man! Loved the ladies, all the ladies . . . until he met me, that is. My father told him no, he couldn't have me, that he wasn't good enough for me. But I told Papa I'd have no other."

"What happened?" murmured Isabelle.

"He never looked at another woman. If he had, I would have . . . but I didn't have to. He loved me . . . my word, how he loved me," said the duchess, patting Isabelle's hand.

"I don't think I can ever forget . . ." said Isabelle.

"Probably not, but if you could forgive yourself, Isabelle, perhaps then you could listen to your heart." The duchess pulled herself up with her cane and hobbled to the door. "Come here and let me out. You'll want to lock it again when I've gone."

Isabelle got to her feet and went to the door, turning the key and stepping aside.

"You think about it, child. Think and listen."

* * *

"Get ahold of yourself, man!" said Lord Dunham, grabbing Alex by the shoulders and giving him a mighty shake.

The marquess let go, and Alex swayed, but he didn't fall down. Neither did he appear to come to his senses.

"I give up! You try," said the marquess to Alex's brother.

The vicar sat his brother down and began to talk, his voice rising in volume as Alex closed his eyes and drifted off to sleep.

"Bah! It's hopeless!" exclaimed Adam, allowing his brother to fall back on the bed.

"Father, I think she's going to come to the ball!" yelled Phillip, bounding into his father's bedroom and skidding to a halt. Robert, following on his heels, nearly knocked him over.

"What's the matter with him?" asked Phillip.

"He's drunk as an emperor," said Robert in disgust. "And just when our problems might be over."

"Again? Can't you . . . fix him or something, Uncle Adam?"

The vicar ran a hand through his copper curls and said, "I've done everything in my power. I'm sorry, boys."

The door opened, and Tompkins minced into the room, carrying a tankard. He stopped, looking from one gloomy face to the next before crossing the room and putting the tankard on the table next to the earl.

The marquess leaned over the concoction and took a deep breath. "Whew! What the devil is in that thing, Tompkins?"

"Just a tonic, m'lord, something to set Lord Fox-worth to rights," said the valet, rolling up his sleeves.

The others looked at the slumbering earl doubtfully.

"Are you sure, Tompkins?" asked Robert.

The valet grabbed his master and pulled him into a sitting position. "Now, don't you fret, young master. I can take care of his lordship. He'll be right as rain in plenty of time for the ball, you just count on me."

"We'll have to. Come along, boys. Let's leave Tompkins to work his magic. I have to get home and dress for tonight. If I am late, your aunt will be in high dudgeon for a fortnight. Work your magic, Tompkins," said the vicar.

"That's what it will take, strong magic," said the gloomy marquess, following them out of the room.

"No, Jane, I do not wish to hear a word about what has been going on in the past day and a half," said Isabelle, holding her hands to her ears. She cast a significant glance at Beth, who was seated at her dressing table, opening jars of cosmetics and dabbing them on her face.

The maid looked at the child and said, "I wouldn't say anything unseemly in front of the child, my lady."

"Nevertheless, I don't think we should . . ." Isabelle's eyes grew wide as the sound of someone shouting next door seeped into her room.

"What's that, Mama?"

"Someone must have stubbed her toe," she said, her voice growing in volume as the shouting next door did likewise, but it was no use. She could not drown out the angry voices.

Beth climbed off the stool and scurried across the bedroom and into her mother's sitting room, pressing her ear to the door that connected to the twins' bedchamber. Her mother was right behind her.

"Beth, come away from there this instant," she hissed, but the child ignored her.

Crossing the room, Isabelle didn't even have to strain to hear Lady Amelia ringing a peal over the heads of her twin daughters.

"And I tell you, my fine girl, you *will* go next door and apologize for all the terrible things you have been saying about Lady Isabelle," shouted Amelia.

"Beth," said Isabelle, but she stood rooted to the spot, spellbound like a charmed snake, unable to move of her own volition.

Listening unabashedly, the shouting match continued with Abigail responding in full force. "Why should I? I haven't said anything that isn't true!"

"Wretched girl! None of it is true, and so the earl told me this morning."

"And you believe him?"

"Abigail, perhaps we should apologize," said her sister, her voice not as loud but full of emotion.

"I won't!"

Isabelle smiled when she heard the sound of heels being drubbed against the floor.

"Fine, then remain unwed! For if you refuse to apologize, do not expect Foxworth to stand the expense of a Season for either one of you!"

"He wouldn't!" shrieked Amanda.

"Then you'll just have to pay for it," said Abigail.

"I'll not spend a single groat on you, you unnatural hoyden!"

A door slammed, and Isabelle dragged Beth back into her bedroom while the sound of wailing and moaning rose. She shut the door to the sitting room and sat Beth down on the bed.

"Darling, I hope you are not upset by what you heard. I am sorry I didn't . . . I should have made you come back in here."

"Oh, I could hear every word, my lady, all the way in

here," said the abigail gleefully. "And I must say, I hope the earl holds fast to what he said."

"That is quite enough, Jane," Isabelle said, frowning sternly at the gray-haired maid who had served her since she had outgrown her nurse.

"It would serve that high-and-mighty miss right, after what she said about you, m'lady," said the unrepentant maid.

"What did she say?" asked Beth, slipping off the bed and tugging at the maid's apron.

"Never you mind, miss," the maid and mistress replied in unison.

"Beth, I think you should go back upstairs to the nursery," said Lady Isabelle.

"But, Mama, I want to watch you get ready for the ball," whined Beth.

Isabelle looked at the green silk gown, saying softly, "I may not go to the ball. I mean, the duchess meant well, but . . ."

"But you have to, Mama! I told Maggie and Dillie you were going! I told them you weren't going to let those nasty twins keep you from going!"

"You don't understand, darling. It's not that easy to ignore . . ." Isabelle looked into those dark eyes and fell silent. She massaged her forehead, all the while searching within for strength.

Then she felt her daughter's hand slip into hers.

"I'll be right there, Mama, watching from the gallery."

Isabelle knelt down, giving Beth a fierce hug before she rose again, her back stiffened by resolve.

"Send for hot water, Jane. You cannot expect me to attend a ball without having a bath."

"Huzzah!" said Beth, jumping up and down.

* * *

"My head is going to split wide open, Tompkins, and when it does, I just want you to clean up the mess and stick what is left of me in the chamber pot," said the earl, holding his head in his hands. "Argh! Damn you!"

"Yes, m'lord," said the valet, putting down the empty pot and picking up another to pour its contents over his master's head.

"You always have those vile tankards of tonics handy to cure me after I have had too much, why the devil can't you just take the brandy . . . oh, blast, it makes me ill just to say the word. . . ."

"Another cold can, m'lord," said the valet.

"Don't warn me, you thatch-gallows! Just pour the demmed stuff! Argh!"

"Very good, m'lord," said the valet, appearing completely unruffled by his naked master swearing at him like a drunken sailor from the copper tub.

"What time is it?" asked Alex, massaging his temples cautiously.

"I believe it is just past eight o'clock, my lord," said Tompkins, dousing his master with the cold water yet again.

"Argh!" yelled Alex, grabbing the empty can and throwing it across the room.

"You told me not to warn you, m'lord," said the valet.

"Well, I lied. I want you to tell me before you pour that blasted cold water over my head, and I want you to tell me before you pour the hot water."

"Time for some more tonic, my lord?"

"No, devil take you and your vile tonic," said Alex, rising in the tub and standing still to see if his legs would support him.

Tompkins wrapped a towel around the earl and provided his shoulder for support while his master stepped out of the bath.

Alex shivered and tottered toward the fire, where the

valet helped him don a silk banyan. When the servant would have tied the sash, Alex pushed him away and sat down in the chair, not caring for the moment if he was decent or not, alive or dead.

"Shall I ring for some tea, my lord?"

"Yes, I think I'm ready for the next phase," said Alex.

"Very good, my lord."

Silence reigned for several moments while they waited for a footman to answer the bell.

Finally, Alex remarked, "You'll have to fetch it yourself, Tompkins. Everyone is busy getting ready for the ball downstairs." Tompkins pursed his lips and stalked toward the door. Chuckling at the indignant valet, Alex said, "It serves you right for making that tonic so demmed loathsome."

When he was alone, he ran his hands through his wet hair, wishing he didn't feel so dashed foolish. He might have been able to justify getting roaring drunk after that fiasco in the village. She had made a laughingstock of him in front of everyone—his guests and the people of Pixley. If he hadn't gotten drunk, he might have set matters to rights immediately by denying everything—that Isabelle was his mistress, that Beth was his by-blow, that he loved Isabelle with all his heart. But he had sought solace in the bottle and that had led to his second fateful mistake when he had gone to Isabelle's room and pounded on her door, shouting at the top of his lungs for her to let him in. That had done the trick, thought Alex, shaking his head and then wishing he hadn't.

He took a slow, deep breath, expelling it while the pounding in his head subsided.

"I hope you are kicking yourself properly."

The shock of hearing his mother's voice in his bedchamber caused him to slew around, sending new waves of pain and nausea rollicking through his head and stomach. He grabbed his head and held it steady.

"Yes, I see that you are," she said, closing the door and crossing the plush carpets, taking the chair closest to his and sitting down before lifting her lorgnette and studying him coldly.

"Hmph, looks as if you have already kicked yourself. Good."

"How maternal of you, Mother."

"Do you have any idea what you have done, Foxworth?"

"Didn't we have this conversation yesterday when I was . . ."

"Drunk? Well, one of us did. Good heavens, boy, what set you off today? I thought you would come to your senses today and speak to Lady Isabelle."

"As I am sure you are aware, Mother, as everyone in the household is aware, I tried to speak to her yesterday, and she would have none of me."

"What do you expect? She has more sense than to open her door to a drunken fool."

"Would that the drunken fool had locked his own room," muttered Alex.

"Here is your tea, my . . ."

"Not now, Tompkins," said the countess.

"Yes, now, Tompkins," said Alex. The valet hovered on the doorsill, tray in hand, while mother and son held a silent battle of wills.

Finally, the countess said, "Oh, very well, Tompkins. Bring in the tray, but leave it. I shall pour the tea."

"Very good, my lady," said the valet, hurrying about his business and vacating the room.

When she had served the hot liquid, and Alex had downed one cup, the countess started in again.

After a moment, Alex held up his hand, saying,

"Mother, if you are going to run down the entire catalogue of my sins, we will both miss the ball."

"Are you going to the ball?" she demanded.

"Of course I am going to the ball. Do you think I would miss the Christmas Eve ball? It is tradition. We may be at the Manor instead of Foxworth Court, but it is still tradition."

"Do you know what time it is?"

"Eight o'clock," he said, focusing on the clock on his dressing table.

"Eight? It is closer to nine! Why do you think I came up here? I thought you were not going, that you were sending Isabelle to the wolves by herself."

Alex grabbed his mother's hands and his eyes bore straight through her as he breathed, "She's coming to the ball?"

"Yes, yes, the duchess convinced her."

Rising, Alex practically shoved his mother toward the door, saying, "Mother, if you do not wish to be shocked, you should leave immediately! Tompkins! Get in here!"

Beth held her mother's hand, leading her to the door of the ballroom. Servants carrying trays of glasses stopped mid-stride to watch. The guests nearest the door—Miss Silverton, the squire, Lady Brisbane—all of them stopped and stared.

"Isn't it pretty, Mama?" said Beth, pointing at all the greenery that decorated the room, giving it a festive feel.

Trembling, Isabelle glanced down at her daughter, who smiled and winked at her. With an imperceptible nod, Lady Isabelle squared her shoulders, raised her chin, and entered the crowded, silent ballroom. No one spoke or moved.

Isabelle wondered desperately how so many people

could remain so very still. Her taut nerves ready to snap, she became suddenly aware of one sound—a dull tap . . . tap . . . tap.

"Good evening, Lady Isabelle. Won't you take my arm?" asked the Dowager Duchess of Charlton.

Isabelle gave the duchess a brittle smile and took her arm, starting a painfully slow circuit of the room. All eyes followed, and no one dared give her the cut direct by turning their backs to her—they might miss something. Mr. Pennywhistle sketched a little bow. The Marchioness of Dunham and her sisters nodded.

Alex, she noted, was not in the room.

"Good evening, Lady Isabelle, how wonderful to see you," said the Dowager Countess of Foxworth, taking her other arm and joining her and the duchess in their ponderous promenade.

They made the entire circuit, arriving back at the door where she had entered. They turned to survey the assembled guests.

Isabelle looked up to see Beth with her cousins, waving wildly from the gallery. She fought back tears and kept her head high.

"I believe the first dance, a waltz, is mine, my lady," said Alex, his deep voice in her ear.

Slowly, she turned to face him, her color high.

He bowed to his mother and the duchess. Looking up, he waved to the little girls and his sons, who had joined them. With another wave, he signaled the musicians to begin.

Taking her hand in his, he led her to the middle of the ballroom floor. One hand on her waist while she placed her hand on his shoulder, their waltz began.

Her eyes filled with tears, and Alex arched one brow, saying, "Keep your eyes on mine. We don't want to give them another show, do we?"

"Oh, Alex . . ."

"No! No recriminations," he whispered, bringing the hand he held to his lips and kissing it. He grinned at the collective gasp that rippled through the room.

"That's better," he said, his eyes twinkling when she smiled back at him. "For this dance, we will be the perfect couple, in perfect harmony with each other. Later, we can decide what is to be done . . . if anything."

Their steps took them past the door of the ballroom, where an army of smiling servants had gathered to watch too. The two housekeepers sniffed into their handkerchiefs. Even Tompkins was there, proud as a mother hen. Alex smiled and nodded to them all, making Finley remember his position. Turning, the butler shooed his underlings back to their duties.

Isabelle saw none of this, keeping her eyes on his, gathering strength from him. Her gaze wavered, and she looked away, saying softly, "Alex, I am sorry."

He bent his head to look into her eyes, smiling and giving her the strength to hold her head high once again.

"No, my dear, tonight you are not allowed to be sorry for anything. Tonight you are simply beautiful. And I?" he added, waiting for her response.

She chuckled and replied, "You, my lord, are an utter rogue . . . but a very handsome rogue."

He swept her into a dizzying turn that threatened to overset his sense of balance. Slowing down again, he lifted his hand from the small of her back, and suddenly, they were not alone. Isabelle looked around her to find other smiling faces—Grace and her vicar, Lord and Lady Dunham, Grace's dapper little uncle and his wife, even Mr. Pennywhistle and Miss Brisbane. Gradually, others joined in, and Isabelle began to breathe again.

The music finally stopped. Their dance was done.

Without the protection of his strong arms, Isabelle

lost her courage, suddenly sure that she would be ostracized.

"Here is Adam, come to ask for the next dance, no doubt," said the earl, his deep voice soothing her fears.

"Good evening, Lady Isabelle. Might I have the honor of the next dance? It is the quadrille, and I believe we can join the group forming just there," said the vicar, taking her arm and guiding her to the square of allies. "My dear wife has taken pity on her brother-in-law, I see."

And so the evening proceeded. Isabelle passed from the vicar to the marquess, then on to Mr. Deal, and afterward, Mr. Pennywhistle and Mr. Dodwell, and once more with the earl, until she had danced twice with each of them.

A third dance would be shocking, as everyone in the room knew. One didn't dance a third time with a gentleman unless he was your husband or fiancé. Isabelle saw the earl push off from the wall, where he had been lazing. She willed him to turn away, but his intent was clear. Everyone in the room watched and waited. Isabelle wanted to run. She was not about to accept a third dance with the earl, but to turn down her host, when he had been so kind to her, was the height of discourtesy.

"I don't care, Charlotte, I'll not stand idly by and . . . Lady Isabelle, I was beginning to think I would never be fortunate enough to find you free for a set," said Colonel Sutter, giving her a deferential bow. Over his sparsely covered head, she saw Lady Brisbane silently fuming. "May I have the honor?"

"Yes, colonel. Thank you," she said, taking his hand and accompanying him to the floor.

As they passed the earl, she heard him say, "Good show, colonel."

From that point on, Isabelle never lacked for a partner. The squire, who had become quite good friends with the colonel, took his cue and asked for the next dance. He was not as elegant as the others, but Isabelle knew that being partnered by the local squire would go far to restore her reputation in the neighborhood.

Twelve

It was long past midnight when the last guest departed, leaving only the members of the house party. Most of them had gone to bed, planning to rise in a few hours for Christmas services at the little stone church. Isabelle waited expectantly near the stairs, hoping to speak to Alex, but others persisted in hanging about, making a quiet tête-à-tête impossible. With a sigh, she climbed the stairs to her room.

Inside, her breath caught in her throat. Jane had followed her orders and had finished packing her things, leaving out only the necessities. It was Christmas Day. She and Beth would be leaving in a few hours.

Isabelle dropped into the chair beside the cold fireplace, too weary to change her gown. Tucking her feet under her, she rested her cheek on her hand and fell asleep.

"Oh, who . . ." Isabelle blinked and shook her head. He was there with her, in her sitting room, his strong hand on her shoulder. She must be dreaming.

"Isabelle."

She shook her head again and sat up. "I thought it was a dream," she said, putting her feet on the floor and yawning.

He settled onto the settee and said, "No, I would not describe the last two days as a dream. A nightmare, perhaps."

"Definitely," she replied, trying to tuck in stray curls and smooth her hair. Alex, she noticed, had removed his coat and cravat and was wearing a silk banyan over his shirt. He had changed his dancing shoes for slippers. He looked infinitely more comfortable than she felt, shivering in the cold room.

"Let me make up the fire while you change," he said, turning and setting about this chore as if his command were law.

She thought about disputing his right to come into her room and order her about, but she was too tired to come to cuffs with him—especially since she was freezing in her fine gown.

It took her longer to remove the gown than it would have taken Alex to build a dozen fires, she thought, as she finally stepped out of the garment. She had toyed with the idea of asking him to assist her, but had dismissed this as being too absurdly dangerous—and not only because someone might discover them in that compromising position. No, after the way he had saved her at the ball, she found him more attractive than ever, and, therefore, more dangerous.

"Better?" he asked when she returned to the sitting room, joining him on the settee in front of the fire.

"Yes, much better," she said, hiding her trembling hands in the folds of her wrapper. "Alex, I'm glad you came."

"Are you now?" he asked, brightening.

Isabelle pursed her lips and said repressively, "I wanted to thank you for making sure this evening was not a disaster. I know it was you who instructed all the others to dance with me."

"Actually, I did not. They are all just capital fellows who saw what needed doing and didn't hesitate to do it."

"Then perhaps you will thank them for me," she said, "after I am gone."

"Are you going someplace?" he asked, trying to find her hand, only to have her withdraw it again.

"Yes, Beth and I always spend Christmas Day together, cooking a Boxing Day feast for our servants. It is a silly tradition, perhaps, but she looks forward to it, and I promised her we would be home to do it as usual."

"I see," he said slowly. "Then perhaps I will say what I want to say now. I had thought to wait a few days, after the other guests have all gone away."

"Alex, I wish you would not," she said.

"Belle," he said, capturing her hand and bringing it to his lips for a chaste kiss. "I love you. I don't know precisely how or when it happened, but I do love you."

"Alex, no . . ."

"Belle, yes," he said, releasing her hand and moving closer. "I know it is not what I said I wanted. I know you will never be a biddable wife, and I do not care one whit. Just say you will make me the happiest of men."

Isabelle shook her head, bowing it to avoid looking at his face while she told him the truth. He deserved to hear it, to know the type of person she really was.

"Alex, I cannot marry you. I . . . I do care for you, but you are not the type of man I could ever wed."

He sat back with a whoosh of breath, as if she had hit him in the stomach.

"Why?" was all he said.

She chanced a glance at him, her heart melting at the pain in his eyes. Then she looked away, beginning her tale.

"When I was four and twenty, I had been through several London Seasons. My father was pressuring me to marry a wealthy older man, a merchant. He was not a bad man, but he was not the man of my dreams. And then I met *him*." With a hollow little laugh, she added, "The man of my dreams."

"He was everything the man my father had chosen was not. He was young and handsome, daring and romantic. Even my mother thought him perfect. She would help me arrange our innocent little assignations—in the garden at a ball, intermission at the theater."

"The rogue," said Alex. "You don't have to say anything else, my dear. I know what he was like. I can imagine how he charmed you."

"He seduced me." She realized the deep breaths she was taking were sobs. Alex dried the tears that fell on her primly folded hands, then he cupped her chin, lifting it so he could dry her eyes.

"The bastard," he growled.

Isabelle shook her head, giving him a watery smile. "No, he was only a rake—a rogue, as you said. When my father discovered what I had done, he called the man out. Fortunately, the coward fled the country, so at least I do not have my father's blood on my hands."

"Isabelle, you were young."

"I was not, Alex. I was not some green girl. I had turned down any number of offers. I had been on the town for five years, and still I was fooled by his practiced charms."

"So you married Fanshaw."

"Yes. The wealthy merchant got wind of my condition and he withdrew his offer. Howard had been in love with me for years. When he discovered my predicament, he spoke to my father and we were wed by special license. My father refused to allow me to see my mother again. She died last year, never having seen her only grandchild."

Alex put his arm around her and pulled her close, letting her rest her head on his shoulder. They sat in silence, watching the flames flicker in the darkness.

Finally, he pulled back enough to look into her eyes.

"Belle, my beautiful Belle. You have every reason to disbelieve me when I say I love you. I have kept nothing from you. You know my past, but you hold my future in your hands."

"Alex, I can't . . ."

"No, no, I will not ask you, not right now. Neither of us is a lovesick child. We have lived long enough to know that we will not perish if we cannot be together immediately. I love you, and I think you may cherish the same sentiments for me."

He paused, smiling down at her when she did not deny his claim.

"Very well, then we will spend time together—a month, six months, a year. Whatever it takes to prove myself to you, I will be patient."

"I can't make any promises, Alex. I don't know that I can ever forget your reputation."

"I'm not asking you to forget the past, Belle. I'm asking you to consider the future, our future, however long it takes."

He leaned over and kissed her on the forehead. Then he put his arm around her again, settling against the back of the settee with her head on his shoulder, her hand in his.

"Mama, I think it is done. Come and see."

Isabelle wiped her hands and hurried to peer into the oven to see if the sponge cake was properly baked. She touched the top and it sprang back.

"Perfect," she said, reaching in and pulling it out with her apron. "We must let it cool completely before we can put it with the custard."

"Should I see if the custard is cool enough?" said Beth.

Isabelle laughed and shook her finger. "No, you may

not. If you, Little Miss Sweet Tooth, keep checking on the custard, there will be none left to make the tipsy cake. What we need to do is put the cloth on the table."

They went into the dining room and spread the best cloth on the table. In the middle, Isabelle placed the silver candelabrum that had belonged to her late husband's mother. Beth twisted sprigs of green ivy around each arm and put new candles in each socket. While Isabelle put out the best plate, Beth came behind, arranging the silverware. When they were finished, they stepped back to admire the table.

"I think it looks quite nice," said Isabelle.

"It's wonderful," said Beth.

"Oh, we need the wineglasses. Will you get them out of the cupboard, sweeting?"

"Yes, Mama." She wrinkled her nose and said, "What is that smell, Mama?"

"Good heavens! It's the partridge pie!" said Isabelle, hurrying back to the kitchen. She threw open the oven and pulled out the dish, burning her hand before she could set it down on the big table in the center of the room.

"Ow! Ow!" she screeched, sticking her thumb in her mouth.

"You should try putting butter on that," said Alex, chuckling when she nearly jumped out of her skin.

Whirling to face him, Isabelle demanded, "What are you doing here?"

He put his finger to his lips to silence her and pointed to the doorway where Robert and Phillip waited respectfully.

"Boys!" she said, opening her arms. They ran to her, receiving her hugs without reservation.

"Where is Beth?" asked Robert.

"She's in there, getting the wineglasses."

The boys disappeared, leaving her alone with Alex.

"You were telling the truth," he said, walking up to her and rubbing a spot of flour off her cheek.

"Of course I was," she said. Her eyes narrowed as she added, "I am torn between exasperation and pleasure at seeing you."

"I am just happy you didn't throw me out," he said, putting his finger in the edge of the partridge pie and tasting it. "You are a decent cook."

"You needn't sound so surprised, my lord. Here," she said, thrusting an apron into his hands. "As long as you and the boys are here, you can help."

"We are at your service, my lady," said the earl, removing his coat and tying the apron around his waist while he looked around the kitchen, his dark eyes coming to rest on the kissing bough hanging over the large kitchen table.

Frowning, he looked from Isabelle to the mistletoe and back again. She waited, bracing herself for some outrageous comment.

Finally, he shook his head, saying, "I want to compliment you on the way you have decorated for Christmas, even in the kitchen."

"Thank you."

"But I can't help wonder if the purpose of placing the mistletoe up there is so a fellow has an excuse to drag his beloved onto the table before he can kiss her. I mean, I applaud the idea, but it doesn't seem quite practical."

"You are being absurd, my lord."

"No, no, word of a Fox. I am merely being observant."

Ignoring this, Isabelle said, "We are almost ready to announce dinner. I usually let Beth do that."

"What is the first course?"

"Nothing as grand as you are used to. It's a Hessian soup and the partridge pie. The remove is spiced beef, which I must admit Cook has been preparing for the past ten days, and steamed cabbage and potatoes. The final course is the tipsy cake."

"Tipsy cake?"

Isabelle giggled. "That is what Cook calls it. You'll see. Would you go into the larder and get the blue, covered bowl in the far corner."

When he returned, she had taken the cooled sponge cake and sliced it in two, forming two layers.

"What is this for?" asked Alex, taking a taste of the custard in the blue bowl.

She slapped at his hand and said, "Are you that hungry?"

"I am," he replied simply, fixing her with a steely gaze. "We left the house before luncheon."

"Well, you may eat after the staff has had their dinner," she said tartly. "That is our Boxing Day tradition. We give the servants their dinner and their gifts."

She placed one layer of the cake in a glass bowl.

"What else can I do?" he asked.

"While I am putting the soup in the tureen, I want you to fill this teacup halfway with brandy and pour it over the cake. Then measure out a quarter of a cup of the sherry and do the same."

"Ah, hence the name—tipsy cake," said Alex, leaning back as he performed this task, trying to avoid the scent from the liquor.

Isabelle, her hands on her hips, watched him, a bemused expression on her face.

"Do not laugh. I never want to do so much as smell brandy again."

"You are looking a little pale," she said, her green eyes dancing.

"Very funny. Now what should I do?" he asked.

Isabelle hesitated. He had offered to help, but she didn't want to take advantage of him. She also wasn't certain she trusted him in a kitchen.

"Do you think you could estimate half of that custard and spread it on top of the cake?"

"I believe that is within my capabilities," he replied dryly.

"Good. And when you are finished, repeat the whole process with the second layer of the cake."

"Very good, m'lady."

"I will go and tell Beth to announce dinner."

"Leaving your minion to labor in the kitchens," he said, pretending to wipe perspiration from his brow.

Isabelle returned a moment later to fetch the soup and pie. Placing them on a big silver tray, she prepared to lift this, when Alex took it from her.

"Oh, Alex, I think you should let me do that."

"I think not," he said, picking up the heavy tray with ease. "Just tell me where it goes."

"Very well. Let me hold the door open for you; it swings closed very easily," said Isabelle. "Only, I hope being served by an earl does not ruin their appetites."

"Are you serious, or are you simply trying to destroy any vestiges of self-respect I might have remaining?" He raised his brow when she giggled, and added, "Exactly as I suspected."

Isabelle needn't have worried about her servants being too overawed by the earl's presence. Benton, Isabelle's elderly butler, had selected and served bottles of wine in the drawing room before the meal, so the servants were quite relaxed.

While Alex held the tureen for Isabelle to serve the soup, Robert and Phillip served the partridge pie. They left the servants to enjoy their meal while Beth, the boys, Alex, and Isabelle waited in the kitchens.

Benton served more wine with the second course, and opened two bottles of champagne for the final remove. When Isabelle entered with the tipsy cake, all the servants stood up, drinking her health, Beth's health, and the earl's and his sons' too. After Beth brought in the small tray that had several cheeses and delicate apricot tarts, the servants invited them to take dessert with them in the dining room. The children remained, but Isabelle and Alex returned to the kitchen.

"Would you like some of the partridge pie, Alex?"

"No, I have tasted every dish, and I am not even hungry anymore."

"Oh, well, thank you for your help," she said, growing suddenly shy to be sharing the large kitchen table with him.

After several minutes of silence, she blurted out, "I thought you said you were going to be patient and give me time, Alex?"

"So I did, my dear. But I forgot about one thing," he added, disarming her with a boyish grin. "I have little to no patience. And as for my being grown and not swept away by passion, well, I may be able to control my animal urges, but to think of going an entire twenty-four hours without seeing you is outside of reason."

"Alex, you are being nonsensical," she replied, smiling all the same.

"Am I?" he said, rising and pulling her to her feet. "Then let the nonsense begin!"

He pulled her into his arms with such force that he lost his balance, staggering back and hitting the door.

"Ow!" "Ow!" "Ow!" The sound echoed as one eavesdroppers after another fell into the person behind him. The door flew open, its well-oiled hinges doing their job too well.

Alex tripped over the first eavesdropper—Robert. Trying to catch himself and not crash into his son, he put his hand back to brace himself, still holding the laughing Isabelle with one arm. His hand hit the edge of the tray, catapulting the apricot tarts into the air, over Alex's head, and into Isabelle's face.

Her laughter ceased abruptly, and everyone waited—Alex, the servants, the boys, and Beth—all silent and wide-eyed.

Scraping a blob of whipped cream off her nose, Isabelle popped it in her mouth and said, "Hmm! I am an excellent cook!"

Her entire audience erupted in hysterical guffaws, Isabelle included.

When the hilarity subsided, and Isabelle had wiped off most of the tarts, Alex picked up the near-empty bottle of champagne, lifted it high, and said, "To Lady Isabelle!"

They followed suit with their glasses.

"To the Earl of Foxworth!" said Benton, and another round of taking wine ensued.

Alex put one arm around Isabelle. Leaning closer to her, he whispered, "To us?"

She gazed into his eyes and found love there. She realized suddenly that the pleasure of being with him was worth the risk that he might someday forget his pledge to leave his old ways behind. She could not imagine living anywhere else but in his arms.

Putting her arms around his neck, she stood on tiptoe and kissed him, forgetting everything and everyone else.

"To Lady Isabelle and Lord Foxworth!" announced the butler.

"Huzzah! Huzzah!" they shouted, downing their champagne and holding out their glasses for more, saying, "Merry Christmas!"

Isabelle felt a tug on her skirt. Reluctantly, she leaned back and looked away.

"What is it, sweeting?" she said, kneeling down to be at Beth's level.

"Are you going to marry Lord Foxworth now, Mama?"

"Yes, my sweet, I think I will."

"Aha! I win, Phillip!" she shouted. "You owe me ten pence!"

"What is the meaning of this?" demanded Isabelle, spearing her daughter and future stepson with an admonitory gaze.

"We had a wager, Mama, and I won. I said you would agree to marry Lord Foxworth, and you are, so I win!"

"Phillip, you are not to teach your little sister to gamble," said Alex, taking Isabelle's hand and leading her away from the crowd. He took her into the drawing room, where he sat down on the sofa and pulled her onto his lap.

He looked up at the ceiling hopefully, but the kissing bough in the room was above the pianoforte. Chuckling, he said, "I don't think you quite understand the purpose of having a kissing bough, my love."

"Oh, I understand perfectly," she said. "But I hardly thought it was necessary in order to receive a Christmas kiss."

"True, I am more than willing to overlook the lack of a sprig of mistletoe above us."

He kissed her the way he had in her dreams, and Isabelle sighed happily when it was over.

Looking around the cozy drawing room, Alex said, "It seems ages ago that I came here, trying to persuade you to reform me."

"Yes, and I am not at all certain that I succeeded. Really, Alex, a boy of eleven making wagers with a girl of seven!"

"Don't blame me for that one. Gambling has never been one of my vices," said the earl, taking out his handkerchief and wiping whipped cream from her ear.

"So, my lord rogue, what do you consider your vices?" she asked.

"Haven't you heard? I have been reformed. All my

vices have been cured. I have become as respectable and dull as my little brother, the vicar."

Isabelle silenced his nonsense with a kiss—brief but full of promise. "Oh, Alex, you are the very best Christmas present I have ever received."

"I feel the same," he said. "Christmas will always hold a special place in my heart." He kissed her again, the thorough type of kiss that left her aching for more.

When it was over, she licked her lips and said, "I am glad to know that you have not forgotten all your vices, my love."

Alex grinned down at her and teased, "If I do, I feel certain you will be able to jog my memory."

"One can only try, my dear rogue. One can only try."

When she kissed him this time, they forgot about vices and memories, words and the world around them.

Finally, his breathing ragged, Alex leaned his head against her cheek and murmured, "I love you, my darling shrew."

"And I love you, my dearest rogue."

ABOUT THE AUTHOR

Julia Parks lives in Texas with her husband of thirty-one years. She teaches high school French when she is not writing or playing with her grandchildren. If you would like to contact her, please write to the publisher or send her an e-mail at dendon@gte.net.